# PROTECTED HEARTS

CISSY MECCA

Boldwood

First published in Great Britain in 2025 by Boldwood Books Ltd. This edition published in 2025.

Copyright © Cissy Mecca, 2025

Cover Design by JD Smith Design Ltd

Cover Images: Shutterstock

The moral right of Cissy Mecca to be identified as the author of this work has been asserted in accordance with the Copyright, Designs and Patents Act 1988.

A CIP catalogue record for this book is available from the British Library.

Paperback ISBN 978-1-83656-267-2

Large Print ISBN 978-1-83656-266-5

Hardback ISBN 978-1-83656-265-8

Trade Paperback ISBN 978-1-80656-067-7

Ebook ISBN 978-1-83656-268-9

Kindle ISBN 978-1-83656-269-6

Audio CD ISBN 978-1-83656-260-3

MP3 CD ISBN 978-1-83656-261-0

Digital audio download ISBN 978-1-83656-264-1

This book is printed on certified sustainable paper. Boldwood Books is dedicated to putting sustainability at the heart of our business. For more information please visit https://www.boldwoodbooks.com/about-us/sustainability/

Boldwood Books Ltd, 23 Bowerdean Street, London, SW6 3TN

www.boldwoodbooks.com

# 1

## BECK

*Cedar Falls, Finger Lakes Region, NY*

The world was my oyster.

It was one of those nights, a Friday to be specific, when everything just fell into place. It was spring, the unofficial start to tourist season, and the bar had been busier than usual since opening. The tips were flowing with at least two prospects to cap off the night. One brunette. And her friend, a blonde. If I were lucky, I wouldn't have to choose.

"Have you decided?" Cole asked dryly as I slid my friend's Scotch across the bar. He was in a good mood, courtesy of the secret stash of Macallan I'd kept on hand behind the bar, just for him.

"Maybe I'll let them fight it out. Or not," I added with a laugh, my meaning evidently clear. Cole only shook his head back and forth like that when he thought one of us, usually me, was being absurd.

Leaving him, I made my way down the bar, humming to the music. O'Malley's Pub and Eatery wasn't a huge place. Our dance floor was only made possible courtesy of a few tables which I shoved in the back room on weekend nights. Bands with more than three members found it a tight squeeze. But what we lacked in space we made up for in an intimacy that came from being the only "Irish"-style pub in our small town. Plus good food and cold beer, of course.

"Hey, man, can I get a round for my friends?"

Before I could respond, the douchebag shoved himself in front of an older woman who'd just made her way to the bar. She reminded me of my Aunt Kay, the only family member I liked besides my sister, so I noticed her right away.

"Sure," I said, more good-naturedly than I would have if I weren't behind the bar. "As soon I get the young lady's order first."

I simultaneously made her smile and pissed off douchebag. Good.

"Martini, extra dirty, please."

"How dirty would you like it?" I asked suggestively, her smile widening. She was way too old for me, and married by the looks of it. I only had two rules when it came to picking up women. That they were over twenty-one. And single.

"As dirty as you can make it."

Winking at her, one I'd perfected working behind the bar since college, I made an extra-dirty martini. Serving her, and pissing off douchebag even more by handing him his drinks with a "here you go, *boss*," I headed back to Cole just as Parker sat down.

"I heard you were up here already. When did you get in?" Parker asked Cole, who looked as approachable as a professor mid-lecture... brilliant, unreadable, and not in the mood for small talk. Since he *was* actually a college professor—an Ivy League one at that—the shoe really did fit.

"About an hour ago."

We, of course, were an exception. Parker, Mason and I had no qualms about pushing Cole's buttons. It was a favorite pastime of mine.

"Don't let him fool you," I said, pouring Parker's beer. "He's excited to be home for the weekend. Right before you came in he was telling me how much he missed us."

"Like I missed grading forty-three essays on the symbolism of the American dream."

Parker chuckled. "Better you than me. I still think the whole thing is pretty cool."

I left them to tend bar, not needing to be in the conversation to already know how it would play out. Cole hated any mention of the scholarship that brought him to Cedar Falls for the weekend. He would try to change topics, and Parker would continue to bring it up for that reason.

I shook my head. Even after all these years—Mason and I met in Kindergarten and we picked up Cole as a friend a year later—I couldn't quite figure him out. Why offer a college scholarship to his hometown high school, one Cole hadn't even graduated from since his family moved away Freshman year, but then refuse to accept accolades for it? I was surprised he agreed to come in person to present it to the recipient this weekend.

A problem for another day.

"Refills, ladies?"

Time to seal the deal.

They looked at one another. One that didn't bode well for going home with both of them. There was a competitive glance in the brunette's eyes and a deferential one in the blonde's. So they'd decided.

"Sure." The brunette gave me a smile. *The* smile.

I grabbed their glasses, refilled and returned a few minutes later. "This one's on the house," I said to her specifically. "You ladies aren't from around here?"

I already knew they weren't. Born and raised in Cedar Falls, only leaving for four years of college, I knew everyone in this town.

"We're from PA," the blonde said. "Here for a girls' weekend."

As if I hadn't figured that one out already. I was about to ask their names when Parker called my name. That fucker had been my wing-man for as many years as I could count. What the hell was he thinking?

"Be right back," I said, grabbing some empties and a tip along the way.

I tossed the empty cans, about to lay into him when I realized why he'd failed in wing-man duties.

Every muscle in my body tensed as I spotted her making her way toward the bar. It would be impossible not to notice the boss's daughter, no longer the girl who'd grown up next door to me. Mae O'Malley had always been the cutest kid on the block. The darling in elementary school. Prettiest girl in middle school. But then in high school, something else blossomed in her. An awareness of her inherent goodness and intelligence so that, by the time she left for the Culinary Institute, her confidence matched her beauty.

Mae's long dirty-blonde hair was tied in two loose braids, one thing that hadn't changed since it had always been a favorite hairstyle of hers. It ended just above her full breasts, and she managed to look both innocently girly and impossibly sophisticated all at once. Her flawless complexion glowed, the minimal makeup she wore enhancing a natural beauty that was without compare. After two years in France, she sauntered toward us with a confidence and sophistication that screamed "not from Cedar Falls."

Except she was. But now she was back, with a French fiancé. Frankly, I wasn't ready for this.

"How about a round of shots?" Cole interrupted my thought, forcing me to tear my gaze from Mae. Parker and Cole waited for my reaction.

I immediately headed for the tequila, poured one for myself, downed it, and poured three more for Cole, Parker and me.

It was gonna be a long night.

# 2

## MAE

"Surprise!"

Before I could respond, Jules tossed her arms around me. I had no idea why she was yelling surprise, but it was so good to see a familiar face. I held on, probably a little too tight, because when my long-time friend pulled away, she already looked concerned.

"Mae?" she asked, staring at me like she was trying to solve a puzzle and I was the last stubborn piece.

"What's the surprise for?" I asked, avoiding the question which I'd eventually have to answer.

Jules pointed to a corner table. It was hard to tell with a crowd in the way who was exactly sitting around it, but there were at least seven or eight people.

"It's not like a welcome home party or anything, just a few people who can't wait to see you."

Inwardly groaning, I was about to plaster a smile on my face and suck it up but instead I found myself being pulled toward the entrance of my parents' bar. Resisting Jules was like standing in front of a tidal wave and expecting to stay dry. As the chatter and laughter of O'Malley's Pub died away and the door closed behind us, I found myself back on the sidewalk. As always in May, especially with good weather, the small-town square was filled with locals and visitors alike. Some sat in the gazebo in the center of the small park in front of us. Others wandered in and out of restaurants and the few shops that were still open.

Good ol' Cedar Falls. For how much I'd wanted to get out of this town, there was something oddly comforting about being back. Maybe not so odd. Only someone that you'd known since middle school would look at you with the same concerned expression as Jules wore right now.

*I will not cry. He isn't worth my tears.*

"It has something to do with you ghosting me for the past few weeks, doesn't it?" Jules and I moved away from the entrance of the bar as a couple made their way inside.

"I didn't ghost you," I argued. "As if I'd ever..."

Jules crossed her arms. At all of five foot nothing, her pitch-black hair and wispy bangs didn't hide one of my friend's most unique features. Light green eyes blazed, Jules daring me to refute her.

"Okay, okay. I get what you mean."

"Spill. Now."

She was as much as a spitfire as the day we met. Thinking of how to say it, not having told anyone except my parents when they picked me up from the airport last night, I went for the direct approach.

"We broke up."

Jules's jaw dropped. Her eyes widened. She was no longer crossing her arms, which flew to her mouth. "Oh my God, Mae. What the hell happened?"

I took a deep breath, steeled my shoulders and started from the beginning.

"About a month ago, literally the day after I got the job at La Petite Miette, we went to dinner to celebrate. I wanted to go to Maison de Lys where he works, my favorite restaurant since it was where we met. But Mathieu convinced me to try Bistro Éclipse, a new place just down the street from my apartment. When I made an offhand comment about not being at Maison de Lys, he acted... strange. I don't know how to explain it, but something was just off. One second, we were toasting to my new job and our future in Paris, and the next, he admitted that we couldn't go to Maison de Lys because a new waitress had started a few weeks earlier and the two of them—"

"No. Oh my God, Mae."

"Yeah. But the absolute worst part was his attitude about it. As if it were somehow my fault for wanting to go there and was it 'really a big deal?' since we weren't married yet."

"Are you shitting me? You are *engaged*," she said with as much antagonism as one would expect from a good friend.

"Were engaged."

Jules looked as devastated as I felt.

"That's why you went MIA for weeks."

"And delayed my return. Instead of packing for a one-week visit, I cleaned out my apartment and took everything I could fit in two suitcases."

If I surprised her with the Mathieu announcement, Jules was positively shocked now.

"Your job?"

I shook my head, tears forming in the corner of my eyes despite me willing them not to. Without a word, she put her arms around me. I hugged my friend, wishing I hadn't given in to her when Jules begged me to meet her at the pub. I should have had her over to the house, or gone to hers, but my mother insisted I should get out.

Maybe I shouldn't have told my mom when she'd asked what my plans were now that my life, and future, had gone up in flames, "To lie in my bed and cry for the next week."

"What a lying, gaslighting, narcissistic asshole. I'm not going to say a word about how I thought he was love-bombing you or that I never liked how he treated you."

Smiling against her shoulder, I pulled back.

"I'm glad you're not going the 'I told you so' route."

"I would never."

My chest still hurt. From a broken heart. Or crying so much over the past few weeks. Who knew? But for the first time since I made the decision to break off our engagement and come home, rather than making a life in Paris as I'd planned, I could breathe. I should have leaned on my family and friends as soon as it happened. Instead, I retreated into a black hole of despair that was almost embarrassing to think back on.

"This has been the worst month of my life," I admitted.

"Of course it has. Everything has been completely uprooted at once. Your relationship. Your career. Your future. But the most difficult thing is the decision to act, the rest is merely tenacity."

"I like that."

"Can't take credit. Someone said it. Just don't remember who. Anyway, you're home now and I got you."

"Thank you," I said simply, wanting to express how much that meant. "I'll be taking you up on that. My life is pretty much a wreck right now."

"Like I said, I got you. And we don't have to go back inside. I will text them saying I got sick and you took me home. It's not a total lie since I've had a headache for two days that won't seem to go away."

"Really?" The thought of going back inside and facing questions about the French fiancé I was supposed to be coming home with actually did make me feel physically ill. "That would be amazing."

"Really. Come back to my place. We can open a bottle of wine and bash that French fuck for the rest of the night."

Jules had always talked like a sailor. "Sounds like a plan." I hesitated. "Although I did want to see Beck."

"You go in there," she warned, "and there'll be questions. Totally up to you."

Questions I wasn't ready to answer without breaking down just yet. As good as I felt, getting that scholarship at CIA to École Lenôtre and spreading my wings to Paris, tonight was just the opposite. Back home, no job, no fiancé, no job prospects or plans... pretty much bottom of the barrel.

Beck could wait.

"Let's go to your house," I said. "I'll catch up with him tomorrow."

Before the words were even out of my mouth, Jules had her phone out to text the others. Besides, from the brief glimpse I'd gotten, it looked like Beck was busy planning his weekend hookup anyway. At least some things hadn't changed.

Beck and I had always been best friends growing up together, and we'd stayed close since. He was probably wondering, like Jules, if I'd fallen off the face of the earth these past few weeks. Only my parents knew what happened, and it had been hard enough telling them.

"Done. Let's go," Jules said, linking arms with me. She lived within walking distance, one of the few benefits of living in Cedar Falls.

Heart heavy, I took one last glance at my parents' bar. Tomorrow, I'd face the questions. Tonight, I just needed to breathe.

# 3

## BECK

"Need help behind the bar?"

"Nah, I'm good. You can head," I told Spence. With Cole in town, the four of us would be lingering for a while.

Mason, who showed up after his wife had fallen asleep, spun around on his stool to answer Spencer, or Spence, as we called the kid.

"How's the geometry coming along?"

Spence made the same face I did when someone ordered Brussels sprouts. How the hell anyone could eat those things was beyond me.

"Better than my love life," Spence quipped.

Parker chuckled. He was the one who got Spence this job after working a few construction jobs with him. Nineteen at the time, now twenty-one, he quickly learned homebuilding wasn't his thing. But Spence was good with people and thrived here. Even so, I finally convinced him to go back for his GED.

"Bring your geometry to the bar," Mason said, waving toward me. "This one will help you."

My hand moved in circular motions as I wiped down the bar, lingering over a beer ring. People really needed to learn to use coasters.

"Beck?" Spence asked, incredulous.

"Don't let the glasses," Parker quipped, nodding to Cole, "and yuppy clothes fool you. Everyone assumes he's the smart one of our bunch—"

"Because I am," Cole said as if it were a foregone conclusion.

"But your boss has a higher IQ than all of us."

Though I was technically the manager, I considered Mr. O'Malley the boss. Not me. Also... "How the hell do you know my IQ?"

"Jesus." Cole took a sip of whiskey. "He doesn't even know what a metaphor is yet you think he's the smartest of us?"

"I know what a metaphor is."

Mason sat back in his seat, eyeing toward the door. A former NYC cop and army ranger, he still looked for threats around every corner, forgetting we were in Cedar Falls.

"So what is it?" Cole asked me.

"It's like... a simile, but without the training wheels."

Cole let out a bark of laughter.

"I don't get it," Spence said.

"Join the club," Mason assured him.

"Beck's been reading again," Cole muttered. "Next thing you know, he'll start quoting Shakespeare."

"You can head out," I told Spence, attempting to spare him any more of the guys' quips.

"You sure? The chairs are stacked—"

"I'm positive. Go ahead. We'll close it down."

He didn't need me to tell him again. As the guys said their goodbyes, I pulled out my phone. I'd texted Mae earlier, but she'd never responded.

"Still nothing?" Mason asked.

I looked up. All three of them stared back at me. Time for a drink. Taking out Cole's secret stash, I poured myself a Scotch and raised it up, hoping to avoid the topic.

"To Cole, who's like a rare book—hard to find, impossible to replace, but somehow always makes you feel like you should've read more."

"That's a simile, asshole."

"No shit."

"Welcome home," Parker said as all four of us drank.

"Well?" Parker prompted.

"Nothing," I confirmed, knowing I couldn't avoid it. These guys, with the exception of Parker, who we met in college, had known me since we started school. There was no avoiding the fact that I'd had a crush on Mae since, well, always. When we made a pact in college never to marry—our bachelor pact as Cole, whose idea it was, called it—one of the rules was made specifically for me. Never date your neighbor. Although it had been a long time since we were actual neighbors, since my father's business boomed and we moved to Mill Creek, one of those gated neighborhoods where the lawns practically mowed themselves and the mailboxes were all designer.

Mae and I stopped being next-door neighbors, but somehow, she never stopped feeling like home.

"That's so strange," Parker said. "Why would she walk in and then leave?"

"I thought you said she was coming back a few weeks ago?" Cole asked. Since he didn't live in Cedar Falls, our Ivy League college professor gracing us for the weekend from Manhattan which he now called home, he was sometimes more out of the loop than the others.

"I thought so too. She was bringing her"—the word fiancé got stuck in my throat—"*friend* home to meet the parents."

Mason looked like he was about to bust my chops, but thankfully, refrained.

"And?" Cole prompted.

"She ghosted him," Mason finished. So much for a reprieve.

"She didn't ghost me," I argued. "She just went dark for the past few weeks."

"Went dark? Mae wasn't in a black site on some covert mission." Mason pushed his beer mug toward the edge of the bar.

"I should let you go dry," I said, heading to refill it. "People get busy."

Thankfully, Parker kept his mouth shut. He knew full well it had bothered me. Mae had never not responded to a text before. But letting Mason and Cole know that was like declaring open season on myself. Those two would never let me live it down.

"Something's up," I said, sure of it.

"If Mason refilled," Parker said, "I will too. Figured you'd be kicking us out." He motioned to where the two women had been sitting.

"Oh, yeah." Mason took the drink I handed to him. "I forgot about those two. Which one did you pick?"

If they got wind that, after one look at Mae, neither of the women were remotely appealing anymore, I'd be crucified.

"The brunette," I lied, having already tossed the napkin she gave me with her number. "But figured she could wait. Honored guest for the weekend and all."

Cole made a face as the others ribbed him, thankfully moving on from Mae.

Why hadn't she texted back? Either tonight or in the past few weeks? Why did she leave without saying hello? And where was the fiancé? I hadn't seen any French-looking dude with her.

Most importantly, why did I care so much? Mae was my friend. She'd always be just a friend, having made it abundantly clear, more than once, "a guy like me was the last one on the planet she'd ever date." Not that I blamed her. My track record with women didn't exactly align with being the relationship type. It's why I made the pact. Mason and Parker might have fallen, but Cole and I would hold true.

Fact was, I should be happy for my friend. That Mae had found the guy of her dreams.

But I wasn't.

Not even a little.

# 4

## MAE

"Mae?" My mom's voice accompanied her knock at my door.

"Come in," I yelled from the small bathroom adjacent to my bedroom, as best I could with a mouth full of toothpaste. It had been a rough morning. After drinking way too much with Jules, I'd passed out at her house and only stumbled into my own a half hour ago. Showering and changing into my favorite old sweats and tee, I felt marginally better than I had twenty-four hours ago, flying across the Atlantic with my tail between my legs.

Closer to thirty than twenty. No job. No fiancé. No future plans, back in my parents' home.

Yeah, maybe not all that much better.

"Hey, sweetie. Beck's downstairs. Should I send him up?"

Spitting out toothpaste and rinsing my mouth, I proceeded to brush my hair.

"Sh—" I caught myself. "Shoot. I never texted him back. Yeah, tell him to come up."

"I'll make some extra eggs. Does he still only eat them with cheese?"

Good question. "I think so, yeah. Knowing him."

Beck ate like a twelve-year-old boy. It had always been a joke between us, me getting him to try new things and Beck resisting. In my opinion, it was just one more way to give his parents the middle finger. He lived to embody the opposite of pretentious, of everything he thought they stood for, to a fault.

I finished brushing and braiding my wet hair, bending down to grab the brush I'd knocked onto the floor. When I stood up, my reflection wasn't the only one in the mirror. As it always did when Beck was around, my stomach did a little flip seeing him. Beck leaned against the door frame, dressed in a pair of jeans and navy tee. His floppy dirty-blond hair was longer than usual and though I couldn't see them clearly from this angle, a pair of light brown eyes stared at me in the mirror.

Impossibly handsome. A rogue of the first order. Jokester. Serial dater. And my oldest friend. I spun around, straight into his tattooed arms. Beck held on to me, smelling just like I remembered. Woodsy and clean, he was like breathing in comfort and safety.

I should have called him. Told him weeks ago. But every time I thought of it, saying the words out loud made it seem so real. When I finally told my parents, I'd broken down like the old pickup Beck bought and relished parking in his parents' driveway, one of many things he'd done to send them over the edge.

Not that they didn't have it coming. But still.

"Hey." He pulled back, looking down at me. "What's the matter?"

I swallowed, trying to find the words.

"Mae?"

I could see them now. Beck said he had hazel eyes, but I never saw blue or green flecks in them. Just various shades of brown, or maybe gold. They were usually lit up as he delivered a joke or busted someone's ass. But now they were filled with concern.

I didn't want to leave the safety of his arms just yet, so instead of responding I stood there, staring up at him. I always fancied Beck was the older brother I never had. After I was born, Mom's ovarian cancer dashed her hopes for more kids.

Except... my feelings for him had never been completely sisterly.

Acknowledging I was making it awkward, I pulled away, headed to my bed, and flopped dramatically down onto it, wishing I could stay in its cocoon of goose-down softness forever. Beck sat on the edge of the bed, as he'd done a million times growing up.

I stared up at the ceiling where glow-in-the-dark stars were still stuck there from my celestial phase. It was easier to talk to them.

"I'm sorry for not texting back. I was at Jules's and crashed there. And never plugged in my phone."

Pulling myself upright, I propped two pillows on the headboard and sat cross-legged against them.

"I saw you in the bar."

"Really?" I asked, surprised. "From my vantage point, you looked pretty busy."

Busy picking up beautiful women, Beck's favorite pastime with that very smile he was giving me now.

"Not too busy to notice my friend, one who was supposed to be home weeks ago and ghosted me."

I winced. "Sorry about that. I—" *Just say it, Mae.*

"Where's the fiancé? I didn't see him last night. Or downstairs. Is he under the bed?"

"I don't have a fiancé."

Beck's smile disappeared.

"Excuse me?"

"I don't have a fiancé. Or a job, or an apartment in Paris."

Obviously, he was shocked.

"Okay... start at the beginning."

And so I did. I told Beck what I had to Jules, and he took it way differently. When I explained how I found out about Mathieu's side-chick, Beck's chiseled jaw, one of his best features in my opinion, clenched. Beck wasn't as big as, say, Mason, but he was big enough, and way more muscular than Mathieu. In short, he'd kick his ass, and Beck looked as if he wanted to do just that.

"What a flaming asshole."

"I won't disagree with you there."

"I get calling things off with him, but why did you quit your job? And leave Paris? I thought you loved it there."

"I did," I admitted. "But we met not long after I arrived. Everything about it reminded me of him. I honestly don't think I could live there and work two blocks away from him."

"Sure," he said, running his hand through his hair. "It would be hard initially, but eventually you'd get over him. And still have your dream job and be living in, what did you call it? 'The most beautiful city in the whole wide world.'"

I had said that.

"My parents said the same thing. They thought I made a hasty decision. And honestly, that's why I didn't call you, or Jules, or anyone back home. I knew you'd try to talk me out of coming back for good."

While I waited for him to respond, I peeked at the tattoo snaking down from under his tee. Unless I was mistaken, he'd added to it.

"Mae..."

I would not cry, even though Beck's uncharacteristic seriousness brought home that this was a heady discussion.

"First of all, I support whatever decision you make. If it felt right to come back, great. Of course I'm thrilled to have you home. Second, I know it's way too soon to tell you how lucky you are to find out before your wedding what a prick this guy is. Fact of the matter is, you'd committed to him, and a life in France, and his selfish decisions fucked it up for you. I'm sorry you have to deal with this, but you're not alone. You know that."

I wiped away a tear at his words. Knowing he was right didn't take away the pain. But having Beck in my corner meant a lot to me.

"I know. I'm lucky to have such good family and friends. And my health. It feels so silly to be this broken apart when I have so much to be thankful for."

"Two things can be true at once. Don't beat yourself up too much. This is a big deal."

"It's just..."

He waited. I felt like a broken record, having gone over this all last night with Jules. But Beck was different. Being a man and all.

"I just don't get it. How does someone declare you the love of their life and say they've never met anyone like you before and stage an elaborate engagement on the Seine and then go screw around with a coworker? Honestly. I really don't understand."

"I assume you asked him that question?"

"Pfft. More than once. Every time, he deflected, or stonewalled me or turned it around, making me feel crazy. I swear, at the end, I didn't even recognize myself. You know me, Beck. I'm not some simpering weeping willow. With him, I became... I don't know. Not me."

He shifted on the bed, toward me.

"What exactly is a simpering weeping willow?"

I smiled, despite myself.

"I have no idea," I admitted. "I don't even know up from down anymore. Since high school, I've had a plan. Life goals. And it was going better than expected. Now I have no idea what I want. Actually," I amended. "I do know one thing."

"What's that?"

"I don't want a boyfriend. Ever again. Men suck. Big time."

Beck cleared his throat.

"Sorry, but not really. You would make a horrible boyfriend, and you know it. You don't count."

He was serious again. Intense, even. "I don't cheat."

I rolled my eyes. "Of course you don't. I know that."

It was one of the things he hated most about his parents' marriage. First his dad cheated. Then his mom, in retaliation. And then they divorced. Were with other people. Got remarried. Cheated more, or at least Beck suspected as much. Honestly, they could be on a reality show of their own, the two of them.

"So why don't I count?"

"Because you don't suck. But also because we'll never be boyfriend and girlfriend. Actually, none of my male friends count. Only the single ones I don't know."

"So." He stuck out his hand, as if counting on his fingers. "Single men suck. But I don't count. I assume single men you would never date, besides me, don't count either."

"Exactly. Like your friend Cole. He's much too serious for me."

"I think I'm following."

I leaned forward and swatted his hand down. "Stop it. I'm serious."

Laughing, he relented, pretending to wipe the smile from his face. "I'm being serious now."

"For like three point eight seconds?"

I counted silently. Waiting. One. Two. Three.

He grinned.

"You're a goofball."

"A hungry goofball. Your mom said something about eggs."

"With cheese?"

"You know it."

Beck stood, reaching out for my hand. I took it, glad to have that off my chest. Two people knew now, and if I wanted to hide out for a few days before telling the world, at least I'd have some company.

"I should have called you sooner," I said, letting go of him as my feet hit the ground.

"Yes, you should have."

We made our way from the bedroom into the hall.

"I'll make it up to you."

He bounded down the stairs like a teenager. "How?"

"I dunno," I said, surprisingly hungry all of a sudden. I hadn't been eating all that well lately. "I'll think of something."

# 5

## BECK

"There's my girl. Lookin' a little rough today."

Mason's wife Pia sat at the kitchen stool of the "old house," the part of their inn that Mason grew up in. When Mason's dad died and he decided to leave law enforcement and take it over, Parker moved in to help renovate. And since Parker and I were roommates at the time, we both ditched our shared apartment and were now one big cozy family.

With renovations nearly complete and Parker now owning his own building company, he and his fiancé Delaney stayed between the inn and her apartment in town while he worked on building them their "dream home," a log cabin with a lake view.

As for me? It was my turn to go too. Especially since Pia was very pregnant. In the meantime, while searching for an apartment, I liked walking up the hill to work, being on the lake and, frankly, always having someone around.

Pia looked up from her sandwich.

"I wasn't until you ruffled my hair."

"True," I admitted. "But that's neither here nor there."

I took a water from the fridge. A confused-looking Pia stared at me.

"What?"

"Something's... weird about you."

"Thanks," I said, sitting on the other side of the island and taking one of her chips despite just having eaten brunch at the O'Malleys'.

"No, seriously." Putting down her phone, Pia waited for me to incriminate myself. She must have been taking lessons from Mason.

"I don't know what you're talking about."

"Stop stealing my chips."

"Someone's gotten food territorial," I said as Mason walked into the kitchen. "Since getting knocked up."

"Nice." Pia made a face at me.

"Cole left already for the ceremony?" I asked.

"Yeah. He had to get there early." Mason took one of Pia's chips too and she promptly slapped his hand. "After reminding me we were not allowed within fifty feet of the place. Apparently he doesn't trust us to behave."

"So obviously we're going?" I asked.

Mason looked at Pia.

"Go ahead," she said to Mason. "I'll stay here for check-ins while you boys torture Cole."

"Sounds like you don't approve." Mason kissed the top of her head before heading to the fridge himself.

"As if it matters. So what's up with him?" she asked her husband, who looked up, as if assessing who she was talking about.

"Good thing you left the NYPD," I said. "Your deduction skills are lacking."

He ignored me. "Whadya mean?" Mason asked Pia.

Her eyes narrowed. "Something's... off. Like there's an extra spring in his step. And I know for a fact he came home alone last night because I was up early and didn't see anyone slinking out."

"Uh, I'm right here. You can ask me."

"Already did. You didn't answer. So?"

"Did I say I liked her?" I asked Mason. "Is it too late to change my mind?"

Pia threw a chip at me. It landed on the counter after bouncing off my forehead, so I ate it. "Thanks." Unfortunately, Mason was looking at me with his detective hat on. I knew exactly why there was an extra spring in my step but wasn't about to admit it even though Mae said I could tell the guys. Apparently she wanted word to get out, rather than having to tell people herself which, in her words, "was torture." Although I'm certain it wasn't as torturous as what I would do to the French prick if I ever got my hands on him.

"That's weird." Mason put the ham and cheese on the counter. "Pia's right. What's with the shit-eating grin?"

I couldn't help it. Although part of me felt horrible for Mae, another (big) part of me was elated. Not only was she no longer engaged, but Mae wasn't just back for a week. The whole way home I tried chastising myself, being happy when my friend was so clearly upset, but I had a hard time pretending I wasn't glad her fiancé had outed himself as a total dickhead.

"Mae's back," he said to Pia. "She was at the bar last night. But it was strange. She came in and left before saying anything. And then never texted Beck back. So I have no idea what's gotten into him."

Now they were both staring at me. Waiting.

"Fine," I said, taking a swig of water. "I just came from her house. Long story short, Mae came in last night but left when she found out Jules had a few people at the bar to surprise her. Mae isn't home for a week. Her asshole fiancé, or ex-fiancé I should say, was screwing around with a coworker so the whole thing's off. She didn't want to stay in France, despite the fact that she'd just accepted her dream job. That's why she's been MIA for the past few weeks."

Mason and Pia stared at me. I didn't blame them. It was a lot to take in.

"She gave me the go-ahead to tell you guys. Mae would rather it be out there than her having to start from scratch and retell the story. But she's not going into specifics about the reason for the breakup, so that's between us."

"No need to," Pia said. "It doesn't matter and is nobody's business. What a jerk."

"Wow." Mason continued making his ham and cheese sandwich. "That's insane."

"Poor girl." Pia lifted a chip to her mouth. "I can't imagine how she must be feeling." I didn't have to wait long for the reprimand. "And that's why you were smiling? Jesus, Beck."

"What?" I attempted to defend myself. "I didn't smile in front of her. I'm devastated for Mae, seriously."

"Sure you are," Mason said sarcastically. "You look it."

"Beckham Claymont, if you dare hurt her after what she's been through..."

"I have no intention of hurting her," I said, ignoring the fact that—thanks, Mason—Pia knew and used my real name to try and irritate me. "I care about her."

Love her.

"I know you do," she said. "But guys sometimes think with their dicks and not their heads."

Mason pretended to be offended but Pia knew better. She was right.

"Mae has zero clue I think of her as anything other than a friend. There are exactly three people—well, five now that you and Delaney are clued in—that know about that. And it's gonna stay that way. I'm the last person in the world Mae would ever date. She knows me too well."

"Then why do you look like the cat who ate the canary? If she stays here, you'll have a front-row seat to her next relationship. Or are you hoping she'll become a nun?" Pia asked.

"You're starting to sound like him," I accused, although that seemed to make Mason happy, as if Pia was his sarcastic wit protege.

"Beck," she warned.

"I know, I know. Be nice."

"The best thing you can do is stay away from her right now. Let her female friends, the ones who don't have complicated feelings for Mae, pick her up. That's a lot to handle all at once. And why do you already look guilty?"

"Small problem. I invited her over tonight. Promised her we could get good and drunk together."

"Don't you have work?" Mason asked.

"Her dad thought my plan was solid. He's covering."

"Her dad thought it was a good idea for his daughter get good and drunk?"

"I didn't put it quite like that."

Mason laughed. "I'm sure you didn't."

"So what's the plan?" Pia asked.

"Plan?"

"Yes, plan. As in, what are we doing for her?"

Mason and I exchanged a glance.

"Oh my God, the two of you. Never mind. Delaney and I will handle it. Go clean up, both of you. You can't go to Cole's ceremony like that. And tell Mae to come over any time after six."

I saluted her. "Yes, ma'am. You really are the best."

"Yeah, yeah." Pia shooed us out of the kitchen. Mason snatched his sandwich first, and I snagged one last chip. Thankfully, my back was to Pia so she couldn't see me smiling.

I wasn't sure what came next—hell, I barely knew what I wanted tomorrow to look like.

But with Mae back in town and no ring on her finger, for the first time in a long time, something felt... possible.

# 6

## MAE

"Thanks for picking me up."

I jumped in Beck's faded blue pickup before he could open my door, which I knew he would do. It had been a habit of his since that day he'd asked my father why he still opened the car door for my mother. We were ten or so, a few years before his parents moved outside of town.

"I was just thinking of when you asked my dad why he still opened the car door for my mom."

Beck waved to Maggie, the owner of a local restaurant who lived across the street. He looked in his rearview mirror as we started down the street.

"He said it made her smile." Beck pulled his truck to the side of the street. Slamming it in park, he jumped out. "Be right back."

What the heck?

I turned around in my seat to see what was going on. Beck was helping Maggie load something into her van. He disappeared into her house and came out with his arms loaded. I was about to get out and help when Maggie gave him a hug, and Beck jogged back to me.

"Sorry about that."

"What's Maggie up to?"

"The Big Easy is hosting a graduation party tonight and one of her ovens crapped out so she made some of the dishes at home. Smelled really good. Now I want jambalaya."

I laughed. "Funny thing to crave for someone who doesn't like seafood."

"She makes it with just sausage and chicken for me."

I rolled my eyes. "Of course she does." Beck had women of all ages running circles to please him. Nothing had changed there. Not that I blamed them. He had always been the hottest guy in Cedar Falls. Some of my friends argued that honor went to Parker or Mason, but there was no contest in my eyes.

"Do you find it strange," I asked as we headed to Heritage Hill, "that the hottest guys in Cedar Falls all became best buddies?"

Beck looked at me strangely. "What prompted that?"

Oops. I really need to learn to think first and talk second. "Just the three of you, not to mention adding Cole in college."

"You think Cole is hot?"

"Obviously."

"Huh. Didn't think he was your type."

"He's not. You know I like guys with a sense of humor. But on a purely molecular level, he's hotter than hell."

Why Beck frowned, I had no idea.

And then it hit me. I hadn't thought of Mathieu in all of four minutes. So much for that streak, which was now over.

"Go ahead, say it."

I sighed. "The last thing I want to do is bring everyone down with my moping."

"I'm not everyone."

True.

"Mathieu's sense of humor was what had first attracted me to him. He waited on Colette and me."

"The one with the big tits?"

Beck was impossible. "Yes. And also an incredible pastry chef, thank you very much. Her boobs are not her best asset."

"If you say so."

I ignored him. "Anyway, he had us laughing all throughout dinner. Colette did warn me, that very night and when we started dating, that Mathieu was a charmer. But I didn't necessarily see that as a bad thing. Looking back, I should have listened when she told me to 'watch out for that one.' Maybe if she'd stayed around, things would have been different."

"Where did she go?"

"Colette was accepted into the spring program and graduated last December. We still stay in touch online, but I haven't seen her since. She probably won't be shocked when I tell her what happened."

Parker pulled into Heritage Hill, parking his truck and turning toward me.

"Hindsight is twenty-twenty, Mae. You can't beat yourself up for not seeing signs, whether they were there or not. That's not how love works."

I couldn't help laughing. "How the heck would you know? You haven't been in love a day in your life."

Beck's smile told me he hadn't taken offense, which was good, because I hadn't meant any. I knew he was capable of love. He adored his younger sister and loved my parents, especially my father, like his own. But romantic love? Not so much.

"Because I have two hot friends who both fell in love this past year who told me so."

I could always count on him to lighten the mood.

"Who do you think is the hottest of the four of you?"

"I am not answering that question."

We got out of the truck, me goading Beck into answering all the way into the house.

I was amazed at the renovations. Heritage Hill looked totally different. Beck told me that they'd been working hard on it since last summer and had sent some pics, but the transformation was even more impressive in person.

"You guys did a great job on the inn," I said as we walked into the kitchen. On the island, everything for a taco bar was laid out, the smell of seasoned beef coming from the stove. "Now there's a sight to behold. Mason Bennett, cooking. You're just missing an apron."

He hugged me with one arm as a beautiful, and obviously pregnant, brunette came into the kitchen.

"You must be Pia," I said as she smiled warmly and hugged me. "It's so nice to meet you."

"Same. I've heard so much about you."

"Mae O'Malley."

I turned toward the voice. "Delaney Thorton. It's good to see you. Congratulations, by the way," I said, hugging my old classmate. She was a year ahead of me, and though we were friends, Delaney and I hung out in different circles and were never close. I'd always liked her though.

"Mae, you remember Parker?" Beck asked.

I stuck out my hand, and he shook it. "Nice to meet you, Parker," I teased as if we hadn't partied together the weekend of his college graduation.

"Nice to meet you too," he teased.

"Very funny," Beck said. "I was being polite. Where's Cole?"

Parker shrugged. "No idea. We were just out at the lake. Mason gets cranky when he's cooking."

"Do not," he grumbled, proving Parker's point.

"As you can see," Pia said, "it's a taco night. Beck's on margarita duty but we also have Corona and—"

"A margarita is perfect," I assured her. "What can I do to help?"

"We've got it under control."

"I could use a lime cutter," Beck said from the side counter where tequila glasses were already lined up. Having worked in my parents' bar since before I was legally able to, I could easily help Beck and keep up with the chatter.

"Question. I am fully aware of the bachelor pact," I said. "So I'm curious how all of this"—I waved my arms, indicating the two couples—"happened."

I tried not to think of Mathieu as they told their stories. It was impossible not to notice the similarities, and differences, as both talked about the challenges they'd faced before ending up together.

Grabbing each glass and salting them, Beck poured the margaritas as I added a lime to each and passed them out. Pia had a non-alcoholic version, and Mason drank beer, but the rest of us were about to toast with our fresh margaritas when Cole stepped into the kitchen.

Unlike the others, he shook my hand in greeting, and from what I knew of Cole and my interactions from the few times we'd met, it tracked. He wasn't the warm and fuzzy type. Then again, neither was Mason, but there were differences between them too. Mason was hard in a "former army ranger, NYC cop" sort of way. Cole, on the other hand, was just... unapproachable. Nice enough when you got to know him, and clearly smart, but more buttoned-up than the others.

"We've been blabbing about us," Pia said as Mason finished cooking and Delaney added bowls of meat to the counter. "Tell us more about you, Mae. What was it like growing up next to this one?"

I regaled them with stories of Beck as we ate and drank. One margarita became two and, by three, I was glad I'd brought an overnight bag. The inn was sold out this week, Beck said, but there were still extra rooms in the house side, so I wouldn't have to worry about getting a car back.

Already knowing I liked Delaney, and hearing so much about Pia from Jules who'd gotten to know her a bit, by the time the taco bar was cleaned up, I felt as if we were all old friends.

"I needed this," I said as Beck and I worked on the third round of drinks. "Thank you."

"Want to talk about it or nah?" Delaney asked.

I scanned the room. Even Cole smiled encouragingly at me. Beck's hand moved to the small of my back, as if to support me. Taking a deep breath, I shared my story. Told them about our whirlwind meeting and engagement, the fateful dinner and my decision to come back home, permanently.

Having sufficiently brought down the room, I ended on a more positive note.

"Enough of Debby downer. Will you guys help me force Beck to answer a question I asked him on the way here?"

"Oh, no, Mae," he warned.

One I didn't heed.

"I made a comment that it was strange, or maybe not, that the three hottest guys in Cedar Falls all became friends. And then picked up hot guy number four in college."

Cole's small smile deepened. If I didn't know him better, I'd think it was almost a secret, borderline flirty, smile. Get a few drinks in the guy, and he turned into a different person.

"What's the question?" Mason asked, obviously curious.

"I tried to get Beck to tell me who he thought was the hottest of the four of you."

Everyone laughed. Pia called out Mason's name as Delaney did with Parker. All eyes were on Beck.

He sighed. "Alright, alright. So let's look at this clinically."

"Ah, fuck." Mason went to the fridge. "I need another drink for this."

"If we're talking classically handsome, probably Cole. I mean, look at his bone structure. At least, what I can see under those glasses."

Cole removed them, gave Beck a smolder, at which everyone laughed.

When I'd asked Beck in the past how he fit into the group, Beck always said he had a fun side. Guess I never had a chance to see it.

"On the other hand, if you like ex-military types, rough around the edge, if you know what I mean—"

"Oh my God." Pia howled with laughter.

"Then clearly Mason's your guy."

Parker made a face, knowing he was clearly next.

"And Parker, my man. Rugged good looks. Good with his hands. All around nice guy. He's a tough one to beat."

Parker lifted his drink. "I'll take it."

"You're such a cheater," I said. "You can't choose everyone."

"Hold up," Beck said, as the gang all agreed with me. "I'm not done."

This oughta be good.

"If we're talking all around hotness, a little bit of the best of each, but adding in a touch of humor, which the ladies like..." He winked at me. "Hands down, I'm the winner."

A round of boos and "cheater" and "you can't choose yourself" greeted his announcement. As they did, I stared at him. My best friend. My old neighbor. Of course, I could never admit it out loud, and certainly never to him, but...

He was right.

# 7

## BECK

"Fresh cup?"

I turned from my view of the lake to see Cole walking toward me. As always, he looked crisp and fresh, as if we hadn't been drinking half the night. I rarely got hung over, but I also didn't usually drink copious amounts of tequila.

"Thanks," I said, putting my coffee mug on the table between the two Adirondack chairs positioned perfectly for the view. Handing it to me, he sat.

"Mighty considerate of you." I took a sip of hot coffee as he sat.

"Was Pia's idea."

"Of course."

We sat in silence, one benefit of a long friendship. Breathing in the fresh spring air, I thought of how much fun I'd had last night. Of driving Mae home earlier. Of the tinge of sadness that surrounded her. And of the guilt of being glad Mae was back, without a fiancé, knowing how torn up she was about it. Despite the show she put on for the others, Mae wasn't herself last night. Made me want to kill the asshole that caused it.

"Now I know why Mason insisted on that rule."

Broken out of my reverie, it took me a second to follow.

"Never date the neighbor," I said finally. "I'll say the same now as back then. It wasn't really necessary. Mae would never go for a guy like me. She's said as much, outright, more than once."

"Even so, I get it. She's sweet."

My head whipped in Cole's direction as I remembered what Mae had said when I asked if she thought Cole was hot.

Obviously.

"Down, boy. Not my type. And I'm certainly not hers."

"Meaning? There's literally nothing wrong with her."

Why was I trying to talk Cole into liking Mae? Idiot.

"Meaning, she said last night that it's been years since she wasn't in a relationship."

"Right." I took another sip of coffee. "And you're not into relationships either."

"About as much as you are."

"True," I offered. "It's just the two of us now."

Cole seemed more annoyed by the fact than me.

"Don't get me wrong," he said. "I like Pia. And Delaney. But I stand by the reason we agreed to it in the first place."

"Same. My parents are more of a shitshow now than they were back in college."

"What's up with them these days?"

I shook my head in disgust. "More of the same. Beck, why did you even go to college? Beck, you're wasting your life away. Beck, when are you going to settle down? Beck, you're an embarrassment to the family," I said in my mother's voice.

"Did she really say that?"

"Not in so many words," I admitted. "So when are you heading back?" I asked, more relaxed now that I knew Cole wasn't interested in Mae. Talk about a disaster of epic proportions.

"Parker's taking me to the train station at one."

"It was nice of you, what you did for that girl."

"It's just money."

Cole wanted everyone to think he was some cold-hearted piece of stone. I knew better, but for some reason he didn't want to be reminded.

"When you coming up again?"

When he didn't immediately answer, I looked at Cole's profile. Something was off with him, but opening up wasn't Cole's strong suit. If anyone got it out of him, it would be Parker. I'd have to talk to him about it.

"Mace mentioned something about a summer wine event they're co-hosting with Casa Di Vino which coincides with my summer break. I'll probably come up for a few weeks then."

Cole loved the outdoors, probably as much as Parker. To say we were surprised he ended up at Columbia, in the city, was an understatement. Unless you factored in Cole's drive to be a tenured college professor, like his father. I guess those jobs were few and far between, especially at that level.

"We should be completely finished with the renovations by then."

"And then what?"

"For me?"

He looked at me like I was daft. It was my least favorite "Cole" look.

"I dunno. I'm thinking to move out sooner rather than later. Give Mason and Pia their space."

"To where?"

I shrugged. "Somewhere within walking distance of the bar, I guess. Speaking of." I pulled out my phone. "Lunch shift today. I'm on borrowed time."

"So that's it for you, then. O'Malley's for the rest of your life?"

Groaning, I tilted my head back. "Not you too."

"Hey, I don't give a shit what you do. You know that. I'm just asking."

I sighed. "I like it. Maybe it's not everyone's dream, but I have no desire to sit in an office somewhere. I like talking to people, for real, and not in some artificial space with artificial lighting."

"And you like talking to women."

"That too." Though one in particular. "I just don't have some burning desire to change the world. I like the idea of making people happy in my own way. Wouldn't have gone to college if my parents hadn't forced it. But I'm not telling you anything you don't already know."

"Works for me. I'm not trying to bust your chops. You do you, Beck. As long as you're happy."

Was I happy? I thought so, before Mae announced she was getting married. Since then, I wasn't so sure. Until she came back and unannounced the engagement. Now I was happy, at her expense. What an asshole.

"What?"

"Nothing." I had no desire to get into it.

"Okay."

And that was that. No more questions, which was one thing I liked about Cole. Surprisingly, he was one of the least judgmental people I knew.

Groaning, I stood up. "Time to hit the shower."

Cole stood with me, shaking my hand.

"See you soon, Beckster."

"Save travels, you bastard."

Cole sat back down, obviously intending to eke out the last bit of outdoor air he could before heading back to the city. For my part, I needed a shower and something to eat, not necessarily in that order.

My phone buzzed with a text.

It was Mae's dad.

> Any chance you can come in a half hour early?

I looked at the time. I could always eat at the bar.

> Sure. What's up?

> I need to talk to you and Mae, together. It's important.

My stomach dropped. What the hell did that mean? Was he sick? Was Mae's mom?

> You ok?

> Fine. Nothing like that. See you soon.

Whew.

Well, that was stranger than hell. What could Mr. O'Malley possibly have to talk to both Mae and me together about? He didn't mention anything yesterday when I'd eaten breakfast at their house. Why not tell us then?

I picked up the pace. Curiosity might've had the wheel, but the thought of seeing Mae was definitely riding shotgun.

# 8

## MAE

When Dad and I walked in, the bar was already open. Beck must have gotten ready in record time. I hadn't bothered texting him myself; everything happened so fast. Sure enough, he was already behind the bar, opening up.

"Mr. O'Malley," he said, refusing to call my father by his first name, as always. "Mae."

I ignored the fact that my heart skipped a beat when he smiled like that at me, not a new phenomenon but an inconvenient one, given the circumstances. And given my own circumstances as a newly non-engaged person.

*Not appropriate, Mae.*

"You look awfully chipper given last night's state of affairs," I said.

"Heard you two had your fill of margaritas." Dad hopped onto a stool. He was in good shape for his age. Thirteen years older than my mom, he was almost seventy-one. Why his retirement announcement had surprised me, I wasn't sure. I guess I thought of him as much younger, sometimes.

"You could say that." Beck closed the register and turned toward us, leaning against the back bar.

"Whelp." Dad looked back and forth between us. "I hadn't planned on having this conversation yet, with Mae's circumstances and all."

"Blowing up my life, he means," I clarified.

"Mae Day." Beck laughed at my father's inside joke, but I just groaned. It was as corny now as it had always been, my father's reminder to not put bad energy about myself into the universe. Yes, he was a hippy at heart.

I cleared my throat. "I meant to say... Mom and Dad apparently had a trip to Florida planned for next week that they were going to cancel. Thankfully, I overheard them and told them that was ridiculous."

"You were planning to cancel?" Beck asked. He apparently already knew about the trip. But I was certain, after talking to my parents, he didn't know the reason they were going.

"We were talking about it. We originally planned it for after Mae was due to head back to France. But now that she's home—"

"They're worried about my mental state," I finished.

Dad gave me "the look." "We are not worried about your mental state. We just want to be supportive and now didn't seem like the right time to tell you."

"That you were going to Florida?" Beck was clearly confused.

I let my father take that one.

"We'd planned on talking to Mae first and wanted to do it in person before coming to you. Then she delayed her trip, so we were unsure what to do."

Now he was really confused. Poor Beck.

I waited for his reaction. Despite knowing him my whole life, I honestly couldn't predict what it would be. His life aspirations were not something Beck liked to discuss. His parents had put way too much pressure on him to live up to their lofty standards and high-society ideals, apparently forgetting they also came from humble beginnings.

"Ray Adams," Dad announced.

Beck blinked, more confused than ever. Ray was one of my father's best friends who up and took a heart attack in January despite being a marathon runner and one of the healthiest people we knew.

"We're on borrowed time. Mae's mother and I have busted our tails at this bar, and don't get me wrong, we loved every minute of it. Being our own bosses. Working together. Meeting a lot of good people. But we're tired of New York winters and don't want to wait until life catches up to enjoy some sunshine."

"Their Florida trip is to look for a condo," I finished, knowing my father's propensity for dragging out stories. "They want to retire."

"Mae has said in the past she wasn't interested in owning the bar," my dad added quickly. "But we wanted to be certain before coming to you."

Beck was finally getting it. He pushed up from the bar, stood straight, and ran his hand through that gorgeous head of hair.

"It's yours if you want it, Beck. It'll be the best price we can offer without taking too much of a hit since we're using those funds, or part of them, for the condo."

"You want... me to have the bar?"

"Of course. Who else? Take some time to think about it, and if it doesn't line up with your goals... well, I'd be sorry to see it go to someone outside the family. But our time has come. No use working our whole lives if we can't enjoy the fruits of our labor."

My father was so corny. But also, such an awesome man. It suddenly occurred to me the one thing that had always bothered me about Mathieu... how different he was from my father. They were polar opposites, which was fine, I supposed, but I always thought I'd end up with someone like him. My mother never questioned his devotion to her.

It also just occurred to me that he considered Beck part of the family. That was kinda cute.

"That's why Paul Baker was in here sniffing around?"

My dad frowned. "Yeah, he must have gotten wind I'd had the place appraised."

"You don't want it?" Beck asked me.

He already knew the answer. "I never minded working here, but owning a pub doesn't exactly line up with my skill set. No offense to either of you, but I didn't go to CIA and study at the best pastry school in France to make chicken fingers and fries."

My dad smiled at me. "I didn't pay for you to attend CIA and help fund your trip to France for you to make chicken fingers and fries either. But you could do anything you want with this place."

We'd had this discussion many times. "I know, but it still takes a lot to run a bar. You and Mom had the benefit of doing it together. I don't think this"—I waved my hands around, admiring the renovated oak and attention to detail my parents had put into O'Malley's—"says mille-feuille."

"Mille what now?" Beck asked.

Dad chuckled.

"If you want it," I reiterated to Beck, knowing it was the right decision, "it's yours."

Beck exhaled. Clearly it was a lot to take in. And neither of us wanted to pressure him. But my parents would be keeping their trip to Florida. The last thing I wanted was them putting their dreams on hold on my behalf.

"Listen, we know this was just sprung on you." I turned my attention to my father. "You and Mom go to Florida. I'll help out while you're gone. I need something to do, and a source of income, while I figure out next steps. We got this. And it'll give Beck some time to think about it."

True to his easy-going nature, Beck shrugged. "Works for me. And I agree with Mae. You guys deserve it." He made his way over to my father to shake his head. "Whatever happens, I appreciate the confidence in me with your legacy, Mr. O'Malley."

Seeing the two of them together made me all warm and fuzzy inside. They were very different in so many ways—as far as I knew my dad wasn't a ladies' man like Beck, even back in the day—but they were both kind at heart, respectful and… it just made me happy that someone believed in Beck.

"We can talk more when I get back. The books—"

"Don't worry about them. I got it," Beck said.

"Uh huh," I said. "By 'I got it' you mean, 'Mae will do it.'"

Beck had always hated math. I'd done pretty much all of his math home-work in exchange for him writing my essays throughout school.

"That's exactly what I meant."

"Dad," I teased. "I'm not sure about leaving Beck as my boss."

He laughed. "You are co-managers," he said. "How's that?"

"Oh, gawd." Beck rolled his eyes, and head, backwards. "Lord help me."

"Not sure about the lord," Dad said to Beck. "But Mama finally sprang for that online program for bookkeeping you've been after us about. We can access it remotely, so if there are any problems, we can help."

Wow, my parents were joining the twenty-first century. Refreshing. "Remote access. Fancy. Do you even have a laptop?" I asked him.

Dad looked at Beck in mock horror. "Do you hear that? The girl goes to a fancy school in France and suddenly thinks her father is a country bumpkin."

"To be fair, I've never actually seen you or Mrs. O'Malley using a laptop. Or a computer, for that matter."

It was true. They liked to live as if we were still in the 1950s and probably wouldn't even have cell phones if I hadn't gone away to college. Never mind how long it took them to learn to video call me in France.

"As a matter of fact," my dad said, looking sheepish now, "we're going shopping for one today."

"I knew it. Country bumpkin my..." Smartly, I stopped before finishing that sentence.

"Speaking of." Dad looked at his watch. "I'm picking your mom up from the hairdressers soon. Do you need a ride back?"

"Could you use an extra hand today?" I asked Beck, to which he grinned.

"You're the manager. You tell me."

My dad stood, chuckling. "Wish I could stay for the fireworks, but duty calls." He kissed me on the cheek. "Take it easy on him, will you?"

"No chance," I said as Dad walked away. I watched him, noticing how he glanced around at the bar. It must be strange, to give your entire life to a place and have to walk away from it. Part of me felt guilty for not keeping it in the family, taking it over. But O'Malley's was his dream, not mine. With luck, Beck would buy it and keep things mostly the same.

Speaking of Beck, he was looking at me strangely.

"What?"

"We have a lot to discuss," he said, in a rare moment of seriousness.

"Yes," I agreed. "We do."

# 9

BECK

My life was a living hell.

Nearly two weeks of working side by side with Mae, and nothing was right anymore. I watched her weave effortlessly through tables, wing night notoriously busy, as if she'd been waitressing her whole life. When Jenn called off, Mae stepped right in. No job was below her, despite her crack about chicken fingers. In fact, she was one of the least pretentious people I knew, and I knew a lot of them courtesy of my parents.

"He's not even looking at them," Parker cracked, referencing the fact that there was a pair of good-looking women sitting across from him that I had barely talked to. He and Delaney were sitting at the bar with their usual—one order of hot wings and one of boneless honey mustard. That comment was one of the many reasons everything felt topsy turvy.

"Zip it," I said with half a mind not to refill Parker's beer.

"I noticed." Delaney offered me her most innocent smile.

"He's a bad influence on you," I said, grabbing Parker's empty glass. "You used to be nice."

"I'm still nice," she said as a familiar face came up to the bar.

"Hey, Jules."

"Sup, Beck? Anyone sitting here?" she asked Delaney.

"All yours. Mae said you might be stopping by so I saved it for you."

I pulled the tap, only glancing over at the two tourist women, one who hadn't stopped staring at me since she sat down. Unfortunately, that brief glance was enough to have her raising a hand at me. Two weeks ago, I'd have sauntered over there gladly. Now, handing Parker his beer, I made my way over but watched Mae instead. She already thought I was an incurable flirt—which was mostly true. The last thing I needed was to cement Mae's bad opinion of me.

"Need a refill?" I asked blandly.

"Yes, please." Her full-tooth grin revealed pearly whites as perfect as the rest of her. Too perfect, in fact, as if she put in way too much effort. Unlike Mae, who woke up looking like a ray of sunshine.

Ray of sunshine. I did smile, then, thinking of what the guys would do if I'd said such a thing out loud. They'd fall off their barstools laughing.

Giving the ladies their drinks, I wasn't surprised when one of them made her move.

"Don't see a ring on your finger," she said.

"I'm in witness protection," I dodged. "'Scuse me."

It was only as the dinner crowd died down and the bar crowd thinned that I got to catch my breath. Mae joined me behind the bar, doing the same.

"Busy night," Jules said.

"Did you know wings weren't actually invented in Buffalo?" Parker took a swig of beer.

"Yes, they were," Delaney countered.

"Anchor Bar, 1964," Mae agreed with Delaney.

"Mason told me they came from a southern barbeque restaurant in Memphis."

"Mace was yanking your chain." I started cleaning glasses now that the bar was so thin. Mae picked up a rag and began wiping it down. "The girls are right on this one."

The last word caught in my throat as Mae slid behind me, our bodies touching ever so briefly. She was killing me. Absolute and complete torture.

"So what's the word?" Parker asked. "Any more thoughts on the bar?"

They all knew the state of affairs. After talking it through with Mae, though, I still wasn't sure what to do. Her parents were in Florida, and we hadn't had any problems, payroll or otherwise. Working alongside Mae felt natural, as if it were meant to be. But this was only temporary for her. And as for me? I rubbed the back of my neck, trying not to look as tangled up as I felt.

"I don't know. O'Malley's is good. Things are good. But is that only because it's temporary? Or am I just afraid of what it means otherwise?"

Parker raised a brow. "What would it mean?"

That maybe I finally found something I actually want. And I'm not sure I knew how to want something without screwing it up.

No way in hell I was going to say that out loud, though.

"Maybe it's easier to be restless than responsible," I said instead. "Don't quote me on that."

"What about you, Mae?" Jules asked. "You look pretty comfortable behind that bar."

"I'll admit, I don't hate it. But I'm starting to miss the kitchen. I'm looking around for pastry chef positions, but they're few and far between. At least locally."

Mae had said as much yesterday. The thought of losing her from Cedar Falls just after I got her back didn't sit well. But at least she'd shown some interest in staying, which was surprising.

"I hate how sad you sound. It's not you," Jules said to Mae.

"You know what we need?" Delaney asked. "A proper girls' night."

"Totally," Jules agreed. "As the saying goes, the only way to get over a guy is to get under another one."

Everyone laughed, including me, even though it was almost physically painful. Having a front-row seat to Mae getting back in the saddle told me all I needed to know about my feelings for her, as if they were ambiguous.

"You have the bar?" I asked, anxious to move away from their discussion.

"Yep," she responded, oblivious to my discomfort.

Thankfully.

I closed down the tables, sent the kitchen home, waved goodbye to Parker and Delaney and only headed back behind the bar as Jules was leaving.

"Maybe you should ask the boss first, for the night off?" she said in parting to Mae, waving goodbye.

And then we were down to two.

"Nightcap?" Mae asked, not waiting for my response to make herself a drink. Cosmo. Classic Mae.

"Sure," I said, pulling out Cole's secret stash.

"Where did that come from?"

"Wouldn't you like to know," I teased.

Heading around the bar, Mae sank onto a stool, sighed and lifted her glass. "Sláinte."

"Or as they say in America, cheers."

We clinked glasses.

"So, boss. Can I have Friday night off?"

I rolled my eyes. "Depends. What's it for?"

I knew exactly what it was for. Wished I could say "no" but since I wasn't really her boss—it was the other way around, actually—that wasn't an option.

"Girls' night with Jules and Delaney and maybe Pia."

"What's on the docket?"

"As luck would have it, Jules found the perfect spot. Boots and Brews in Kitchi Falls has line dancing lessons once a month on Friday. We're thinking of an overnighter there."

I lost whatever else she might have said with a sudden vision of Mae in a pair of daisy dukes and cowboy boots. I took a sip of whiskey, attempting to concentrate. Somebody knew the owner of the country bar, Mazzie.

I hated everything about this plan.

"Sounds great. Just what you need." I plastered a smile on my face.

"Speaking of needs, I saw you working the bar earlier."

"The redhead? Nah. Not my type."

Mae chuckled, taking a sip of her drink. I tried, and failed, not to notice as her lips delicately touched the chilled martini glass.

"That's a blatant lie. She's exactly your type."

Belatedly, it occurred to me that... Mae had noticed me talking to the redhead.

"Oh, yeah?" I pushed. "Then why did I give her the witness protection line?"

"Not that one. It's so lame. What does it even mean?"

"That—"

"Never mind, pretend I didn't ask."

She was so effortlessly pretty. And kind. Mathieu was the stupidest motherfucker in the world.

"Except, you did."

As soon as the words were out of my mouth, I regretted them. Smiling to deflect the actual meaning of my words, I took a sip of my drink.

Too late.

Mae's eyes narrowed. "What does that mean?"

"Nothing at all."

She might be nice, but that didn't mean Mae was a pushover. She could be a pitbull when she wanted.

"Interesting."

"What's interesting?" I asked.

She continued to watch me. "Nothing."

"I must be exhausted. I've totally lost track of the conversation."

"Classic dodge."

Like I said, a pitbull.

"So... back to the redhead."

"Do we have to?"

"Why brush her off? And don't say she's not your type. The second I saw her I figured you'd be all over her. Pretty. Nice legs. And of course—"

"Big tits."

"Exactly."

I shrugged. "Not in the mood."

"Hmm." Her eyes widened. "Is there... do you have someone in your life you're not telling me about?"

I made a sound in my throat, tossing out, "Like a girlfriend?" before I thought better of it. If I was trying to clean up my image for Mae, that wouldn't help.

"Never mind. Stupid question."

"Not necessarily. I'm not opposed to having a girlfriend."

Mae laughed so hard, I thought for a second she'd fallen off the stool. In reality, she'd hopped off, apparently headed to the ladies' room.

Stupid question.

Was it? Playing fast and loose with tourists wasn't as fun as usual, even more so now that Mae was back to compare them to. But that was a far cry from her taking me seriously. A few minutes later, she slid back onto the stool, Cosmo in hand. "Still here?"

"Didn't want you to drink alone."

"How noble of you."

"So... Boots and Brews Friday?"

She grinned. "Yep. And I hear there's a mechanical bull."

Great. I took a long sip of whiskey.

"You okay?" she asked, quieter now.

"Fine." I looked at her. "Why?"

"No reason. You just... looked like you remembered something."

I did.

And if she asked the next question, I wasn't sure I could lie.

# 10

---

## MAE

"Can I please tell you how much I needed this?" I asked Jules.

Boots and Brews was just what the doctor ordered. I especially loved the fact that it was a woman-owned bar which was totally different than any in Cedar Falls or even on the lakes.

"It reminds me of that bar we went to in Nashville, off the strip."

Jules joined me at a hightop I'd scored. Delaney was grabbing new drinks.

"It does. What was the name of that place?"

"Are you kidding? I can't even remember what I ate for breakfast."

Jules did have a pretty bad memory, but mine wasn't much better. "Mason told Pia that the owner's father ran a honky tonk in Arizona but then she met a guy in Italy whose family runs a local vineyard so they moved here, and Boots and Brews was born."

"Sounds like a Hallmark movie."

"Right?"

"What vineyard?"

"Grado Valley."

"Two vodka sodas and a Surfside." Delaney passed out the drinks. "How'd you get the table? This place is packed."

We'd already taken line dancing lessons after each taking a spin on the mechanical bull that was apparently only a few-times-a-year thing. I hadn't even thought of Mathieu until now.

"It's a secret talent of mine," I answered.

"Stalking tables?" Delaney laughed.

"Yep. I have a sixth sense when people are about to abandon."

"She really does," Jules verified. "Speaking of Pia, I'm sad she couldn't come."

"I know." Delaney took a sip of her drink. "But I can't imagine this is a fun scene while preggers."

"Also, speaking of getting under guys, the dark-haired hottie in a white tee hasn't taken his eyes off you." Jules looked in the opposite direction to not be obvious, but I saw who she was talking about.

Disturbingly, an image of Beck popped into my mind. This guy was good-looking, for sure, but he didn't compare. Part of me wanted to tell the girls about the strange vibe I got from him the other night, but I also didn't want to make a big deal out of it, especially with Delaney being engaged to Parker and all. I knew better than anyone that the guys talked about everything, including women. And the last thing I needed, especially given our current work situation, was any strangeness between us.

Never mind the dream I had two nights ago.

"He's alright," I said, trying not to sound nonchalant. "Not totally my type."

"Um, really? What's your type, exactly?" Delaney asked.

"Beck," Jules blurted.

I stared at her in horror.

"Looks-wise," she added. "The opposite of him, personality-wise."

The two of them laughed, and I breathed a sigh of relief, picking up where Jules left off. "I won't disagree he's cute. And actually has a great personality. It's his dating history and general thoughts on relationships that would make him a terrible boyfriend."

"Agreed," both of them said at the same time.

"Okay, so someone who looks and acts like Beck but doesn't sleep with a new girl every week?" Jules asked. "Got it."

I swallowed. If Beck still was sleeping with a new girl every week, Delaney would know since they lived at the same place. Part of me wanted to ask but that would be way too suspicious. Also, I really didn't want the answer.

As the two of them scoped out the bar, I pulled my phone from my jean shorts pocket as it buzzed. Speak of the devil.

> How's Kitchi Falls treating you?

My pulse raced. Bad sign.

> So far so good. Line dancing. Bull riding. Can't go wrong.

> Three of you out there breaking hearts, I bet.

> Just two of us. Delaney is out of commission, obvs.

Pause.

> Obvs. Doesn't mean she isn't breaking hearts.

> True.

Nothing else came through.

> Busy tonight?

> Weekend in May? You betcha.

> Can't be too slammed if ur texting me.

> Priorities.

Another flutter. What the hell? This was *Beck*.

"Who you texting?" Jules asked in a sing-song, "innocent" voice.

"Just Beck."

Delaney was looking at me a little too closely. I put my phone back in my pocket. When another text came through, I didn't answer and took a sip of my drink instead, pretending to look around. But really, I wondered what he said next.

"Is one of you ladies Delaney?"

The pretty redhead came out of nowhere.

"I am." Delaney stuck her hand out. "You must be Mazzie."

"Guilty as charged. Sorry I wasn't able to greet you guys. I was next door with a friend of mine who just got her first tattoo."

"I saw that place when we got here," I said. "I've always wanted a tattoo."

Mazzie smiled at me.

"I'm Delaney's friend, Mae. And this is Juliette." For some reason, I always introduced Jules using her full name.

"So nice to meet you guys. And welcome to Boots and Brews."

"This place is awesome," Jules said. "We're having a blast."

"Good to hear it." She looked at me. "So if you've always wanted one, what's stopping you?"

It took me a second to focus. A tattoo, right. "Honestly, I'm not sure. Just the permanence of it, I guess. But I even know exactly what I'd get."

"Tell me," she said. I immediately liked her.

"*Fearless*. Down my spine. Dainty but with curves on each side of the word. There was a woman in my pastry class with one that started at the base of her neck and down her spine, and it was so pretty."

"Fearless. I love that," Jules said. "I could use a new one. I'd get it on my rib, just below the bra line. I've always wanted one there but am a big chicken. I hear it hurts like hell."

"Let's do it." Delaney was looking at us with big wide eyes that said, "Let's go!" "I'd get the same word to match you guys, right here." She pointed to her forearm.

"Are you being serious?" I asked.

"Totally."

Mazzie looked at our drinks. "How long are you guys in town?"

"Just for the night." Delaney took a sip of her drink.

"Lucas is usually closed in the morning, but he'd absolutely make an exception. If you want, I can take you over there to talk to him. He's about to close down so we'd have to run over now."

The three of us looked between us. Clearly Delaney was in. For someone who didn't have any ink, she seemed pretty sure of herself. Jules would do it for sure. She had four or five already and was due for a new one.

It was completely not me, to do something so permanent impetuously. On the other hand, I knew exactly what I wanted. When I first heard the quote, "Doubt kills more dreams than failure ever will," I loved it. Made it my phone background and tried to remember it when the inevitable doubt monsters peeked out from under my bed. And the fact that the girls were willing to get matching ones was really cool. But lately, nothing about my life had gone according to plan, and maybe that wasn't such a bad thing. Maybe spontaneity didn't always mean recklessness. Maybe it meant saying yes to the life I actually wanted.

I looked at Jules, then Delaney. Their eyes were lit up with the kind of thrill I hadn't felt in a long time.

Screw it.

"I'm in," I said, surprising even myself. "Let's get fearless."

"I like you ladies already," Mazzie said, echoing my thoughts. "Take your drinks."

Each of us grabbed them and followed her from the bar right next door. I honestly couldn't believe this was happening. But aside from that brief hesitation, I wasn't second-guessing it. As we walked into Grunt Ink, Mazzie called for the owner in the back room. Jules and Delaney chatted excitedly, looking at the various pictures on the wall. For my part, I sank into a leather chair and grabbed my phone, putting the drink on a coffee table.

Finally, I was able to see Beck's last text.

You're always #1 Mae Bae.

My heart raced. Impending tattoo and all.

It was the kind of thing he'd said a hundred times. Beck's nickname for me wasn't new, and neither was the sentiment. But for some reason, it hit differently tonight. I tried to think of a response.

*Since when did you agonize over a response to Beck?*

Since tonight.

"I hear we might be interested in getting some tattoos?" a deep voice asked.

Time to go. I stood, heart still pounding, sliding my phone away, like if I waited long enough, maybe I'd figure out why I needed to think about what to text him back.

# 11

## BECK

"You're home early."

"You're up late," I responded, not expecting to see Pia at the kitchen island, drinking tea. Decaffeinated, I assumed.

She checked her phone. "Eleven thirty. Yeah, Mace conked an hour ago. Has he ever actually finished a movie at night that you know of?"

"Good question. That's the problem when you're programmed to wake up when it's dark like a maniac."

Grabbing a water from the fridge, I sat across from her.

"Jenn closing tonight?"

"Yep. Whatcha reading?"

"*Big Magic* by Elizabeth Gilbert. My friend Madeline gave it to me."

"Trying to manifest some five-star Yelp reviews?"

"Funny."

"Thanks."

My phone dinged.

> Apologies for going MIA.

I shot back:

> Again.

Lol when your life falls apart it doesn't count.

That's your one pass.

While Mae typed, I looked up. "Does it suck, missing things like the girls' weekend?" I wondered.

Pia's hand moved to her stomach, probably without her realizing it. "It does. I could have gone but... I'm not feeling the best. I honestly don't get people who say they love being pregnant. It's damn uncomfortable."

Alarm bells went off in my head. "Are you alright?"

Pia's soft smile was reassuring. "I'm fine. Relax. Just normal 'growing a human in my stomach' things. Nothing to worry about."

Thank God.

Mae texted:

Anyway, take a guess what I'm doing?

"Is that Mae?" Pia asked.

"Yep," I said as Pia went back to reading her book.

Let me guess. You and Jules started a wine flight war and now the bar's on fire?

Nope.

Writing my name on a bathroom wall?

Lol, no.

I paused. And decided to push the envelope a bit.

Thinking about me and trying not to admit it?

You wish.

Yes, actually. I did. Teasing Mae over the years about a pretend crush on me that she didn't have was nothing new. Neither were her comebacks. They just never bothered me as much in the past.

Deciding not to push my luck any more, I texted back.

I give up.

Just got a TATTOO!

"Holy hell," I said. Pia looked up.
"What is it?"
"Mae got a tattoo."
"Are you serious?"
"I think so."
I texted back:

Didn't see that one coming.

Actually, all three of us are getting them. There's a tattoo shop next to the bar and one thing led to another... the owner of Boots and Brews brought us over to meet the owner. We were going to get it tomorrow morning but the owner said let's just do it now since we're not inebriated. Apparently he won't do tattoos on you if you're drunk. Anyway. Can you believe it?

I fucking loved Mae's paragraph texts. She teased me about my short, one-word ones, and I teased her back for writing dissertations over text message. But I could literally feel her excitement through the phone.

Also, an impromptu tattoo was not Mae. Which I loved for her.

Spread your wings, girl.

Sounds like fun! Show me?

Pia's phone buzzed. She picked it up, laughing.
"Guess they're getting matching ones?"
"Who texted you?" I asked.
"Delaney. She just showed me hers and informed me we're all heading to Kitchi Falls after the baby so I can get one too. They're cracking me up."
"Maybe it's good you didn't go with them," I teased. "What did they get?"
"*Fearless*. Delaney's is on her forearm. It's red as hell but looks amazing."
Pia showed me her phone.

"Nice."

Mae's pic came through.

Catching my breath, I reminded myself it wasn't my first time seeing her bare back. She was in a bathroom, presumably in the tattoo studio. No shirt, or bra. Just Mae's bare shoulders with a dainty "fearless" in cursive starting at the top of her neck and running down her spine. The ink looked fresh, slightly raised, reddened, and covered in a thin layer of clear film, the edges secured with medical tape. Still, it was sexy as hell.

"You okay?" Pia asked.

Shit. No. I wasn't.

Swallowing, I gathered myself back together and showed Pia the picture.

"Oh, wow, that's hot."

Tell me about it.

I texted Mae back those exact words to which she replied:

> Thanks.

Then:

> TTYL, Jules is almost done.

"I can't believe they got tattoos."

"Especially Mae," I said. "Does Delaney have any?"

"Not before tonight." Pia closed her book. "But she's talked about it."

I couldn't get that image out of my mind. Even after Pia went to bed. Or after I headed up myself. Or undressed and stepped into the shower.

*Don't do it, Beck.*

Mae, sliding behind me at the bar. Her fingers brushing mine as we washed glasses. Her laughing, drinking a margarita. Mae's sidelong gaze, sitting in the passenger seat of my truck.

The picture of her new ink.

She'd be standing in my bedroom as I approached from behind. Wearing her white, short puffy-sleeve top with red polka dots and buttons all the way down the front, cutoff jean shorts and cowboy boots, and her hair would be in two loose braids. I would unbutton her shirt. Slowly. Methodically. Tension building with every slip of a button through its hole.

I reached for the soap, lathering it in my hands while pushing aside the promise I made to myself to not get off thinking of a woman I could never have.

*As I slip the shirt from her shoulders, Mae's bare neck gives way to her new tattoo, no longer raw but healed, the delicate black line unfolding down her spine. I trace it with my fingertip, relishing the way her body shivers as I arrive at the bottom, not stopping but dipping below the waistline of her shorts. Mae tries to turn around, and I want to see her face. I want to kiss her, feel her breasts press against me for the first time. But not yet.*

I pumped my hand, faster and faster, the vision so clear in my mind it could have been real. I could see her, smell her.

Taste her.

*I lean down, letting my tongue tease the delicate flesh of her lower back, Mae's bold new ink a guidepost for my exploration. Moving upward, inch by inch, her soft moans encourage me to move ever so slowly even though I want to pick Mae up and toss her onto the bed. My hands hold her waist steady, fingers gripping soft flesh as she calls my name.*

I was so damn close. The vision just real enough, if elusive, for the pressure that continued to build to find its natural end. With a few last pumps, the money shot came as quickly as if Mae was standing in the shower with me. Holding myself upright, water raining onto my head and down my back, I relished its aftermath, reluctant for the sensation to end... for the throbbing to ebb and the reality of the situation to sink in.

She wasn't here.

Wasn't in my bedroom.

Mae would never be in either place, not like that. She wasn't the kind of woman you fucked around with, not that I'd risk our friendship by trying. But damn, it had been a long time since I let myself come, thinking of her. Knowing it was a bad idea, like playing the slot machine despite the fact that the odds were stacked against you... but that picture of her... damn.

Mae.

She'd be the death of me.

# 12

## MAE

"It doesn't hurt, but it's itchy," I said, blissfully drowning myself in coffee.

We gathered around a plate of cinnamon buns, apparently a specialty at the cutest bakery on Main Street in Kitchi Falls. After returning to Boots and Brews post-tattoos and showing them off to Mazzie, we closed the place down.

"When you take off the tape later," Jules said, "just be sure to use the balm to keep it moisturized."

"And keep out of the sun and hot tub?" Delaney asked.

"Who has a hot tub?"

She scrunched up her nose. "I mean, no one. Just in case."

Jules and I laughed. At least she was smart enough to have drunk water in between drinks last night. I, on the other hand, was so excited about the tattoo that responsible all-night drinking flew out the window. Shots to celebrate, way too many vodka sodas, and I was paying the price.

"So what did Pia say about getting one too?" Jules asked, popping a bun into her mouth. She'd already eaten eggs, saying she needed protein to start the day. For me, carbs would do just fine.

"She just laughed, so not sure if she's on board or not." Delaney looked at me. "What did Beck think?"

"How do you know I told him?"

"Because you tell him everything. Or was that picture for your parents?"

Jules laughed. "Wonder what Mr. and Mrs. O'Malley will say?"

I was more concerned about the way Jules was looking at me when she asked the question. I knew her. That was a very suspicious-looking expression.

"What?"

"Nothing."

"Jules?"

I was going to kill her. Delaney was looking on with interest, and this was not a discussion I wanted to get back to Parker.

"Fine. I know you. Something is... off with Beck."

Yep. She was dead.

"Is he okay?" I asked innocently, trying to deflect.

Too late. Delaney was also now looking at me as if I was the latest installment of a relating dating show.

"I don't know. You tell us."

I wiped my sticky fingers on a napkin, dredging up my most nonchalant tone. "I think so. I mean, the whole selling O'Malley's thing was a shock to him. And to me too, actually. But he's seriously considering buying and I hope he does."

"Not what I'm talking about, and you know it."

I looked pointedly to Delaney and then back to Jules.

"If you want this convo in a lock box, just say the word," Delaney said.

I had the subtlety of a marching band. So much for my spy career.

Jules raised an eyebrow. "You've been smiling at your phone like it holds the meaning of life since last night."

I sipped my coffee slowly. "Maybe I just like cinnamon buns." I leaned back, trying to play it cool, but the truth was apparently broadcast through every text notification.

Jules wasn't wrong. I reached for a bun, despite vowing not to eat any more. Now it was just stress eating.

The two of them waited.

Screw it. My life was complicated enough without trying to figure this all out on my own.

"Lock box?" I asked Delaney.

She inserted an invisible key in the air, turned it and tossed it into thin air.

"I have no idea what's going on but it probably has to do with my life blowing up in my face. But with Beck and I working side by side..." I shrugged. "I don't know. Something's... weird."

"By 'weird' do you mean you're attracted to him?" Delaney asked, her voice lacking judgment, which I appreciated. Because honestly, I would judge me. Nothing could be a worse idea than being attracted to a guy like Beck.

"I guess?"

Jules sat back, as if she was about to deliver a UN speech. "Okay, here are the facts for the uninitiated," she said to Delaney. "The two of them have been dancing around each other since middle school. When his family moved outside of town, she was devastated. Cried for a week. And then Beck's family went from well-to-do to high society, and he hated it and rebelled. About that same time, all the other girls started to notice him too, and he's been a man whore ever since, totally turning Mae off to him as anything but a friend. Then he was off to college, she was off to CIA and later France; never the twain shall meet, for any extended period of time, until now. Obviously Beck is still hot, and charming, if you like that sort of thing. You're welcome."

I'd have loved to argue with Jules's version of events, but that was pretty accurate.

"If you like that sort of thing?" I focused on the part of her story not involving me. "Who doesn't?"

"Me," Jules said. "People who smile too much make me nervous."

I laughed. "How many times have you said my positivity is your favorite thing about me?"

"You're different."

"Hold up," Delaney interrupted. "I think we're getting off track. Thanks for the background, Jules. But we're missing a major piece of the puzzle. Namely, Beck's feelings for Mae. The whole 'never date the neighbor' thing."

I froze. Put down my coffee mug. Stared at her.

"The whole... what, now?"

Delaney's hand flew to her mouth. "Oh my God," she said, her words muffled behind her hand but still clear enough. "Shit." Heard that too.

"Delaney?" My pulse raced.

Her hand dropped. "You obviously know about the bachelor pact. I thought you and Beck were"—she crossed her index and middle finger—"like this."

"I do know about it."

"And the rules?"

"Yes, I know about the rules. All three of them. Never stay the night. Never fall in love. Never say 'I do.'"

Jules watched us go back and forth as if watching a ping pong match.

"Four of them," she whispered.

This couldn't be happening.

"I am so sorry. I had no idea you didn't know. Parker never told me not to mention it to you."

"He is a guy," Jules offered. "Details aren't their strong suit."

Delaney didn't appear mollified. In fact, she seemed properly horrified so I tried to reassure her.

"It's fine. Honestly, you didn't do anything wrong. Lock box, remember?"

She exhaled, clearly not convinced. "Beck will kill me."

"Not before I get to him first," I teased. "Tell me what you know."

"Weeell." She took a deep breath. "Just that one of the four rules is 'never date the neighbor' which was made specifically for Beck who, let me see if I remember what Parker said exactly... something about the fact that if you were ever into him it would be 'game over.' Which I took to mean Beck would break the pact."

Not possible. "I don't... this doesn't make any sense. Beck doesn't see me like that at all. He's always treated me like a sister."

"Wonder if that has anything to do with the fact that you've been saying," Jules added, "since high school you wouldn't date him if he were the last guy in the world?"

I had been known to say that.

"Only because he's slept with every pretty girl in Cedar Falls. And not to mention most of its pretty tourists. And has a thing against commitment, hence the pact and all."

"Not to state the obvious"—Delaney shifted in her seat—"but Mason and Parker took the pact too. Things change after college."

"For most guys," I said. "Not Beck."

"And the other one, Cole. He's still all in, I assume?" Jules asked.

"You haven't met Cole?" Delaney asked her.

"No. Not yet."

"Now that one probably won't ever fold. According to Parker, it was his idea in the first place. But Beck?" She shrugged. "I just think he has a little maturing to do."

"A lot of maturing to do. Emphasis on a lot." Jules didn't seem as shocked as me by this fourth rule revelation. I said as much.

"Eh. I always thought he had a thing for you."

"You did?" I asked, incredulous. "You never mentioned that."

"Didn't seem to matter. I always just took the two of you as good friends at face value. Until now. I could tell something was up."

She seemed very proud of her investigative prowess.

"Is something up?" Delaney asked.

As if on cue, my phone buzzed. It was upside down on the table.

"Get it," Jules said.

"No."

"Go ahead," Delaney prompted. "Now I'm fully invested."

They were looking at me like I was about to crack open some long-buried secret.

I sighed and flipped the phone over. One new message. From Beck. I opened it, expecting a meme or some dry sarcasm after I'd sent him a selfie of the three of us in front of the bakery.

Instead:

Kitchi Falls looks good on you.

Short. Casual. But my stomach did that annoying swoop anyway.

I didn't respond right away but just stared at the message a little too long. And then looked up.

"Damn," Jules said, watching me carefully. "That bad?"

I shook my head. "No. Just... Beck being Beck."

But even I didn't believe that anymore.

## 13

### BECK

I sensed her before seeing her. My Mae-dar was firing on all cylinders. Striding toward me, fresh from her weekend trip to Kitchi Falls, Mae wore a pair of jeans and an O'Malley's tee. She smelled as fresh as she looked.

"Reporting for duty," she said, saluting me and heading behind the bar. "You can take off if you want. It's looking slow for a Sunday."

*Get a grip, Beck. There's work to do.*

"Not gonna happen. Guess who I just got off the phone with?"

"Hmm. My dad?"

"Nope."

"Your dad?" She laughed at her own joke.

"Uh, no."

"Yeah, that can't be right. You're smiling. I give up. Who?"

"Someone from the Finger Lakes Flavor Fest. They had a cancellation and wanted to know if we were interested. Apparently the smash burger is"—I grinned—"a smash."

Mae rolled her eyes. "You're ridiculous. But seriously? Dad's been trying to get in there for years."

"I know. Although he didn't even apply this year. Was a little salty about being rejected so many years in a row."

"They're really picky, especially with pub food."

The Finger Lakes Flavor Fest had become iconic in just seven or eight years, thanks to its selective vendors. When I visited a few years ago, I was impressed by the scenic lakeside park setup—food trucks, local businesses, live music, wooden picnic tables, string lights, and waterfront views—attracting locals and tourists alike. For O'Malley's, this was a perfect chance to establish a reputation beyond being Cedar Falls' drinking spot.

Despite myself, I'd begun to start thinking like an owner and not just the manager of the pub. The more I thought about it, the more I realized that maybe the carefree lifestyle I'd held on to wasn't as appealing as I'd always convinced myself it was, and this opportunity to take ownership was starting to feel like something worth considering.

"Exactly. Which is why we have to do it."

"When is it?"

This was the bad news part of the call. "Next weekend."

"Next... what? You're kidding me?"

"Wish I was. We'll need a setup, menu, coverage for the weekend—"

"Holy shit. Beck? In less than a week?"

"Excuse me. Can I get a Yuengling draft?"

The bar was picking up. Dinner crowd.

"Sure thing."

By the time I got his draft, and served a new couple that just sat down, Mae was already running the floor. It went from slow to packed in fifteen minutes, and we didn't get a chance to catch up for over an hour. That wasn't to say I didn't notice her.

Challenging myself to keep my eyes from her, I lasted all of about five minutes when she dropped her pen and bent over to get it, right in front of the bar. Talk about torture. Finally, she disappeared in the back as things slowed back down, presumably to look at the books, something she mentioned doing on Sunday.

"Mom is on the ball," she said finally, re-joining me. "Payroll looks good. I took care of a few invoices but... we really need to talk about this festival. What did you tell them?"

"That we'd do it. Obviously."

"Good."

And that was it for another good hour. May wasn't usually as busy as the summer, with the exception of graduation weekend. The local college always brought in more than a few extra visitors, and I was suddenly glad to have

Mae around. It was too bad she didn't want to take over the bar. She was really good at it.

All of it.

Not just serving. Or maintaining the books. But greeting customers, handling the needy and ornery ones with as much grace as her father. It shouldn't have been any surprise that the service business came so naturally to her.

"Alright," she said, coming behind the bar. "It's apparently gonna be one of those nights. Since we're closed tomorrow, what if we get together and hammer out the details?"

"Sounds good. Come to the inn when you get up?"

"Too much going on there. Come over to me when you're up. 'Scuse me," she said, reaching for the fountain soda.

"I can grab that."

"No worries, I got it."

How I'd forgotten about her tattoo after the shower episode last night, I had no idea.

"How's the new ink? Can't wait to see it."

An understatement.

"Itchy. I'd tell you to pull my shirt down in the back to see it, but I'm pretty sure that would illicit some strange looks." She laughed. "Will show you tomorrow," she called back, carrying a tray of sodas away from the bar.

*Good idea, Beck. Arrange to be alone with her. Ask to see her back tattoo. Maybe I could just tell her that I jerked off thinking about her last night. And add that it wasn't the first time, while I was at it.*

"What's that face for?"

Parker and Delaney. Hadn't seen them come in. I was slipping.

Plastering a smile on my face, I headed over to them.

"You're lucky to get seats. It's been nuts the past few hours."

"Graduation weekend," Parker said. "Delaney was craving a burger."

"What a liar. This was all him," she said.

"All the same to me. You guys can come in every day if you want."

"There's a word for people who drink every day."

"Who says you have to drink? What'll it be? The usual?" I grinned at Delaney. "And a water?"

"With a burger? Get outta here. I'll have an Ultra draft."

I slid their drinks toward the couple.

"Lemme see it?"

Delaney grinned and lifted her left forearm.

"Nice," I said. "Great detail."

"Lucas is a gem. I already have an idea for another one." She looked at my arm. "Is it true what they say, about not being able to get just one?"

"Was for me."

"You're off tomorrow, yeah?" Parker asked. "I'm heading to a new potential site on Seneca, shouldn't take long. Up for some trout fishing?"

"Can't," I said, grabbing an empty from nearby, catching the customer's eyes and raising his glass. He nodded. "Got a call earlier from someone at the Finger Lakes Flavor Fest. They had a last-minute cancelation, so we're in. Only a few days to prep." I slid the guy's filled beer to him. "Heading over to Mae's tomorrow to plan a menu and start securing supplies."

Was it me, or did Delaney's eyes widen?

If there was one thing I knew, it was when a woman was up to something. And Delaney definitely had a look about her all of a sudden.

"That's great. I know you guys have been trying to get in with them for years."

I looked at Parker while he spoke but watched Delaney from the corner of my eyes, a sneaking suspicion making me want to test a theory.

Jenn slipped me a drink order. While I made it, I said to Parker, "We're pretty stoked. Would have come over to the inn but Mae suggested it might be too busy. She has a point."

*There!*

While pretending to concentrate on the drink I was making, I watched Delaney, who definitely looked suspicious, especially when she sought out Mae five minutes later, saying that she wanted to say hello.

When the two of them disappeared into the back, I was convinced.

They'd talked about me on the trip. I'd have bet a hundred dollars on it. The question was... what did they say? More importantly, what did Mae say about me?

Maybe tomorrow would be the perfect time to find out.

# 14

## MAE

I stared at my laptop screen, the words all running together and blurry. Giving up, I closed it and looked out my parents' front window just as Beck pulled up. Watching him stride up the walkway, as I'd done a million times growing up, it was clear something had... shifted between us. Or maybe just me. But there was an awareness that had never been there, or maybe had lurked beneath the surface, which was undeniable. Yesterday at the bar the air had been thick with tension. Not a bad kind of tension, like waking up on the day of a dentist appointment. More like the seconds before you reached the top of a roller coaster hill, knowing the next few moments would be exciting and fun, but also a little scary too.

He wore a hat this morning, always a good look on him. I smiled when Beck adjusted the rim, something he usually did when he was nervous. Not that Beck got nervous all that much. He was one of the most laid-back guys in the world, maybe with the exception of Parker. Sometimes, too much so.

But man, he looked good in a hat.

The front door opened.

"That anxious to see me again, huh?"

"Obviously not."

"Then why you waiting at the window with bated breath?"

"You're impossible."

We headed into the kitchen. It was small but functional, and we'd spent many days in here studying, swapping notes and being fed by my parents.

"Mom and Dad think they found a place," I said as Beck opened the cupboard and grabbed a coffee cup. I turned away before I bored a hole in the back of his jeans. Beck had always filled them out well, but the last thing I needed was him catching me staring at his ass.

"Whereabouts?"

"Well," I said, sitting and wrapping my hands around my own still-warm mug. "They're a little north of where they originally started looking in a town called Delray Beach. They fell in love with the downtown, though I guess it's a little pricier so their dream of oceanfront might not be possible. They have an appointment with the realtor tomorrow to look at a few places."

"Good for them. They deserve it."

I agreed, pushing the box in the center of the kitchen table toward him. "You have to try one of these. There's a bakery in Kitchi Falls known for their cinnamon buns, and they're amazing."

"High praise from the master pastry chef. How can I say no?"

He took one out of the box, and I watched as Beck bit into it, staring at his lips. Blinking, I turned away, opening my laptop.

"Holy shit, you weren't kidding. These would be worth a day trip."

"Right?"

"Speaking of Kitchi Falls, let's see the tattoo." Beck was out of his seat and walking around the table toward me. I shifted so he could lift my shirt, pretending it was no big deal. This was Beck. He'd seen me plenty of times in a bathing suit.

"It's probably easier to lift it up."

He squatted down behind me, smelling distinctly... Beck.

As he lifted up my t-shirt, I wondered if he would touch it. Imagined him tracing the ink with his fingers.

"Oh, wow, Mae, that looks incredible. Hasn't started to peel yet. Nice lines."

"You like it?"

"Love it."

"You can pull my bra strap down to see it better." What the hell was I thinking?

Beck did exactly that. Deep breaths.

"He did a really nice job. I may have to pay this guy a visit."

Letting my bra strap go, Beck released my shirt too. Finally, I could breathe again as he stood up and made his way back around the table.

We needed some sanity here. Normalness. "Okay, so I've been doing a bit of research, and we'll need a temporary food permit from Lakeshore Haven's health department—already emailed the form. We'll need to finalize a menu by tomorrow to get the ingredient orders in, and figure out what we can prep ahead versus what needs to be cooked fresh. Also, we'll need signage, a printed menu, and something that makes the booth stand out. Oh—and do we even have a tent?"

"Whoa, didn't even finish my breakfast."

I gave him a "be serious" look.

"We do have a tent. Remember your dad sprung for that custom pop-up one for the Cedar Falls Brew Bash? The one with the logo and those ridiculous side panels that zip shut like we're running a secret speakeasy?"

"Oh, yeah, you sent me a picture. I was—" Nope, not going to get nostalgic. Mathieu wasn't worth pulling on even one heartstring for. "In France."

"Right. It's in the storage room behind the walk-in. I saw it last week when I was digging for the holiday lights."

"Holiday lights? In May?"

Beck popped a second cinnamon bun in his mouth. "Mmm, these are good." He licked icing from his bottom lip. I bet he was really good with that tongue.

*Yeah, Mae, because of all his experience. You'd do well to remember that.*

"Had the idea of a Christmas in July and wanted to take stock."

He pulled the box toward him. "Only one left." Because of his regular workouts with the guys, Beck had no worries about his physique. "Want it?"

I shook my head.

That smile of his was dangerous. Always had been.

I cleared my throat.

"I sent Pia a text, asking who she uses for their signage. I'm hoping to just get it to someone without having to design ourselves. Will probably have to pay a rush fee."

"That's not a problem," he said, washing a third bun down with coffee. "Thanks for taking care of that. I can check with Pia later too. Either way, we'll need the menu sooner rather than later."

"I have some thoughts on that too." I opened my laptop. "Take a look?"

Beck grabbed the back of his chair and slid in half beside me and half behind me.

"Did you change colognes?"

His expression could only be described as suggestive. "You noticed."

"Only because you've been wearing the same one since sixth grade."

"Not true." He pretended to look injured. "Seventh, maybe."

Laughing, I navigated to the screen with a sample menu and was about to share my ideas when he stopped me.

"Like it?"

I turned my head from the computer to him, wondering if I should be honest or give him the kind of smart ass remark he'd give me.

"Yeah," I said, choosing honesty.

Our eyes met for the briefest of seconds before I chickened out, afraid to hold his gaze, and turned my attention back to the laptop.

"What do you think?"

He scooted forward.

"That you did a lot of work while I slept in this morning."

"It's fun. I like planning events like this. Doesn't feel like work."

I tried not to notice the fact that he was leaning forward to see my laptop screen and only inches away from my face.

*This is Beck. Get a grip.*

"Definitely the pub burger since that's our specialty. And I like the idea of loaded fries, especially the way Rick seasons them, but I don't think they'll be memorable enough. What about the bacon-wrapped jalapeño poppers instead?"

He was right. "Good idea."

"And what the hell is tarte tatin?"

"It's sort of a caramelized upside-down apple tart, served warm with a scoop of vanilla ice cream."

I picked up my coffee mug to distract myself from Beck's nearness.

"Nice. Though I'm partial to whipped cream myself. Especially when it's strategically applied."

I choked, nearly spitting out my coffee.

"You okay? Need the Heimlich?"

Now I was choking and laughing at the same time and couldn't catch my breath.

He picked up my phone from the table and pretended to talk on it. "Need an ambulance right away. My friend is suffering from an innuendo-induced choking fit."

"Beck," I managed. "Stop."

"Yeah, a whipped cream one. Tragic. But honestly, not the worst way to go."

My stomach actually began to hurt, I was laughing so hard, actually imagining an ambulance pulling up to my house.

Beck put the phone down and sat back in his chair, obviously pleased with himself for inciting me to laugh so hard.

"Should I keep going?"

"Please," I begged him. "No."

Catching my breath, I shook my head and gave Beck my best "you're a nut" glare.

"All joking aside, it sounds delicious. I was wondering when I'd get to benefit from this fancy French pastry training you've gotten."

"I made you éclairs when I was back last year, remember? You licked the filling off the spoon before they even cooled."

"I do. But now you're an École Lenôtre graduate. Whole new ballgame."

"Tell me about it. I thought I was coming around to home plate, but I feel like I'm back on first base." He opened his mouth to speak, but I cut him off. "Forget I said anything about bases. Bad analogy."

Beck's grin told me he was indeed going to make another sexual innuendo. One of those for the morning was plenty, thank you very much.

"You'll get there, Mae. It's not a strikeout, just a curve ball. I have no doubt you'll be rounding third base to home, even if it looks a little different than you expected, before long."

I never knew what to say when he pulled out his serious side. Beck was more thoughtful than most people realized.

"Thank you," I said simply.

"Besides, what other choice do you have? With a tattoo that says 'fearless' on your back?"

"True. Seriously though, you should check out Lucas's shop. If you do, we have to hit the bar there too. You'd love the vibe. Maybe the guys would want to come? I could totally see Parker line dancing."

"Sounds good to me. It's a date." He laughed. "I mean, not an actual date."

I was playing with fire, bound to get burned. But since my life was already a dumpster fire...

"Obviously. Can you imagine?"

"You and me?" He shrugged. "Is that so crazy?"

My mouth dropped. "Um, yeah."

Beck crossed his arms. "Because?"

As if we hadn't been through this a hundred times before.

"Because"—I ticked the reasons off my fingers—"one, you're a one-night-stand guy, and I'm a relationship girl. At least, I was. Especially at this stage of my life. Two, we are best friends. Something we don't want to ruin. And three, I am no longer dating anyone. Ever. Too much pain."

He watched me, but said nothing.

I waited.

"Are you done?" he asked finally.

"I suppose."

"One," he started, sardonically. "People change. Two, friendship isn't a bad place to start from. And three..." Beck's impish grin told me the next one would be a doozy.

"*Au contraire, mon amour*. With me, there's only pleasure."

# 15

## MAE

"What are you doing here?" I asked, realizing Beck was a bit of a workaholic. "Thought you were taking the night off?"

Jules was sitting at the bar with a writer friend of hers who was staying in town for the weekend. I'd heard a lot about this guy, Boo, who dressed like a washed-up Oxford professor with Caribbean-blue eyes. Jules told me about his checkered past, including the time he was kicked out of book camp for having sex with the captain's daughter. Although I think she'd phrased it differently. "Porking the captain's daughter," if I remembered right. She'd also left out one important detail... his good looks. I wondered if there was something more than friendship simmering beneath the surface with these two?

"Couldn't stay away," Beck replied.

Jules nearly spit out her drink. Giving her a hard stare, I turned to Beck, who was joining me behind the bar. It had been a bad idea to spill the beans to Jules. She could barely keep a straight face.

"You met with the printer already?"

He jumped right in, refilling a customer's beer without missing a beat.

"Yep. It won't be ready until Saturday morning at eight, but that should be plenty of time. If we're at the park by eight thirty, that gives us two and a half hours of setup."

I'd have preferred to be there sooner, but it would have to do. We'd have a lot of the prep work done already, so as long as we were set up by ten thirty, I'd feel comfortable.

"Hey, Jules." Beck slid past me as she introduced him to Boo.

Only one thing had saved my sanity this week. The distraction of figuring out why my feelings for Beck were complicated as hell had overshadowed my desire to wallow in the black hole that was my life plan. Late this morning, while contemplating Beck's words from Sunday for the umpteenth time, it hit me. I hadn't thought of Mathieu once today. It was a far cry from tossing and turning all night only to wake up, unrefreshed, to stare at the ceiling and think of him some more. Run through the disastrous dinner that changed everything, again. Wonder how I could have been so blind to his narcissistic tendencies, again.

*With me, there's only pleasure.*

"You-hoo? Earth to Mae?"

Beck waved his hand in front of my face. He looked good in navy blue. Always had.

"Sorry, was just thinking of all the things we have to do before Saturday," I lied.

"I'm meeting the suppliers tomorrow morning. If there's anything we can't get or are missing, I'll grab it before heading in."

"I can do that," I said. "You've done so much."

"No such thing. We're a team. Like Tom and Jerry."

I laughed, about to counter that Tom and Jerry were not a team. They were, in fact, enemies. But that was exactly what he wanted me to say. Beck's favorite pastime was goading people.

"Not playing right into your hands," I said instead.

A look flitted across his face, so brief, I could have imagined it. Except, I hadn't. I may not have had the vast experience Beck had with the opposite sex, but I knew enough to be able to decipher *that* look.

I smiled as if I'd won our little battle of wits, but honestly, that round went to Beck. I could feel a fluster making its way to my cheeks and slapped him on the chest with the rag in my hands to cover for it. Then, promptly heading back to Jules, I ignored the fact that Beck was behind me. Talking to a customer. Looking hotter than hell.

"So that's the famous Beck?" Boo asked. "Jules did a good job of describing him."

He'd moved from the bar to the floor. Not that I noticed.

"What did she tell you?"

"She said he was hot, if you liked a cross between surfer dude and Ralph Lauren model type of guy."

That was a fairly accurate description of him, actually.

"But that he knew it, wasn't cocky exactly but didn't turn away from attention. And he got lots of it. And also funny, but with a chip on his shoulder about his family who are filthy rich. Something along those lines."

It was all true. But I knew a Beck most didn't. He was also extremely intelligent and more thoughtful than he let on.

"Sounds about right."

"And that the two of you are in the middle of a"—he cleared his throat—"rediscovery."

"Big mouth."

"As if Boo is going to say anything."

"I wouldn't call it so much of a rediscovery as..." What would I call it? "Maybe me having a midlife crisis."

"At the ripe old age of twenty-six? Pretty sure that's a quarter-life crisis," Jules said.

"Whatever." I wiped the bar under their glasses without much more to do. It had rained most of the day, keeping tourists away. Mid-week it was mostly locals, and they weren't venturing out today.

"So I'm a neutral third party. Give me the scoop. Clearly there's chemistry between you two."

Beck was nowhere to be seen now. Probably in the back.

"There is?" I asked, innocently.

"A hundred percent. I thought the bar might go up in flames a few minutes ago."

Chemistry. Between me and Beck. What was the world coming to?

"The scoop?" What was the harm in laying it all out? "Well, first, we are good friends, and I don't want to ruin that. But more importantly, the reason I never saw him as boyfriend material before, and still don't, is that he has literally slept with half of Cedar Falls and beyond. Beck's a bit of a man whore. On the other hand, I get too emotional, too quickly. It's something I've learned to accept about myself. We'd never work. Also, I was just engaged a few months ago and don't want to jump from that relationship into another one. Especially with someone in the service industry who makes a living being around pretty women. My ex cheated," I added, realizing it was an important point. "I'd like to avoid having my heart broken, again."

"Wow," he said, taking a final sip of his rum and club soda with lime. "That's a lot of negatives."

I took his glass. "Another?"

"Please."

"Bacardi?" I teased.

Boo looked as if he wanted to throttle me.

When I'd asked earlier what kind of rum he wanted, lifting up the Bacardi, Boo had a visceral response that made me laugh when he'd replied, "Jesus Christ, not fucking Bacardi. Mount Gay will do."

I sighed.

There really were a lot of negatives. If Beck was anyone else, I might have agreed with Jules's "get over a guy by getting under another one" advice. Although that would be taking a page more out of Beck's playbook than my own.

Tattoo. Contemplating one-night stands. I couldn't decide if this new Mae was liberated or just repressing her heartbreak in one unhealthy way after another. There was no rulebook on this thing called life. Which was where I started when I returned back to Jules and Boo.

"I wish there was a rulebook on life that could tell me what to do. On one hand, I'm feeling... free. As if I could do anything in the world. On the other, part of me thinks it's just self-destructive behavior to cope with the whole Mathieu thing."

"A rulebook on life." Boo shook his head. "Don't have mine with me, but if you want mine, I'm happy to give it."

"Shoot."

Beck was back. He was talking to Cedar Falls' mayor, smiling up a storm and... Shit. Caught me looking.

"Never get just one tattoo. And as for you and Beck... *memento mori*."

"*Memento*, what?"

He never got to answer.

I nearly fell to my knees at the sight in front of me.

Impossible.

"Mae? What's wrong?" Jules asked, her voice slightly panicked.

"I..." Gripping the edge of the bar, I stared at Mathieu, unable to respond. What the hell was he doing here? In the States? In this bar? I hadn't spoken to him since I blocked his number out of self-preservation when he kept trying to apologize and get me back.

She and Boo turned on their stools just as he approached the bar. Dressed impeccably, as always, he demanded attention... and got it. Every person at the bar was looking at him.

Including Beck.

He wasn't watching Mathieu, though. Beck's eyes were glued to me as he strode toward us. He'd seen pictures of him before, and if there was any doubt Beck knew who he was, it vanished when he stood beside him.

"Are you Mathieu?"

His answer was immediate. "I am."

Without another word, before I could intervene, Beck's arm swung back and then forward, straight into Mathieu's face.

# 16

## BECK

I wanted to go after her.

Truth was, Mae was an adult. If she chose to tend to Mathieu's swollen face, or worse, listen to whatever bullshit he was slinging at her, that was her prerogative. Whether I liked it or not, my place wasn't chasing after her.

It was here, making amends.

"Apologies for what you just witnessed," I said, loud enough for everyone in O'Malley's to hear. "It won't happen again. Drinks on me."

Some went back to what they were doing before the show. Most cheered. One of my regulars said, "He must have deserved it." Their reactions didn't matter though. Owning up to my actions did. Heading behind the bar, now that we were devoid of a tender, I poured myself a shot and downed it. Chatting with my mechanic who was just happy for the free drink, I couldn't say I was entirely surprised when Parker strolled in.

Cedar Falls. You couldn't take a piss without someone getting sprayed.

"That didn't take long." I slid Parker a beer.

"I was already in town. What the hell happened?"

I shrugged. "That French fuck who cheated on Mae walked in here like he owned the place."

Parker waited.

"One punch," Lou called from the other side of the bar, proof no conversation was private in here. "Guy was on the ground. Boy has an iron fist."

Parker lifted his glass as if to thank Lou for his version of events.

"Did he say anything?"

"I dunno. Muttered something in French. Mae didn't give him much of a chance to respond before she dragged him out of here. But not before she screamed at me, ran around the bar and knelt down to assess the damage."

The sight of her expressing even an ounce of concern with the guy who'd ruined her life wasn't one I wanted to dwell on.

"Two Coors Light drafts, one Tito's soda—light ice—and a Jack and Coke," Jenn rattled off at the wait station, already scanning the floor for her next table before flicking her attention back to me. "On the house," she added, teasingly.

While I made the drinks, I caught Parker's curious look.

"An apology to the thirsty folks of O'Malley's."

"Better be careful, Beck, or word's going to get out you're actually a stand-up guy."

"Watch it," I warned him. "I have a reputation to uphold."

"Speaking of which, Mace and I noticed your dry spell."

That was my cue to check on the other side of the bar.

"All good down here?" I asked Lou and the two solo flyers perched at the rail.

Unfortunately, they were all topped off. Reluctantly making my way back to Parker, I tried to strike up a conversation about his fishing trip, something he usually couldn't resist talking about. Until today.

"Tryin' to change the subject. Not suspicious at all. I'm sure your dry spell and Mae's arrival in town, not to mention you clocking her ex-fiancé, isn't at all coincidental."

"Glad we're on the same page. So, about those trout..."

"Sure you don't want to talk about it?"

What was there to talk about? I had it bad for Mae. She saw me as a friend and always would. End of story.

"Nothing to talk about."

"Fine." He gave up. "And the bar?"

A somewhat safer subject.

"I don't know. I've been thinking about some of the changes I'd make as the owner. Has one thing going for it. Doesn't reek of money or bullshit."

Parker laughed. "No one would confuse you and the other Mr. Claymont, even if you owned this place and weren't just a staple behind the bar."

"Don't give a shit about that," I said, flipping a clean rocks glass into my palm and dropping in a cube like muscle memory. I grabbed the bottle of Booker's from the shelf behind me. "Let them think what they want. I know where I belong."

"Not even a little?" he challenged.

Digging in would be lying, something I wouldn't do to Parker, even if I was willing to lie to myself.

"Maybe a little. Now tell me about the trout."

As I expected him to do earlier, Parker regaled me with every detail.

While he talked, I snuck in a text to Mae.

> All ok?

No response.

While Parker waited for takeout that he was bringing back for Delaney, I tried not to think about what Mae was doing. What her ex was saying. What she thought about me, at the moment. Was she pissed? Most likely. Probably should have thought it through first, but honestly... I wasn't sorry. He deserved it for hurting Mae.

Parker was on his phone, likely texting Delaney.

*You know what? Fuck it.*

"The rule was warranted," I blurted.

Parker immediately put down his phone and looked at me.

"No shit, Sherlock."

"Having her home is a double-edged sword," I admitted. "In some ways, it was easier when she was across the Atlantic. And engaged."

"Tell that to past Beck."

I laughed, remembering the night I found out about her engagement. I hadn't taken it well. Dating was one thing. But an engagement, and then subsequent announcement she was taking a job in France? That was an entirely different animal altogether.

Running both hands through my hair, I squeezed my head. Hoping to stimulate some sort of sense out of the whole thing. My brain just wouldn't function properly anymore.

"She's killing me, man." Jenn brought his takeout over. "Nachos won't travel well cold. Forget I said anything."

Parker grabbed his takeout, thanked Jenn and hopped off his stool. "No can do. Off to the house and will be back with reinforcements. Calling an emergency meeting."

Ah, Christ. Parker was all smiles, but it was too late now. I'd shot my big mouth off and, an hour later, wasn't at all surprised to have both Parker and Mason sitting at my bar.

"I know we'd typically call Cole, but this meeting could do without him," Parker said as I served them both.

I agreed. Cole's advice would be as unsympathetic and uncomplicated as my dating life was before Mae came back home.

"What do you got?" Mason asked.

"It's bad," I warned him.

"Worse than having the hots for your new employee? And being the first to break our pact?" he asked.

Fair point.

"I checked my phone at least five times since Parker left to see if Mae texted me back after I clocked her ex a minute after he walked into the bar."

"Ooo," Parker grimaced. "That's bad."

"Agreed," Mason said. "You have a few hundred dollars to spare for the pot?" Mason laughed at his own joke.

"I will if I buy the bar."

"Or take the trust fund you're sitting on," Parker tossed.

"Not a fucking chance. There are more strings attached to that goddamned thing than a puppet show, and I'm nobody's entertainment."

"So give it a go."

Mason really was so black and white that he thought it was good advice.

"Give it a go?"

"Yeah, give it a go. You took a pact. We broke it. You can too."

Was he serious? I looked at Parker, asking the silent question, but he just shrugged his shoulders.

"You honestly think the only thing standing in my way is a pact I took with you dickheads almost ten years ago?"

He shrugged, took a swig of his drink and apparently had nothing else to say.

"Alright." Parker sat up straighter, as if getting serious. "What *is* standing in your way of telling Mae how you feel?"

*Dear lord, give me strength.* I would have been better off getting advice from Jules or her Maine friend. Or my little sister. Maybe should have hit up my mechanic before he left.

"We're listening," Mason said, unhelpfully.

"Let's start with the fact that Mae and I are friends, and that's all she sees me as."

"How do you know?"

"I know."

Parker's hand circled the back of his neck, the way he did when something didn't sit right. "What else?"

"Besides not having Mae's will or consent to date her?" I quipped.

"Yeah, besides that." Mason was in investigative mode now. You could take the cop out of the city, but you couldn't take the badge out of the man.

"I don't want to ruin our friendship."

"Duly noted," Parker said. "What else?"

I leaned back, letting my eyes rest on the bottles behind the bar like they might offer an answer.

"She's been through enough. The last thing she needs is some guy screwing up her peace just because he's catching feelings and doesn't know what to do with them."

Mason raised a brow. "Sounds like her choice, not yours."

"Maybe. But I know myself." I paused. "And I know how this ends if I go in half-assed or still figuring shit out. She deserves better than a guy who's still crawling out from under his family's shadow."

Parker let out a low whistle. "That's poetic. Stupid, since you nearly lost her once waiting for the stars to align. But poetic."

I cracked a grin. "Thanks."

"You want my advice?" Mason asked.

"Do I have a choice?"

Parker made a low sound in his throat, almost a chuckle but not quite.

"I almost lost Pia trying to figure shit out. Don't make the same mistake. Is it a risk, you guys being such good friends? Sure. But what's the alternative, especially if Mae stays in Cedar Falls? Being miserable and punching out every guy she meets?"

Parker picked up what Mason dropped. "You said she sees you as a friend and always has? Could that have anything to do with you chasing every girl but her? Who the hell wants to date the guy who's always chasing tail?"

"What Parker's trying to say is... grow the fuck up, get your shit together and show Mae there's more to you than some smooth lines and a halfway decent pour."

Wincing inside at his words, I couldn't refute them. "Halfway decent pour, my ass."

"Not to mention," Parker added, "sounds to me like you already made your choice. You're just scared she won't make the same one. Which I get more than most. Learn from our"—Parker waved a hand between him and Mason—"mistakes."

"The pact—" I started.

"Was nothing more than four guys who had shitty examples of what being married looked like. Is it a fifty-fifty chance? Maybe," Parker admitted. "But don't throw the whole damn thing out just because your old man couldn't keep it in his pants."

Coming from Parker, it wasn't a dig. His parents split because of his own father's infidelity, and we'd had more than one conversation through the years about it.

I nearly jumped out of my jeans when my phone buzzed.

"Mae," I said, hoping I was right.

I took out my phone, pulse racing at her signature pink icon.

I'm fine. Can you cover tomorrow? I'll text you about Sat. morning to be sure we have everything ready.

"What is it?" Parker asked.

I read them her text.

"Think she's taking off because he's still in town?" Mason asked.

"Why else?"

Neither of the guys said any more. What was there to say? Our entire discussion was a moot point if Mae was taking him back. My stomach turned at the thought. I grabbed a rag and went to work. Didn't really matter anyway. I appreciated the guys' advice, and their perspective having a rocky road with Pia and Delaney to get to this point, but the thought of spilling the beans to Mae... nah. I just wasn't ready to jeopardize our friendship anyway.

*Please don't listen to his bullshit, Mae.*

The next twenty-four hours, until I could see her Saturday, were going to feel like the longest of my life.

# 17

## MAE

The last twenty-four hours had been hell.

After the fiasco at the bar, I dragged Mathieu back to my house and finished where Beck had started. Laying into him for flying here without notice—which would be admittedly hard to do since I blocked him, everywhere—and walking into O'Malley's? I wanted to strangle him.

Against my better judgment, I let him stay at the house but hardly talked to him after our initial confrontation. Yesterday I finally gave in to his pleas and let him say his piece. A flurry of sorrys and I love yous and, "It was the biggest mistake of my life," and after making me feel as if I were crazy for having an issue with him cheating, Mathieu dredged up feelings I'd been trying to bury.

Letting him stay at the house had been a mistake. Between prepping food and coordinating with Beck—my feelings about him were as complicated as ever—I was forced to listen to more of Mathieu's pleas, finally convincing him it was going nowhere. I'd told him I was headed out of town for the weekend, and he had to find alternative accommodations or, preferably, fly back to France, and it was only when his car was on its way that he mentioned taking a train to New York City to meet "a friend." The fact that it really didn't matter to me if the friend was male or female, maybe jumping from trying to get me back one day into another woman's arms the next, told me all I needed to know.

In short, as I'd told Jules last night when she came over to talk about the whole fiasco, it had oddly been a good thing, him pulling that stunt. I was more over him than I'd realized. One of the reasons for it, according to Jules at least, was the very man pulling his pickup in front of my house.

My heart skipped a beat at the sight of him. There was nothing remarkable about his appearance except that he looked... good. In a dark green "O'Malley's Pub" tee and jeans, hair tousled and smile firmly in place, he was just so *Beck*.

"Mornin', Mae," he said, grabbing my overnight bag.

"Good morning," I said, heading back to my front porch to grab the pastry boxes. Meeting me halfway down the sidewalk, he took those from me too.

"Careful. They're tightly packed and can't move."

"Got it."

We loaded up the coolers and stood behind his tailgate.

"I see the flat top strapped down."

"Yep," he replied, all business. "Deep fryer and extra propane are back there. Collapsable prep tables too. All of the coolers are labeled and iced down—"

"We still have an extra-large rental cooler coming though, right?"

"I called them yesterday to verify. Should be dropped off by nine."

"Good. Let's go over the ingredients, just in case." I opened up my notes app and scrolled. "Pastry filling's packed in the cooler, shells are layered with parchment so they don't stick. I've got the glaze in a squeeze bottle, the garnish in a separate container, and enough napkins to run a damn wedding. You grabbed the condiments, right?"

"Yep. Meat and cheese already packed, so we're golden."

"As long as you didn't forget the poppers."

"Poppers are prepped and stuffed and ready to be fried on site."

"You remembered the oil?"

He tapped the dash. "Tucked in next to the propane tanks and flat top. I even brought your fancy sea salt. Don't say I don't love you."

My stomach did a flip. "I'll believe it when the pastries survive the drive."

Business out of the way, I locked up the house and climbed into his truck. He slammed my door closed and joined me.

"Next stop, the printer's, and we'll be good to go."

I gave him a sideways look, not able to recall the last time I'd felt weird around Beck. Between the conversation in my kitchen and Mathieu, my thoughts were a jumbled mess.

"We gonna discuss the elephant in the room?"

Beck looked around his cab. "A, this is a truck, not a room. B, don't see any elephant."

"Be serious, Beck."

"Do I have to?"

"Yes," I said.

He sighed dramatically, as if it was a tough ask. "Fine."

"Maybe start by telling me why you thought punching Mathieu was a great PR move."

"You insinuate I gave it any thought first."

"Beck," I admonished, vowing to take the fact that a part of me relished seeing Mathieu flattened to the grave. "He wasn't worth it."

In response, he closed his right fist, which looked slightly swollen and purple, and shrugged. "It'll be fine. Felt worth it to me."

I refused to smile, even if I wanted to. Encouraging Beck's reckless behavior, even in defense of me, was never a good idea. This wasn't my first rodeo in the "Beck defending my honor" department. I swore it was one of the reasons my dad liked him so much.

"Wait, you said 'wasn't.'"

"Yeah?"

"Not 'isn't.'"

I tried to follow. "Not seeing your point."

"He wasn't worth it. As in, past tense."

"You're kidding, right? Do you seriously think I'd take him back?"

"I don't know. You called off yesterday. Figured it was because he was still in town."

"He was," I said. "Mathieu stayed at my house, begged me to talk. I thought about asking Pia if they had a room, but I honestly didn't want to involve anyone else. What's wrong with you?"

"Nothing."

"Sell that to someone else. Something's wrong. What's up?"

"Would you look at that? We're at the printer's already. Coming in?"

He was frustrating as hell. Thankfully, the signage looked great and was ready as promised. Beck, of course, used the opportunity to change the subject. Or tried to, at least. When he opened my door, I didn't get in. Instead, I propped my foot up on the running board and crossed my arms.

"What?"

"You know what. Spill."

We locked eyes, something shifting in the air between us. It crackled in a distinctively non-"friend" way. This time, I didn't back down. Not that I wasn't scared to explore it, but enough was enough. I was done waiting for the perfect moment, the perfect sign. Because sometimes, the right person was already standing in front of you. Close. Too close.

"I wanted to fucking kill him." Beck's voice was low, gravely. Not at all the lighthearted one I was used to from him. "It was a terrible PR move. Apologized and bought the whole damn bar a drink, on my dime. But I'd do it again, every time. He was an asshole to you, committed himself to building a life with you and reneged before it had even begun. I'm glad he got on a plane to come here, though. Tells me he realizes how badly he fucked up, and I take a perverse sort of pleasure knowing he realizes what he lost."

With every word, my heart rate increased. I couldn't dispute any of his words, and had felt much the same myself. But that Beck had too, on my behalf... I always knew he cared about me as a friend. But...

"Thank you."

His eyes widened.

"You're thanking me for making a spectacle of myself in your father's bar?"

"I'm thanking you for caring enough to defend me. Besides, it won't be my father's bar for long. You're good at so much more than tending bar, Beck. You would kill it as the owner. Why even hesitate?"

I'd managed to surprise him. Beck was never great at taking a compliment, unless it was something superficial, like his looks. But his integrity? Intelligence?

"I can tell you why," I said, Beck not answering. "You care more about playing the irresponsible Casanova bartender than you do letting other people, including your parents, see the real you."

I expected a quip. A joke. This wasn't a revolutionary, life-altering theory I was tossing out, but one I'd offered many times, the new spin being O'Malley's.

But Beck didn't smile. Or laugh it off. Instead, he continued to look at me, dead serious. Before responding, though, his eyes dipped to my mouth. That time, I didn't have to second-guess. Or wonder if I was hallucinating. He didn't even try to hide it.

His gaze lifting back up, Beck parted his lips. But nothing came out. Instead, he did it as if to... entice. Tease. My pulse raced as I waited for him to say something. Core clenching, I caught myself parting my own lips in response.

"You're right, of course."

What had he just said?

No response could have been more of a surprise. It was the first time in our lives Beck had agreed with me or even pretended to have a serious discussion about him or his future. I honestly had no comeback.

"Now let's go, buttercup. Can't be late for our own food tent."

Somehow, I hopped back into the truck. Made conversation with Beck for the rest of the ride, albeit nothing as deep or serious as in front of the printer's shop.

The way he'd looked at me... really looked at me. Listened. And actually agreed with me? I'd been right earlier. Something was up. And tonight, after the day's festivities, in the B&B we'd reserved knowing it would be a late night and early morning, I would find out exactly what that was.

# 18

## BECK

By the dinner rush, we were a well-oiled machine. Aside from a little grill fiasco and me nearly torching my eyebrows trying to fix it, everything ran smooth. We couldn't have asked for a nicer day, and clearly the festival gods were looking down on us. Stationed directly across from a fresh-cut fries stand, after chatting with the owner during setup, we were working together to send customers over and vice versa.

Even better? The company. I couldn't wipe the smile from my face since this morning's drive. Mae wasn't pissed off at me for clocking her ex. And that ex was firmly in the past-tense category.

*If you're not "going there," why does it matter, anyway?*

"Earth to Beck?"

I turned from the grill to focus on Mae.

"Got 'em coming right up," I said as the customer on the other side of the table watched me.

"Add another burger to that order," she said.

"On it."

"And don't forget—"

"The jalapenos," I finished. "Have 'em right here."

A new customer walked up. Cute redhead in cutoff shorts who ordered two smashburgers with extra cheese. "You come with that?" she called over to me.

Mae waited for my response. Her eyebrows lifted in amusement, but something flickered in her eyes... barely there, but I caught it.

I smiled, kept my eyes on Mae.

"Sorry. Already spoken for."

Mae snorted. "By who?"

"Depends on who's asking."

If my response confused Mae, the redhead was even more bemused but got the hint. I had more let-down lines than a tap on dollar beer night.

*Wouldn't need one if Mae was mine.*

A dangerous thought.

Miraculously, as the dinner crowd began to die down, we had a break in customers. Mae wiped the table and made her way over to me.

"This is so much fun. Do you know how many people asked about the bar?"

"Lots, I hope. Come here."

Without hesitation, she took a step toward me. I reached up, wiping powdered sugar from her cheek. "You're supposed to serve your fancy French pastries. Not wear them."

Her skin was so smooth. I imagined cupping that cheek with my hand, just before I kissed her. Turning away from temptation, I used the break to clean my grill.

"I was a little worried about them." She sat on the folding chair beside me. I think it was the first time either of us had used it all day.

"Why?"

"I love them, and knew they'd keep well, but wasn't sure if they'd fly with burgers and stuffed peppers."

"Your dad always thought bringing your talents to O'Malley's would work. Give the guy some credit for knowing his customers."

"I guess. But it's different out here." She gestured to the crowded tents and food trucks surrounding us. With a clear view of the lake and dusk beginning to let the multitude of white bulb lights do their thing, the Flavor Fest could only be classified as a success. We were far enough away from the makeshift stand that the music wasn't overly loud.

"Different than it would be, serving it in the pub, you mean?"

"Yeah," she said, getting up as a young teen couple approached.

"Only one way to find out. Let's get them on the menu as a special."

"Excuse me."

I looked up to find a reporter and her cameraman standing in front of me.

"My name is Krista Loomer with FLR News. Mind if we shoot a live feed from your booth?"

"Hell no. Just give us a sec to fulfill this order," I said, cooking up two burgers. "Mae, want to take these and say hello to the local news?"

The next few minutes were a flurry of camera checks and Mae quickly re-braiding her hair. I could watch her do that all day, her fingers nimbly flying through the golden strands like she'd done it a million times before, because she had. Predictably, she applied lip gloss—Mae was addicted to it and kept them everywhere she went—looking as fresh as if we'd just started serving.

"So are you guys the owners?" she asked.

Mae and I exchanged a glance, smiling at each other.

"Husband and wife?"

"No." Mae explained our situation while I contemplated the idea. We'd be good together, Mae and me. No doubt. Marriage wasn't something that excited me, but with Mae? All bets were off.

"Okay, ready?" the reporter asked, making a motion for the cameraman to begin rolling.

"Good evening, Finger Lakes! Krista Loomer here, coming to you live from the heart of Flavor Fest where the grills are hot, the pastries are sweet, and the local talent is even hotter. I'm standing in front of the O'Malley's Pub tent. Organizers tell me this stand is a late addition but we've noticed it's been drawing major crowds all day. Serving up handcrafted smashburgers, jalapeño poppers, and... get this. French pastries that have festivalgoers telling us it's their favorite dessert here."

I'd wondered why she'd chosen our tent, since we weren't local, and couldn't be happier at the reason.

"I'm here with one of the masterminds behind the menu, O'Malley's manager Beckham Claymont."

Beckham, nice. Mae could barely contain a grin. I should have paid more attention as she talked to the reporter. "Mr. Claymont, can you tell us what inspired this delicious pairing?"

"The smashburgers and jalapeno poppers were no-brainers. The three most popular things at O'Malley's are our ice-cold beers and those two menu items. But the tarte tatin was Miss O'Malley's idea. She received the Jacques

Delacroix Culinary Arts Grant at the Culinary Institute of America and just returned from studying under the world's most famous pastry chefs in France. I'll let her tell you about it."

The reporter moved her microphone to Mae, who talked about tarte tatin and why she loved it. Mae was a natural on camera, as photogenic on video as she was in pictures. Fact was, Mae had very few bad qualities, aside from being more self-sacrificing than she should. For the life of me I couldn't understand how her ex could fumble this woman. He really was the stupidest fuck in the world.

"Luckily for all of you," the reporter concluded with a smile, "there's still one more day to check it out. The festival opens its gates at eleven tomorrow, so come taste for yourself what's drawing such a crowd. That's it from Flavor Fest. Now let's head over to Brett for a look at your Sunday weather."

With that, the camera light went out as the reporter shook both of our hands. "Thanks so much, you guys were great. I'll have to get down to Cedar Falls to check out that menu in person."

"We look forward to it," Mae said as the reporter and cameraman walked away.

"You were perfect," I started. "Except—"

Mae broke down in laughter before I could finish.

"Real funny. Next time we get interviewed on live TV, I'll be sure to mention your first culinary attempt—feeding brownies to the neighborhood."

"You wouldn't dare."

"Oh, look, customers."

Mae frowned before stomping off, apparently not amused, just because the brownies were so undercooked her "customers" needed a spoon to eat them.

Shooting me a glare that was undermined by the corner of her lips lifting ever so slightly, we finished out the day serving mostly desserts. By the time we packed up and jumped in the truck, I was exhausted. Thankfully our B&B was less than a ten-minute drive from the grounds.

"I brought a bottle of wine. Know it's not your favorite, but I can't drink it all by myself."

"If that's an invite to your bedroom, Mae, the answer is yes. I'll drink Jeppson's Malört if you're leaving the adjoining door to our rooms open for me."

I'd never uttered a truer statement despite the fact that Mae took it as a joke.

"How do you know we have adjoining rooms?"

"Asked for them specifically."

"Why? And the real question is why would they give them to you?"

"Said we were coming for the festival and didn't want to walk far between rooms."

Mae snorted. "You mean you didn't trust me not to wander off?"

"No, I didn't trust *me* not to knock on your door."

"You're impossible."

Over the years, we'd had hundreds of similar conversations. The thing was, over time, they lost their effect. Mae always thought I was joking because she'd made her stance on us getting together crystal clear.

*I almost lost Pia trying to figure shit out. Don't make the same mistake.*

*Grow the fuck up, get your shit together and show Mae there's more to you than some smooth lines and a halfway decent pour.*

Except, I wasn't joking. Less now than ever before.

## 19

### MAE

The B&B was much smaller than Heritage Hill, probably a third of the size. But Parker knew the owner and had arranged it for us, which we appreciated since the first few places we called were sold out for the weekend. Technically, we could have headed back to Cedar Falls for the night, but having to replenish a few ingredients in the morning before setup was going to make for an early wake-up call as it was.

"Cute place," I said as we waited to check in.

"Can I help you?"

Beck stepped up to the counter as I wandered around the front room that served as the lobby. The house was on the same lake as our festival, heading south. Reading an article on the wall, I learned it was owned by a husband and wife, the latter of which was helping Beck now. The article, from over twenty years ago, mentioned she was a chef.

I wandered over to the counter.

"And these are your keys," the older woman said. "Up those stairs, the last two rooms on the right."

"The article over there," I said, pointing to the wall, "said you were a chef before you and your husband converted this into a bed and breakfast."

"I was," she said with a friendly smile, the wrinkles at the corner of her eyes a testament to how many times she'd greeted someone like me in her lifetime. "Met my husband at CIA. We ran a little place in New York City, where he's from, until trading the chaos for calm. Bought this place, fixed it up and never looked back."

"I'm a CIA grad too."

Her smile widened as Beck listened, not saying anything.

"Best decision I ever made. Cooking for people. It's still the heart of this place."

I didn't say anything right away, but my chest warmed the way it did when I felt a pull toward something meaningful. Maybe it was this place. Or maybe it was hearing someone speak with certainty about a life she chose and built with someone she loved.

I'd thought I was on that path too.

"How about you?" she asked.

The dreaded question.

"We just came from the Flavor Fest," Beck jumped in. Grateful, I let him talk. "Got in on a last-minute entry."

"The others here tonight are festivalgoers too. But sounds like you had a booth?"

"Sure did. O'Malley's Pub and Eatery, in Cedar Falls."

"You cook there?" she asked me.

"My father owns the pub. I just got back from France where I was training to be a pastry chef. As you can imagine, job opportunities are few and far between around here."

"You'd be surprised," the woman said, settling back into her chair with her tea. "People don't just come to small towns for the views anymore. They come for the experience. The story. A warm croissant from someone who learned in France? That's not just food—it's memory-making."

I smiled. Thinking.

The woman continued. "I had a guest once... a pastry chef from Boston. Burned out. She came here for a weekend, ended up staying six months. Taught a baking class at the community center and said it was the happiest she'd been in years."

"That so?" Beck said, stealing a glance at me.

The woman just shrugged. "Sometimes the dream changes. Or maybe you just find it in a place you didn't expect."

"Cedar Falls would definitely qualify."

"Mae's tarte tatin were a huge hit," Beck boasted. "Even served with burgers and stuffed jalapenos. As a matter of fact, by midday tomorrow we'll most likely be sold out."

The innkeeper looked impressed.

"Is that so?" Her eyes narrowed as she looked at me. "Would you be interested in making some for us? Pastry isn't exactly my husband's or my specialty."

That was an easy one. "Absolutely. I love making them. That sounds great."

"Do you have a card?"

Shit. A card.

"Here's mine." Beck pulled one from his wallet. "I can connect you."

"Claymont. As in—"

"Bottling. Yep." If Beck tried to keep the bitterness from his tone, he failed. Helping him let go of the resentment for his parents had been a years-long quest. Beck thought it equated to forgiving them, but I just wanted him not to hold hate in his heart. He'd never have a perfect relationship with them, and that was fine. He could have no relationship, if he wanted.

"You two must be exhausted. I don't mean to keep you from your rooms. They're just up there." She addressed me. "I'm looking forward to working with you."

"I am as well."

And I really was. At least I'd have a purpose again, even if it was just for one job.

We headed upstairs, Beck grinning the whole way. He was clearly proud of himself for hyping me, and I had to admit to being extremely grateful.

"Still coming in for a nightcap or too pooped?" he asked as we arrived at our rooms.

"I'm tired," I admitted. "But doubt I can go right to sleep. Leave your door open," I teased as Beck saluted. Somehow, as I entered the room, small but lovely and quaint, that quip had felt different. Beck and I had a years-long history of him "hitting" on me, and me turning him down or teasing back. But ever since Kitchi Falls... and then my kitchen... things had been off. It was suddenly hard not to notice him.

So what had changed?

Beck was still the playboy he'd been since girls started to notice him. I saw the way he'd talked to the women at the bar that first night in town. Every time I asked what he'd been up to or who he was dating these past few years, it was never the same name.

Unpacking, I pulled out my yoga pants and tee and headed to the shower just as the adjoining door unlocked. I held my breath, but nothing happened. I told him to unlock it, so why was I standing, frozen, as if some portal to another world had just been opened?

Making my way to the shower, pleasantly surprised by the scented body wash, having forgotten my own, my mind wandered to the next room. Beck was likely showering right now too. I could picture him slicking his hair back with both hands like he did, exposing every inch of his face. What made him so good-looking, anyway? His jaw line? Lips? Or was it Beck's eyes? He'd never been shy at holding eye contact, something I'd noticed way back in high school.

Unbidden, a thought of the rest of Beck popped into my head.

He, Cole and Mason had been trying to one-up each other in the physique department for as long as I could remember, and the friendly competition had benefited all three of them.

Swallowing, trying to push the thought of naked Beck from my mind, I turned off the shower and dried myself.

It was his smile.

That plus Beck's confidence was what made him so attractive. It also didn't hurt that, unlike most of the world, I knew the guy inside who carried wounds he rarely let anyone see. Everyone else knew him as the slick bartender, as smooth with a tossed bottle as he was picking up women. But I knew him as the one who plugged me on the news... who may have gotten me a connection here by singing my praises.

Leaving my hair wet and loose so it could air dry, I made my way back to the room, grabbed the two glasses and bottle of wine and stood in front of the adjoining door, pausing.

*This is silly. It's just Beck.*

Knocking first, I pushed the door open and called in.

"Are you decent?"

"No, but come in anyway."

I wasn't sure if I wanted it to be true or not, but as I stepped inside, zero percent of me was surprised to see him fully dressed in sweats and a white tee.

"You're ridiculous. Oh, shit."

"What?"

"I forgot a wine opener. I swear I was so focused on the festival I left half my stuff at home. No body wash, no toothpaste and now no wine opener."

"No body wash? Eww."

I rolled my eyes. "I used the inn's, you ass."

"I suppose you can borrow my toothpaste," he said, reaching for the wine bottle. "Gimme that."

What the hell was he going to do with it without an opener?

"I can ask—"

"I got it," he said, picking up his sneaker.

"What in the ever-living hell are you doing?" I asked as Beck made his way into the bathroom. I followed.

"Don't want to put a hole in the wall. Or get wine all over the carpet."

Jumping into the bathtub—still wet from his shower—Beck placed the bottom of the wine bottle in his sneaker, lifted it, and began pounding the sneaker against the fiberglass wall.

"Beck," I started, but he wasn't listening.

He pounded again, checked the cork, then did it once more. I was about to stop him when the cork popped out. Beck jumped back from the dribble of wine that escaped and held the bottle upright, completely uncorked. I stared at him, amazed.

"What other hidden talents do you have?"

Beck's suggestive grin told me immediately I shouldn't have asked.

"I'd be happy to show you."

# 20

## MAE

"You're such an ass."

I left the bathroom laughing. But also...

"We are not drinking wine from those," Beck said, catching me as I picked up our glasses.

"What do you propose... Beck? Where did you get wine glasses?"

He proceeded to pour the wine that he'd opened with his sneaker into each glass.

"Ellie."

"Um. Who's Ellie?"

He handed me a glass.

"Your first client."

Sitting in the armchair in the corner of the room, I curled my legs under me, taking a sip of wine. For as hard as we worked, I should be more tired. And I was, but also... content.

"I feel like an idiot. I didn't even ask her name. Some businesswoman I am. She won't be a client for long."

Beck lifted his filled wine glass to me, sitting on the bed, propped up against the headboard. "*Au contraire.* I went down after my shower and asked for proper wine glasses. Made sure Ellie knew how grateful we were for getting us in here last minute and told her you were excited about working with her. All's well."

Air toasting, I took another sip.

"You know, I get it."

"Get what?"

"Why women fall at your feet, despite the fact that you've slept with half of Cedar Falls. You can be extremely charming, Beckham Claymont."

"First of all, you know how much I love that name," he said, clearly meaning just the opposite.

"I do. Which is why I use it. It's a great name."

"My parents don't even pretend it's anything other than pretentious. I swear they found it by looking at Yale attendance rosters. Beckham. Seriously."

"You're ridiculous."

"Second," he said, ignoring me, "I haven't slept with more than a third of Cedar Falls, at most."

"My bad," I said, keeping my tone light despite the sudden, and unexpected, pang in my chest at the thought.

"Third," he said, "I appreciate you're finally getting my appeal."

This was tricky territory. "I always have," I admitted. "To a woman looking for a good time, I get it. You are good-looking, charming, etcetera, etcetera."

He had that "look" about him. The one that drew in countless women.

"Let's explore those etceteras."

"Now you're just fishing for compliments," I accused.

"Maybe."

"Well, you're not getting any more from me."

"No?"

"No."

Shrugging, he took a sip of wine, watching me.

"What?" I asked.

"Nothing."

"You're looking at me weird."

"Anytime I get serious, you think it's weird."

"True. What's with the serious face all of a sudden?"

It was getting harder and harder not to notice Beck, now that I had, in *that* way.

"I can be more than a good time."

The words didn't penetrate, at first. They were so unlike anything Beck had ever said, I had to run the phrase through my head a few times. He needed to clarify.

"Meaning?"

"Meaning, I have real relationships. With you. With the guys. With my sister. I'm capable of them."

"Of course you are. But we're talking about something entirely different. Romantic relationships are a whole different beast, and that's not something you're into."

"People change." Beck downed his wine, hopped off the bed and went for more.

"You do realize wine is meant to be sipped, right?"

"You do realize I've been bartending since college? This is kinda my forte." This time he sat on the edge of the bed with his full wine, closer to me.

"Just checking."

"Mmm hmm."

"So," I ventured. "Have you changed? I thought the whole pact was about you never wanting to get married. Color me confused, but how do you get involved in a serious relationship if you have no intention of getting married?" Then realizing that wasn't quite right, I added, "Unless you're in a relationship with someone who also doesn't want to get married, I guess."

"Mason and Parker took the pact too, and look at them."

"True. But we're not talking about Mason and Parker. We're talking about you."

I was surprised Beck hadn't slipped into "just kidding" mode. He was rarely serious for this long. It was that fact, and something about his demeanor, that told me this wasn't a throwaway conversation for him.

"All I'm saying is that with the right person, I could be more than a good time."

"You'd consider getting married to someone?" I asked, shocked. More than shocked.

"Maybe."

"What prompted the three-sixty?"

He didn't answer. Instead Beck looked at me, like he wanted to respond but... hesitated. Took another sip of wine.

"Must be the wine talking," he said finally. "Or maybe I hit my head in the bathtub."

Beck was back to being Beck.

"I still can't believe you got the cork out that way."

"Like I said, I'm a man of many talents."

A heady thought. What would Beck do if I climbed onto that bed and asked him to put his money where his mouth was? To show me one of those talents. I'd never know. The thought was ridiculous.

"My glass is empty," I said, reaching out my hand toward the wine bottle.

He laughed. "What are you doing?"

"Trying to use the force to bring the bottle to me so I don't have to get up. I'm cozy."

"By 'the force' do you mean me?" Putting his wine on the nightstand, he hopped off the bed again, got the wine bottle and brought it to my uplifted glass.

"Maybe," I admitted.

"Maybe my ass. Definitely."

I looked up at him as he poured, but despite the teasing, Beck wasn't smiling. Instead, he was looking at me, not turning his gaze away.

I stared back, the stirrings of something I promised myself not to go near again bubbling to the surface. It was like when we'd texted while I was in Kitchi Falls. Except this time, we weren't in two separate towns but right next to each other.

In the same bedroom.

He finished the pour but didn't move away.

# 21

## BECK

I envisioned myself squatting down in front of her, eye to eye, and confessing everything. But imagining her look of horror, realizing I'd just ruined our friendship, prompted my legs to finally work. Retreating back to the bed, I vowed no more talk of relationships or people changing, so for the next twenty minutes, we kept the conversation light.

Safe.

The festival. O'Malley's future. Her parents' condo hunt. Mae worked out the kinks of making and delivering pastries here and wondered if there might be other establishments, inns and bed and breakfasts that might want to order too. She nearly spilled her wine twice, her hands flailing around in excitement over the idea.

I loved seeing her like this.

"What are you smiling about?"

*You.*

"Nothing in particular. Definitely not at the state of our wine."

My glass was empty. The bottle was empty.

Mae sighed dramatically.

"Fine. Ugh." She stood. "I could have slept in that chair."

"I wasn't kicking you out."

She put her empty glass on the dresser. "I'm out too. A sign from the universe that we should get some sleep."

I got up from the bed. "What time does the universe think we should get going tomorrow? The supplier is meeting us at nine."

Mae thought about it. "We have to get downstairs for breakfast. So maybe ready to leave by eight which gives us forty-five minutes to eat and head out?"

"Works for me."

She opened the adjoining door, said "good night" as she had a thousand times before, and disappeared through the door. I stood there, wanting to close mine and get some sleep. But I also wanted to call her back. Tell her, despite the empty wine bottle, it didn't matter to me how tired we'd be tomorrow. That I wanted her to stay.

*Idiot. Why are you tormenting yourself this way?*

Instead, I lifted my t-shirt and tossed it on the dresser, reaching over with my other hand to close the door, when Mae's whipped open.

"I almost forget to tell..."

Whatever she was about to say was lost. Mae's eyes dipped down to my chest before flying back up to my face. I could easily break the tension with a quip about not having to pretend to forget to tell me something. That she could admit she secretly wanted to see me undressed.

But the words stuck in my mouth.

I wasn't the only one frozen in place.

"Mae."

Having no idea what I was about to say, I was fairly certain I'd just given myself away. My voice was thick, unnatural. Filled with a need for this woman unlike anything I'd ever experienced before.

She blinked, wide-eyed and as beautiful as ever. Evening gown, sweats and a tee... didn't matter. If it were any other woman, I'd have kissed her by now. The signs were all there. But... this was Mae.

I had to be sure.

Just when I was about to do that, her lips parted in a telltale sign, coupled with the way she looked at me, and her silence... she wanted me to kiss her.

And I was more than happy to oblige.

I took the one step necessary to close the distance between us, reached behind her head and pulled Mae toward me.

"Beck." Her hands shot out, I thought to push me away, but instead lay on my bare chest, as if to brace herself. She would need it.

Bringing my head down, I captured her lips in mine.

They were softer, tasted better and fit more perfectly in mine than I ever could have imagined. Her hands moved from my chest to my shoulders, Mae gripping me as if to hold me in place. As if I was going anywhere.

Tongues tangling, the kiss was frantic and urgent, as if neither of us could get enough.

*I am kissing Mae.*

Surely this was a dream, and I'd wake up any second. Instead, a soft moan that I would hear in every one of my dreams from this day forward came from her mouth.

I'd paid dearly for all the times I'd kissed the wrong women. But if it taught me one thing, it was... when it came to Mae, I would never, ever waste a second.

I would kiss her until she forgot every man before me.

And until the only thing she remembered was us.

My hands moved to the back of her head, pressing Mae against me, leveraging the closeness of our bodies to deepen the kiss. She tilted her head, giving me full access, one I took advantage of, ensuring every moment would be a memorable one.

If we were a cartoon, stars and hearts would surround us, the moment exactly as I dreamt it would be... and more. I could kiss Mae all night.

We fit perfectly together.

Too perfectly.

I pulled away. Not because I wanted to, but because this was getting all too real.

"If I don't stop now, Mae," I murmured, wondering if she could hear the shakiness in my voice, "I'm not gonna be able to."

She stepped back, our arms falling away.

I was struggling to breathe, regretting ending the kiss. But I hadn't been lying. That kiss had escalated to something more so fucking quickly.

"What have we done?"

I hated how stricken she looked, as if Mae already regretted it.

"I'm pretty sure we kissed."

Her smile was back, thank God. "Really? Is that what that's called?"

I smiled back, hoping to reassure her we could be... us. Mae and Beck. That it wasn't the end of anything, but maybe the start of one.

"I don't know... I can't believe we did that."

"Do you regret it?"

She blinked. "No. I mean, I don't know." Mae let out a breath. "I think I should go to bed."

I wanted to disagree, but rushing something as complicated as... that wasn't a great idea.

"Agreed."

"Alright then. Good night," she said, taking another step back.

As much as neither of us wanted this to be awkward, there was no escaping the fact that it was awkward as hell. "Good night, Mae," I said, trying to keep my tone light. Casual.

I stepped away from the door frame, winked like I might have done even without the kiss, as we closed the doors at the same time.

But I didn't move from that spot. Instead I stared at it, seeing us as if I were watching a movie with Mae and me as the main characters.

That was... incredible. Earth-shattering. Perfect.

If I had any doubts, they weren't about our chemistry. Mae deserved more than Mathieu, and I was certainly a step above that French asshole, but I was nowhere close to perfect for her.

I was a loaded gun with no safety, just waiting for the wrong moment to go off. The smart move would be to walk away now, before either of us got hurt. But standing there, heart pounding like a fucking drum in my ears, all I wanted was to tear that door back open and finish what we started.

# 22

## MAE

Knocking on Beck's door after a night of very little sleep was not something I relished doing. But it was five after eight, and he hadn't made a peep yet this morning. Probably because he was as mortified and utterly confused as me.

We hadn't just kissed.

That was, as my mind continued to replay it over and over, an experience.

Lying on my bed last night, part of me wanted to reverse time and have a do-over where I went to sleep the first time. A do-over that didn't jeopardize our friendship. But another part of me, a bigger one if I were being honest, actually wanted just the opposite.

To kiss him again.

The door opened. A smiling, freshly showered Beck, as if he hadn't a care in the world, stood in the same spot as the scene of the crime. Was it me, or had he gotten even hotter since last night?

"Morning, Mae."

"Good morning."

"Ready to rock and roll?"

"I am."

"Cool." He reached out, taking my overnight bag from my shoulder.

"You don't have to do that."

Beck headed to the bed, popped his toiletry bag inside his own duffle, and slung it on his shoulder. "Now what kind of gentleman would I be if I didn't?"

"Who says you're a gentleman?"

"Ouch. You don't play fair."

And just like that, as we headed downstairs, we fell right back into our old pattern of busting each other's asses and being... well... normal. Except, nothing was normal about this morning at all. Apparently we weren't going to talk about the kiss. I certainly wasn't going to bring it up. What the hell would I say?

*Soooo, about that kiss?*

We had a pleasant enough breakfast, Ellie introducing us to her husband and another couple who were already eating breakfast when we got down there. The only exception? When we both reached for the pepper at the same time and our fingers touched, at which point I pulled quickly away. I promised to follow up with Ellie when I got home, and just like that, the day started without any fanfare. On the short drive to the festival grounds, we discussed preparations. We tried to predict when we would run out of pastries... I said after the lunch crowd, Beck predicted earlier.

One thing we didn't talk about?

The kiss.

I couldn't take it anymore. Was Beck seriously going to pretend it didn't happen? Just as he was firing up the grill, I leaned against the table beside it, crossed my arms, and waited.

"Nice day for a festival," he mused, pulling an apron over his head.

"You're seriously going to talk about the weather?"

Beck's laugh always had a way of wiggling itself into my soul. "I don't want to make you uncomfortable, Mae. Just taking your lead."

"Well, it feels like something we should talk about."

"Agreed."

He wasn't making this easy.

"Or..." He was about to say something cheeky. I could just tell. "We could just do it again, instead."

I swatted him on the arm with the rag I was holding as the fry guy across from us approached.

"Morning, guys. All ready for another nice day?"

He was around my dad's age, maybe a little older. Didn't have a brick and mortar but worked festivals and loved it. Apparently "life on the road" was for him. He looked like a cross between Larry David and a weathered rock star, all wiry energy and mischievous grin.

"I can't imagine doing this year-round," I said, shaking my head as I wrung out the rag. "You must really love deep fryers and porta-potties."

"What's not to love?"

Beck snorted as the two of them traded barbs. Two peas in a pod. But really, Beck could get along with just about anyone. I watched as they talked, realizing it really was a strength of his, making everyone around him comfortable.

He was the perfect person to take over Dad's bar. I had no doubt O'Malley's would thrive with Beck at the helm. I had to talk to him on the way back about why he was so hesitant about it.

That wasn't the only thing we had to talk about on the way home, but it was clear our "kiss" conversation would have to wait. After fry guy, one of the event organizers stopped by, along with the owner of a local restaurant looking for partners for a fall festival he was planning. Apparently my tarte tatin was making the rounds.

"Mae O'Malley," a cheerful voice called from behind my current customer.

"Thayle," I exclaimed as she waved excitedly. Standing beside her husband, one of the owners of Grado Valley Vineyards, my long-time friend finally made it to the counter.

"You remember Neo?"

"Of course," I said. "How's GVV doing?" I asked them both, grateful there was nobody behind them yet.

"Couldn't be better," he said. Neo was the winemaker for the vineyard he and his siblings owned. I'd met Thayle over email first. She was a long-time customer, and I'd contacted her with a question about the wine club which she ran. When we finally met in person, we hit it off immediately.

"You have to come down one of these days now that you're back in town. Is it for good?"

I hadn't spoken to her in person in over a year. "Lots has happened since we talked last. Long story. But I'm back from France for good. Just not sure about next steps. Working for Dad until I figure things out."

"I saw the sign and wondered if it was the same O'Malley's." Two teen girls got in line behind her. "Let's catch up when you have time. Actually, we're having a girls' night next Thursday. Come down and bring some friends. I'll see if we have an empty cottage."

"Actually," Neo said, "I know we do. Remember Brooke telling us the bachelorette party cancelled. They were coming Thursday to Saturday and had three booked."

"That's right," she said. "I'll make sure one stays empty if you promise to come."

"Girls' night at a winery. Cottage on the lake. You drive a hard bargain."

Thayle laughed. "Gotta look out for my girls. I'm counting you in. How about two burgers and one of your pastries, obviously?"

"Obviously," Neo quipped beside her.

I called the burger order to Beck, realizing this could be a blessing in disguise. If anyone was perfectly positioned to help me navigate the Beck situation, it was Thayle Burke.

"On the house," I said as Neo pulled out his wallet. I handed the pastry to Thayle who stepped aside, letting the girls order.

Beck slid two burgers to them as I handed back change to the girls as I pushed aside thoughts of the kiss that crept into my head.

"Do you remember Thayle and Neo from Grado Valley?" I asked him. We'd been there more than once together with a few other people, the last time about two summers ago.

"Of course." He grabbed a rag, wiped his hands, and stuck out his right one to one of them at a time. "Good to see you again. Hope you're enjoying the festival."

"I had to pull him kicking and screaming away from the vineyard," Thayle said. "The downside of owning your own business."

"Funny you should say that." I gave Beck a sidelong gaze.

"Don't look at me," he said. "You're the one who got a new client this weekend."

"Client? What?" Thayle asked. "You'll have to tell me all about it Thursday. Go ahead, we don't want to keep you from your customers."

"I'll see you soon," I said, blowing her a kiss and waving to Neo.

They stayed and talked to Beck while I took care of the girls, and then another couple, and before long I couldn't think about anything, even Beck's kiss, for long as the lunch crowd picked up. As he predicted, the tarte tatin sold out before one o'clock which really did surprise me based on our estimates from the organizers' numbers.

Every so often, I'd glance back at Beck, who was either cooking or peeking at me. We kept things light, professional, all afternoon, and it was actually less awkward than I expected.

Until it wasn't.

I couldn't remember having been this distracted in my life, thoughts of our kiss intruding on bits of normalcy.

Dinner was actually less crazy than lunch, just the opposite of yesterday. With less than an hour to go, I'd even begun to start packing up a bit when I saw her.

It wasn't someone I recognized, but the woman was just Beck's type. Legs for days. Extremely pretty. And most of all, staring at him from the back side of the grill as if he were the next coming of Adonis.

I could have been wrong, but it seemed as if they knew each other. Which, since this was Beck, meant they "knew each other" in a very intimate way. Pretending to put away napkins in a big Tupperware bin, I couldn't tear my gaze away.

Confirming the fact that they weren't strangers, the woman reached down to the table beside Beck's grill and grabbed his phone. She brought it to hers, tapped, smiled like she won the lottery, and put it back down.

I couldn't watch anymore.

Heading back to the counter, I saw a new customer. Anything to take my attention away from what just happened. Less than twenty-four hours after Beck kissed me he was re-connecting with an ex, or a fuck buddy, or whatever. I didn't know if that or me being wrong and Beck giving his number to a stranger was worse.

Actually, it didn't matter.

"Can I help you?"

"I was here yesterday with my wife who asked me to grab two more of your pastries to bring home." He pointed up to town. "Just closed my hardware shop for the night and figured I'd come down and see if you have any left."

"Unfortunately we are out of them."

I snuck a glance at Beck just as his "friend" was walking away. He turned to me and smiled.

Ugh.

I gave my attention back to the customer.

"Damn." He looked up at the sign. "Where is O'Malley's, anyway?"

"Cedar Falls," I said with a smile, hoping it looked genuine since I was suddenly not in a mood to smile. Or socialize. Or be near Beck.

Truth was, for half a second, I had actually thought hard about Beck's "people change" and "friendship isn't a bad way to start" comments. Coupled with the revelation that one of their bachelor pact rules had been made for him, for us, I couldn't help but let my mind wander.

Guess Mathieu wasn't enough of a life lesson for me. I could kick myself.

"I don't suppose you have them on the menu?"

It took me a second to re-focus on what we were talking about. Right. Tarte tatin.

Thinking back to Beck's suggestion about getting them on there for a special, I put away my wounded woman hat and put the businesswoman one on instead.

"As a matter of fact, we're going to have them on as a special for the next few weeks. You should stop by with your wife. Cedar Falls isn't that far away."

"It's not," he said. "I think we'll take a day trip next weekend. Get someone to work for a rare day off. Thanks for the tip."

"My pleasure."

I should have been pleased with myself.

O'Malley's food tent was a success. My pastries, which I loved making, were a hit. I had a client, as Beck kept calling her, which I supposed Ellie was. And more of a purpose than I had two days ago.

Except... him.

Angrily packing up, I tried, unsuccessfully, to cool my jets. Remind myself Beck and I weren't a "thing." It was just a kiss.

Except it wasn't just any guy.

It was Beck.

And that made all the difference.

## 23

### BECK

"Tired?"

It was a dumb question. After two long days, we were heading back to Cedar Falls. Evidenced by the fact that Mae had put her seat back and had her eyes closed, I knew the answer already. But she'd also been unusually quiet packing up too.

"Very," she said, eyes still closed.

I waited, considered letting her rest, but also knew I'd be kicking myself when we got back. Since we were closed tomorrow, I most likely wouldn't see her and couldn't wait until Tuesday.

"Still wanna talk about last night?"

At first, I thought maybe she'd fallen asleep. Or was avoiding the discission. But a moment later, Mae's eyes popped open and she turned to me.

I was surprised by her expression. Mae wasn't tired. She was angry.

"What's wrong?"

"Honestly? It's most likely the fact that I haven't healed yet from Mathieu's betrayal."

"Where did that come from?"

Mae did look tired. But worse, defeated.

She sighed. "It came from the fact that you're just being... you. And because of last night's kiss, I took it personally. But that's my problem, not yours."

I drove mindlessly in the dark, having taken this route hundreds of times. Unfortunately, navigating women's feelings? Not as much. I usually bailed if they caught them.

Mae put her seat back up and shifted toward me.

"Promise you won't tease me? This is serious."

I winced. "Not even a little?"

"No."

"Okay," I promised.

"The woman you gave your number to, at the festival. I have absolutely zero reason to care. It was a stupid kiss. And a total mistake, obviously. But still…"

Holy shit. No, no, no, no.

"I didn't give her my number, Mae."

"Beck," she said, reminding me of the time I stole a kid's bike who was bothering Mason and Mae made us give it back. "I have eyes, you know."

I was about to say something smart, but remembering my promise, held it back.

"She took it. Without permission. I swear, I did not willingly give her my number, but my hands were a bit tied up at the time."

"You know her?" It wasn't accusatory, just a fact.

I winced. "Yeah. We"—I cleared my throat—"dated."

"Dated? Or hooked up?"

Again, I held back my immediate response, and instead of saying, "I plead the fifth," said instead, "The latter." Quickly adding, "She came through Cedar Falls. Lives here. Apparently lost her contacts and grabbed my phone before I could respond. When I failed to give her my passcode, and respectfully declined to give it to her, she eventually left."

Mae blinked. Stared at me.

"I've never lied to you once, and don't intend to start. Even if it's self-incriminatory. You know everything there is to know about me, good and bad."

"I believe you."

"Then what's with the frown face?"

"I don't like that I cared whether or not you gave her your number."

Time to clear the air.

"One—"

"Here we go." Finally, a smile. "Why is everything a list?"

"Because that's how my brain works, I guess. One, the kiss wasn't stupid. Two, it wasn't a mistake. And three, I like that you care. Correction, I love that you care."

I couldn't keep the grin off my face if I tried.

Mae processed that information. I could tell the exact moment she understood my implication. More than an implication. A flat-out admission.

"Do you think it was a mistake?"

She was clearly frustrated. "Yes. No. I don't know, Beck. It just... happened. I honestly didn't think it through."

"Neither of us did. But you've thought about it since."

"I have."

"And?"

"Well, obviously it's complicated things. I've never watched you give a woman your number, or take it," she added when I was about to correct her, "and been upset about it."

I would probably regret asking this.

"Never?"

She opened her mouth. And then closed it.

That was a start, at least.

"I know about the rule," she blurted.

Well, shit. "Since?"

"Just recently. Delaney mentioned it. She just assumed I already knew. Delaney wasn't trying to stir up anything—"

I stopped her. "I don't blame Delaney. Honestly, I'm surprised you hadn't heard about it already. Not that I thought one of the guys would mention it but..." I looked at her. This wasn't a conversation I wanted to have while we were driving.

"Where are you going?" she asked as I pulled over. We were between two houses, the lake on our left, in a neighborhood not far from where my parents and sister lived.

"Just pulling over. This is a conversation years in the making," I admitted, turning off the engine and facing her. "The rule was real. We made the pact because we were stupid enough to think we could protect ourselves. And that one was specifically for me because the guys knew if you showed any interest in me, in *that* way, it would be different. But there's no protecting myself from you anymore. I crossed that line the second I kissed you. Hell, probably before that."

"How could we have been so close, me knowing everything about you, like you said, except that?"

Grinning, I reminded her, "I never kept it a secret from you, Mae."

She rolled her eyes. "But I always assumed you were joking. Making constant innuendos because you were teasing me."

"I was teasing you, but the constant innuendos weren't a joke. Why wouldn't you think I was serious?"

"Because you feel the same way about every pretty woman, Beck."

"No." I needed her to understand one thing. "I do not feel the same about every pretty woman as I do you, Mae. Not even a little."

"You want to sleep with every pretty woman who takes an interest in you. Which is, basically, all of them."

Fuck.

"You can't deny that."

Denying it would make me a boldfaced liar. I didn't have a leg to stand on. Except... "You're different."

She clearly wasn't convinced.

"Hence the problem. I am different because we're friends. Crossing the line, like we did, is only going to complicate things. And I really don't want to lose your friendship."

*Now or never, Beck.*

"Like I said, friendship is a good place to start, don't you think? Genie's already out of the bottle." I didn't want to make light of the situation, but I also couldn't resist any opportunity to make her smile. Mae looked genuinely worried. "Can't pretend you didn't like kissing me."

"Ugh."

Mission accomplished. Smile city.

"Obviously, I did."

"And can't pretend you didn't *want* me to kiss you."

"Equally as obvious."

"So what are the options at this point? Go back to pretending we're only friends? That I don't know you know that the guys made a rule specifically for you because that's how different you are, Mae? Ooor... say, 'fuck it,' cat's out of the bag."

"And what?" she pressed. "Go back to my house and jump into bed?"

Although that seemed like a really good plan, I got the sense Mae didn't agree.

"Feels like you're being facetious."

"No," she said, smiling, her tone even thicker with sarcasm than before. "You don't say."

"We could start with another kiss."

Her gaze dropped to my mouth. I held in a groan.

"You're impossible."

I ran a hand through my hair. "I don't know what to say," I admitted. "I'd be lying if I didn't admit to understanding why you'd be skeptical of my intentions. But you have to know you are not just any woman to me, Mae. Not by a long shot."

"I... can acknowledge that might be true."

"Might?"

"Is probably true."

"Thank you."

"Welcome."

"But it doesn't account for the fact that there are still good reasons for some space before we jump into anything." She smiled. "One, I really don't want to ruin our friendship."

Cheeky girl.

"Two, I was just burned pretty badly, and you deserve more than a rebound. And three, I honestly don't believe you *really* want an actual relationship. Friends with benefits is a great movie title, but in real life, it's actually a recipe for a broken heart."

"I'll give you that last point, in our situation at least. As for what I deserve, let me be the judge of that." Never mind I didn't deserve *her*, but that wouldn't bolster my argument here. "And to your second point." I took a deep breath, but had no hesitation in saying this out loud. It was something I'd thought about for a long, long time. "With most women? I'd agree. I'm not looking for a relationship. But with you? I'll clean up my life quicker than you can say 'commitment issues.'"

Mae's mouth twitched like she was trying not to smile, but I wasn't joking. Not this time.

"I'm serious, Mae. You're the only one I'd even think about getting it right for. The only one who makes me want to be better."

She looked down at her hands. Toyed with them. Raised her head.

"I opened the door back up last night," she said quietly. "Partly because I remembered something I wanted to tell you. But mostly because I didn't want the night to end. We're complicated, Beck. Our lives are intertwined. With the bar. Our friendship. Diving into the deep end now feels like a recipe for drowning. I kissed you because I wanted to. Badly. And still do. But that's the problem. There's no turning back for us."

In other words, she was scared. I couldn't argue with that. I was too. Terrified, actually. The guys had it right in college though, when we took the pact. Mae was different. Always had been. For her, I would risk my heart. I would risk everything.

"I'll show you, Mae."

The more I thought about it, the more it felt right.

"You need time? Take it. You want me to prove I'm not the guy you're afraid I am?"

I paused. These weren't words I could take back, but I wasn't backing down now.

"I'll prove it. Every day. For as long as it takes."

"Beck—"

"As friends. No more kisses. No crossing the line."

Her eyes narrowed. "No teasing about getting me naked?"

"Pfft. Let's not get crazy. A no-teasing clause is one step too far."

"Fine," she said, her voice low and reluctant. "Friends."

It would do. For now. And for the first time in my life, I wasn't chasing a good time.

I was chasing Mae. I didn't plan on losing her.

## 24

### MAE

"Okay, what's the emergency? And why are we drinking wine on a Monday? Not that I'm complaining," Jules asked as she approached.

I'd snagged us two Adirondack chairs and a charcuterie board already. And wine, of course. Jules had to run some errands, so we drove to Golden Grove separately, a newer winery that was quickly becoming one of our favorites, behind lakeside.

"Got us white. Figured it was lighter," I said as she sat. "Being it's Monday and all."

Laughing, she grabbed a handful of grapes and the wine. Didn't even ask what it was, but I had more important things to tell her.

"The emergency is that I kissed Beck. Or he kissed me. Whatever."

Jules froze. Clearly, this was a legitimate emergency because she didn't even take a sip of the wine but instead put it on the table between us, turned to me and just stared.

"Yeah, told you."

"Are you serious?"

"Deadly." I took a sip of wine and reached for a piece of cheese.

"Okay." She picked her glass back up. "Start from the beginning, please."

As we sipped wine and tackled the charcuterie board as if neither of us had ever eaten, I started with our late-night hangout in Beck's room and ended with the toe-curling kiss.

"I just... it felt so natural. We just sort of looked at each other and..." I shrugged.

"Was it good?"

"Beyond good. I don't even remember why we stopped. When I think back to what could have happened... honestly, Jules... I am so confused right now."

"Okay, what happened afterwards?"

I was a little fuzzy on the details. Thinking back, I was fairly certain my brain wasn't functioning normally at that point. "We just sort of agreed that anything more was a bad idea and went into our separate rooms."

"That's it? You guys didn't talk about it?"

"Not really. It was actually worse the next morning. Beck acted totally natural. Didn't say a word. And I felt like an idiot, not knowing what to say. So we sort of... ignored it. Went down to breakfast but then finally broke the ice. By then we'd gone into festival mode, though."

I told her about my little jealousy incident and our discussion on the way home. Recalling everything made it seem more real. Last night, after he dropped me off, I figured I'd be too exhausted to do anything other than pass right out. Instead, I lay on my bed, checking my phone to see if he texted. And basically obsessed over every word from the car talk.

"Holy. Shit."

"Exactly. Now you know why we're drinking wine on a Monday afternoon. I really need to dry out this week."

"Same. Delaney and I... actually, never mind. Doesn't matter. We need to figure this out."

I love that she said we. I'd made friends in France, but there was nothing like old friendships with people who you'd known most of your life. It was good for the soul.

"So," she said, as if trying to figure out a math problem. "You pretty much put the brakes on it as Beck is going to prove that he's not the king of one-night stands and can take anything seriously for more than five minutes. Does that sum it up?"

"Kinda. But I'm second-guessing myself."

"What are you second-guessing?"

"Can I get you ladies more wine?" an attendant asked. I hadn't even seen him coming.

"You know what," Jules responded for us. "We'll take a bottle of whatever this is," she said, lifting up her glass.

"Sure thing."

"A bottle?" I asked. "We both have cars."

Jules chuckled, picked up her phone and apparently sent off a text.

"What are you doing?"

"Asking Boo if he can pick us up later."

"He's still in town?"

"Yep. He got pulled into a squash tournament and actually beat the club pro."

"Interesting. As for the second-guessing, I said no because I was scared. But what if I'm more scared of what happens if I say yes?"

"Sounds reasonable to me. I actually think you did the right thing."

"You do? Because Beck is highly unlikely to change?"

"I do. But it has nothing to do with Beck. You have to figure yourself out first. We both know you adore each other, and now it's pretty obvious you have the hots for each other too. So let's pretend Beck really could show up emotionally for you as well."

That was a perfect summation of everything, actually. Jules always did have a way with words. Her being a writer had always made sense.

"Okay." The attendant came back with our wine. We thanked him for the refills as I looked out to the lake. It was always slow on a Monday, even in the spring. But this weekend, we'd be surrounded by people and those calm waters would teem with tourists. "I'm with you so far."

"Best-case scenario, everything works out between the two of you. He buys the bar. Which is likely, right?"

"I think so. We didn't talk about it much, for obvious reasons."

"Let's go with him buying the bar. That ties Beck to Cedar Falls. And now the two of you are in relationship bliss. Get where I'm going?"

"I do."

"A pause button is a good idea, until you figure out what's next. The last thing you want is for the two of you to work out but your dream job is in the city, or whatever."

The idea of Beck and me "working out" seemed so far-fetched. He was more likely to break my heart than heal it.

"Problem with that is... what's my dream job?"

"Are you asking me?"

"Maybe? I've asked myself and don't have an answer."

We polished off the bottle, and the charcuterie board, but eventually got hungry for real food. While Jules went up to the bathroom and texted Boo to pick us up, I closed my eyes and thought about our conversation.

Jules made a lot of sense. So maybe I had done the right thing? Problem was, that didn't help clarify my life path. In the meantime, I completely forgot about Thursday.

"Speaking of wine," I said when she sat back down. "I forgot to tell you. I ran into Thayle and Neo Grado at the festival. She invited us to a girls' night at GVV on Thursday and even has an empty cottage... a bachelorette party canceled. What do you think?"

"I think, sign me up. A lakeside writer's cottage? Sounds like a dream."

"Only you would think of that first. Who works on a girls' night?"

"Writing, at least the fiction, isn't work for me."

Jules wanted more than anything to make that her career. In the meantime she pieced together college writing courses and tutoring and all sorts of soul-sucking things while she worked on her own stuff on the side.

"I'm gonna ask Delaney and Pia. Who else?"

We chatted about Thursday, all talk of Beck and my future over. For now.

Problem was, my phone just buzzed in my pocket, and I reached for it more quickly than I should. When Beck's name lit up and my heart did a little "pitter patter," it was time to face reality.

Like it or not, pause or otherwise, I'd caught feelings for my best friend and would need to buckle up. It was about to be a bumpy ride.

# 25

## BECK

"Yes, sir. No, sir."

Speak of the devil. Mr. O'Malley had just asked about his daughter when the door opened. An unexpected surprise since she wasn't due to work lunch.

"Actually," I said, shifting my phone to the other ear as I put two sodas on a tray for Jenn, "she just walked in."

"We have to run, meeting with the realtor at noon, but tell her we'll text later. Glad everything is going well," he said.

"Will do, sir. Good luck at the realtor."

I put my phone back into my jeans pocket.

"What are you doing here?"

Mae came around the bar, her hair back in a ponytail. An unusual style for her, but I liked it. We weren't very busy, not unusual for a Tuesday at this time.

"What kind of greeting is that?" she teased.

So far, it hadn't been the least bit awkward since our drive home, but this was the first time we were seeing each other. We'd texted a bit back and forth yesterday like normal, but even now, it was just... us.

Except, of course, everything had changed.

I took a step toward her as Mae leaned against the back bar. Leaning in, to make sure I wasn't overheard, I whispered, "Love the pony. Thing is, Mae, I know all of your secrets. So I know for a fact if we found ourselves alone in the back room, you wouldn't mind if I used it as leverage."

Her lips twitched, fighting a smile, but she didn't answer. I left her and turned to Lou, who'd just walked in.

"You're early today."

He grunted. "Hired a college kid to help me out."

Pouring him a beer, only one at lunchtime, I slid it across the bar.

"About time. I've been telling you for years to hire some help. The usual?"

"Yeah," he said. "No fries, though."

That was a surprise.

"I'm cutting back."

I could have commented, but got the sense Lou didn't want to talk about it. He was divorced, had been for years. But I had noticed him looking a little leaner. Was there a woman involved? I punched in his order and stood beside Mae.

"Your dad called. Said they were heading to the realtor but would text you later."

She smelled like lilies. It was a new scent, since France. A pretty one, perfect for her.

"So you're just going to pretend you didn't say... that?"

I looked her in the eyes. "I'm not wrong."

"Not the point."

"Come down to the inn tonight. Mason and Pia have leftovers from a wedding Sunday."

"Um, I'm working."

"I know, you weren't supposed to be in until four. Miss me?"

Mae shoved me away from her, but laughed. "Hardly. You mentioned the supplier shorted us on mixers again. Figured I'd sort that out and take inventory on the wine fridge while I was at it. Thought I'd knock it out before the rush."

"Hmm, likely excuse."

I scanned the bar while pulling my phone back out. Clicking it, I wasn't surprised Tessa answered right away. "Hey, Tess. Any chance you can cover tonight around seven? Shouldn't be a late night. You could close down anytime."

Wondering if Mae could hide her emotions in a high-stakes poker match, I decided she couldn't. "Thanks. I owe you one."

"You're something else, you know that?"

"I do. What other excuse do you have?"

"Give me a few hours, and I'll think of one."

I smiled. She was coming.

"Hang on a sec before you go in the back."

I grabbed a coaster and made my way to the window seat.

"Sorry, folks, this has been giving us some trouble lately. Mind if I fix it?" I asked the couple before proceeding to use the coaster to steady it.

Mae was right where I'd left her, looking perfectly at home behind the bar as she took Lou's order from Jenn and served him.

"Table three's off again. Grabbed a coaster to fix it. Don't need spilled IPAs during happy hour. Really need to get that leg replaced."

"Did you want me to stay so we can talk about table three?" The corners of Mae's mouth tugged upward. I tried not to notice her lip gloss, but the memory of our kiss made it impossible.

"Smart ass. I wanted to talk about your parents. They apparently fell in love with a place. He called to ask about my interest in the bar and where I stood."

Mae crossed her arms. "I was actually going to talk to you about that this weekend. I don't think he means to pressure you. They were just going to look at the area and got talking to another couple who own a condo there, and the next thing you know—"

"You don't have to explain it to me. I know your dad better than that. Funnily enough, he said the exact same thing. That another place would open up but they figured they'd meet with a realtor while they were down there to get the details."

"Exactly. I think they're getting caught up in it, being there."

"Can't blame them. I know they've wanted to do this for years. I just wondered what they told you about this place? Do you really think they'll be able to find another they like as much? Your dad seemed pretty excited."

"You know how he gets. Thankfully Mom is there to temper him. There must be a million condos down there, although they do love its proximity to the town, especially some breakfast place Dad found that he swears will be his new home. It does seem like a great price for ocean view, but yes. I think they'll find another. Why?"

I had some initial thoughts, but not ones I wanted to share just yet.

"Beck, I have a customer asking for the manager," Jenn said.

Mae tossed her hands in the air. "Don't look at me. Not officially on duty yet."

With that, she headed to the back room.

"Coward," I called.

"What's the problem?"

"No problem. Apparently table eleven was at the festival and came to check us out. Said he wanted to talk to the manager to discuss a possible partnership."

From my vantage point at the bar, I couldn't see table eleven.

"Intriguing," I said, tossing a towel on the bar.

Even more intriguing? The thought of ramping up my "Mae campaign" as Parker called it when I told him and Mason yesterday about our talk. They both had a lot to say about the whole situation but thankfully, both fully supported it and were going to help me win her over.

On the bad news side, they also agreed Cole wasn't likely to be very happy about the whole thing. If by some miracle I could convince Mae the womanizing commitment-phobe she knew could sing a different tune if the woman in question was her, he would be the last man standing.

But I had bigger problems than Cole. I put the thought of visiting my parents, and worse, asking them for a favor, out of my mind for now. That was tomorrow's problem.

Tonight, at the gathering I convinced Mason and Pia was a good idea, it was game on.

# 26

## MAE

I hadn't taken two steps inside before Pia and Delaney swooped down on me.

"Hurry up." Delaney grabbed my hand. "He's still up in the shower."

As she pulled me into the living room of the house side of the inn, I couldn't see the kitchen but I could hear male voices. Apparently not Beck's, though.

"He probably got stuck at the bar. When I left—"

"Girl," Pia interrupted me. "We only have a few minutes. Start. Talking."

Our kiss wasn't a big secret, apparently. Not that I expected it would be. If I didn't want the guys to know something, I had to explicitly tell Beck not to mention it to them. Otherwise, pretty much anything I said was fair game, especially with Mason and Parker. But even Cole, although he wasn't in Cedar Falls, stayed in the loop with his bosom buddies.

"As you know, we kissed."

Delaney rolled her eyes dramatically.

Yesterday when I'd texted them to ask if they wanted to go to Grado Valley on Thursday night, I was forewarned that they already knew. I wouldn't be surprised if tonight was either to get the scoop or Beck's doing. Once he put his mind to something, there was usually no holding back. Which didn't bode well for us keeping things in the friendzone.

They exchanged a glance, waiting.

"Please tell me that's not your whole story?"

When I grew up, I wanted to be someone like Delaney. Fearless to say whatever was on her mind. "You crack me up. So." I peered down the hallway. No Beck yet. "It just sort of happened this weekend at the B&B. We had adjoining rooms," I added.

"Beck was convinced you didn't see him as anything more than a friend. He said as much when you came back," Pia said. "I warned him not to complicate things and stay away."

"Honestly"—I couldn't fault Beck—"he did. The kiss was... both of us. He was right, but it wasn't because I never thought Beck was awesome. I mean, he's one of my best friends for a reason. He's funny, and smart, and obviously hot. But that was always the problem. He knows it. And the hordes of women he's been with do too."

"So what changed?" Delaney asked.

Good question.

"I... I don't know," I said honestly. "In some ways, nothing. Which is why I put the brakes on it the next day. Beck says I'm different, but—"

"Party's in the kitchen, ladies."

Caught. Beck's grin told me he knew exactly why we were huddled in the living room.

"Just got here," I said.

"Uh huh." Everything about him was suggestive. His tone. His stance. The way he looked at me was the exact opposite of "friend."

"Shoo," Pia said, waving him away. "We'll be right in."

Which, of course, sealed the deal. He 100 percent knew we were talking about him.

"For what it's worth," Delaney said, "I get the sense from Parker that it's true. You really are in a whole different category than anyone else."

Pia nodded. "Not that we're trying to convince you of anything. The idea of Beck being in an actual relationship..." She made a wincing face. "But there's a first for everything."

"I also have to figure out my own life too," I admitted. "But we can talk more Thursday. I'm so glad you're both coming."

"I got someone to cover the shop in the afternoon Thursday. And we don't open until eleven, so Friday shouldn't be an issue."

"Works for me," I said. "Let's go in there before they get suspicious."

"Oh," Pia said as we walked. "That's a done deal. Beck knows we're talking about him."

As we walked into the kitchen, I saw a plethora of leftovers in tin food trays on the island. How things could change so quickly. Not long ago, it was a taco bar. And my man troubles were named Mathieu, not Beck. Talk about complicated.

"Wine is already opened," Delaney said, a flurry of activity commencing as everyone grabbed drinks and plates.

"Red?" Beck asked me, grabbing a glass.

"Yeah, red," Delaney answered for me when I paused, my thoughts a jumbled mess. "Goes better with the meal."

Laughing, I accepted the glass from Beck as everyone chatted and dug in. Pia and Mason talked about the wedding, and how far Heritage Hill had come now that they were doing events. Parker updated them on the final stages of the renovation which we'd set to be finished by summer, which led to a discussion about his and Delaney's house.

One thing we didn't discuss? Me and Beck.

Thankfully.

But that didn't stop him from not so subtly reminding me things weren't 100 percent normal between us. At one point, Beck caught me watching him eat from across the island and winked at me. At another, when I tried to refill my wine, he took the glass from me, his fingers brushing mine, and did it for me.

Every look, every touch, made one thing clear. We might be in the friend-zone, but now that the cat was out of the bag, so to speak, there was a chemistry between us that I couldn't believe I'd missed.

Or maybe I hadn't.

Thinking back on me and Beck, as I'd done since Saturday night, a lot of things made more sense now. I could even admit, at times, to a slight twinge of jealousy at a few of Beck's stories, ones of second dates and hints he might actually be taking a woman he was with seriously. But inevitably, he would push her away, solidifying his "playboy" persona. One that would never jive with a ticking internal clock of womanhood. I'd always wanted children, a family, and dating someone like Beck? Never a consideration.

Until now.

"You're quiet tonight," Beck noticed.

"Just taking it all in," I said. "You guys really do have a good thing going here, you know that?"

"*We* have a good thing going," Beck clarified. "You're a part of us too now, Mae. Like it or not, you're stuck."

"What's not to like?"

"Exactly," Parker agreed. "Especially now that Mason's less moody, thanks to his wife." He looked at her glass. "How's the iced tea?"

"Zip it." Pia took a sip. "Delicious. Almost as good as a glass of vino."

Mason snorted, earning a look from his wife.

"So word on the street is that we're celebrating tonight," Parker said, looking at Beck.

"You didn't mention a celebration." I twisted my wine glass back and forth between my fingers.

"I wanted to surprise you," he said. "All of you."

So even Parker didn't know what this was about. Interesting.

"Lemme guess, you're quitting O'Malley's and buying that food truck you always wanted?"

Beck's expression made me laugh. "I never once talked about wanting a food truck."

"Nah." Parker stood behind Delaney, kissing her on the head. "He's going to propose a group marriage. Unfortunately, I'm not into that kind of thing. Sorry to disappoint you."

Everyone laughed.

"Ladies? Any guesses?"

By the way Beck was looking at me—expectantly, as if excited—I had one. And I couldn't be more thrilled.

"You're buying the bar?"

His grin deepened. "Bingo."

Something fluttered in my chest, impossible to ignore. Excitement. Elation. Hope, maybe?

"That's fantastic." Pia, the closest to him, hugged Beck. After a round of handshakes and congratulations, I finally made my way over to him. Hugging Beck felt both as natural as can be, but also, at the same time, strange and exciting.

"You sure you want this?" he whispered in my ear.

"Absolutely." I let go, before wanting to. "I am so happy. My parents don't know?"

I'd talked to my mother an hour ago, and she didn't say anything about it.

"Not yet. I'll call your dad tomorrow. But don't say anything yet. I want to tell him."

"No problem," I said, about to go back across the island to my seat when Beck reached across and grabbed my wine, bringing it to me. Subtle, but also I was onto him. I gave him a look that told him as much.

"About time." Parker sat on the stool I'd just vacated. With the smell of leftover chicken parmigiana, mixed with a vanilla coconut candle, the kitchen smelled like warmth, and love.

"That he stopped holding his dick-beater in his hands," Mason quipped, "and is making something of his life? Damn straight."

"Fuck off," Beck tossed back.

Pia, Delaney and I shook our collective heads. When these guys got together, which was almost every day, they really were like a side-show comedy act. Guys could be incredibly immature, and frankly, dumb, sometimes. But there was an easy camaraderie among them too that was almost admirable.

Or, if nothing else, entertaining.

"Having fun?" Beck asked.

"I am."

"Surprised?"

"Honestly? No. I was more surprised you hedged on it for so long. You're a natural and are going to kill it as the new owner. I'm more excited than anything. For you, for my parents..."

"Glad to hear it." Beck raised his chin. "It's a very... mature, responsible decision. Wouldn't you say?"

As the others conversed around us, Beck and I dropped back from the island to lean against the kitchen counter.

"Ahhh, so you had an ulterior motive?"

"Not really. I just needed to be kicked in the ass a bit."

I smiled and took a sip of wine.

"Speaking of asses," he said, leaning into my ear and whispering, "yours is looking exceptionally fine tonight."

I nearly spit out the wine, which would have been a disaster since I was wearing a white sundress.

"Can you not wait until my mouth is full to say things like that?"

He watched me, but remained quiet.

"What are you doing?"

"Waiting until after you take a sip, so I can talk."

"Oh my God, you're impossible. Another option is just not to say anything like that. Just a thought."

I did take a sip then, and as promised, Beck waited until I swallowed. And then he leaned into me one more time.

"One, the thought of your mouth filled with something, and I'm not talking about the wine, is the stuff of dreams. Mine in particular. Two, keeping it PG, now that the secret's out, is not a viable option, Mae."

I waited for the rest, my traitorous body responding to every word.

"And three?"

"And three?"

Beck's grin turned lethal.

"And three... you should probably stay the night. Since you're drinking wine and all."

"Beck—"

"Don't worry, Mae. I meant in the guest room."

A beat.

"Unless you ask nicely."

# 27

## BECK

"Your room, my lady."

Could Pia have escorted Mae? Sure. Did I need to open the door and step inside for her to find her room? No.

"Thank you, kind sir, for your escort."

"This is the Julie room, named after Parker's mom's best friend."

"Really?"

Mae flipped on a lamp, headed to the window and opened the curtain.

"Sorry, no lakeview, those are all sold out. Which is surprising to me, how many people are on vacation on a Tuesday."

She turned toward me.

"Not so surprising. Everyone has a different story. Some are probably still here from the wedding."

"True."

"And maybe another is in town for the whole week."

"A week in Cedar Falls?" I asked, skeptical.

"It's not a bad home base to explore all the lakes."

"Maybe," I said, stepping back, leaning against the door frame. I didn't want to assume too much, having talked Mae into staying.

Putting the kit of toiletries Pia had given her on the dresser, Mae not having come prepared to stay, she sat on the bed.

"You guys did a great job with the renovations."

"It was mostly Pia's good taste. We just grunted and nodded and painted what she told us to."

"Sounds about right. And you can come in," she said. "You'll scare the guests, lurking out there."

I didn't have to be told twice.

Even so, I sat in the armchair. "Reversed positions," I said. "From Saturday night."

"I feel like any response to that is going to be taken out of context and turned against me."

Man, this woman knew me. "Good guess."

Her legs were crossed, but damn if that did little to stop my imagination from running wild. The second I saw her in a white sundress, all coherent thought went out the window.

"So, O'Malley's. That was a nice surprise."

"You approve?"

"Very much. What tipped your hand?"

"You, in part. Despite what you think, I actually have been listening to you. And the guys, honestly. While they've all got their shit together—well, everyone but Cole—I've been screwing around, pretending I'm still in college. Bartending might have started out as a big middle finger to my father..." I smiled, thinking about how much that had pissed him off. Served him right for treating me like a pawn instead of a son. "It's not a life plan."

"Cole? I'd say tenure track at Columbia qualifies as having your shit together."

"Sure. If he actually wanted that. Dumb fucker is trying to impress his father and making himself miserable in the process. He hates it."

"He does? I had no idea."

I shrugged. "Because he hides it well. But we were talking about my suitability as a potential boyfriend."

I loved making Mae laugh. "I'm sorry. Did the conversation veer away from you for a half second? My sincerest apologies."

"No worries. I'll let it slide."

Mae collapsed backward onto the bed, mumbling something about me being ridiculous.

"Tired?"

"I think the weekend is catching up to me."

I stood and sat on the edge of the bed. Everything I'd planned to say flew out the window as I looked down at the familiar face that knew me as well as anyone. She was so goddam pretty. And good. There wasn't a mean bone in Mae's body.

I loved her. The kind of love that changes throughout the years as we grew from children to adolescents to teens to adults. I loved her so much it actually tugged at my chest to think about how close she came to marrying another man. Living in France. I nearly lost her and wouldn't take that chance again.

"I can be a better man for you, Mae. If you give me a chance."

Mae scooted upwards so her legs were on the bed, rolled onto her side and propped her head on her hand.

"I just don't want to ruin"—she waved her hand toward us—"this."

I had no good comeback for that. If we tried, and failed, to turn a friendship into something more, I had no idea if it would be possible to go backwards. Seemed unlikely. I was better off with the plan that the guys had helped me formulate.

Show her.

Show Mae I was serious about getting my shit together. I was serious about her. Words would only go so far after Mae had watched me flit around without a care in the world since, well, always.

"I'm gonna make your dad proud," I said instead. "He won't regret selling to me. I have so many ideas I want to talk to you about."

"I know he won't. My dad adores you. And I've seen firsthand how much you care about the customers. You know that was always his number one."

"What about you? Any thoughts on what's next?"

I wasn't stupid. The answer to that question could very well make or break us.

"A few. I was actually thinking of hashing some things out with the girls Thursday on our overnighter. If my brain was working now, I'd tell you more."

Clearly, it wasn't on full throttle. Couldn't be. The last few words of her sentence were murmured as Mae drifted off to sleep. I'd give her hell tomorrow for falling asleep on me mid-conversation, but it was understandable. She'd been going non-stop.

Slowly, gently, I slipped off the brown cowboy boots she was fond of wearing. Then, knowing she'd wake up if I tried to get her under the covers, I headed toward the closet, pulled out the extra blanket, and gently laid it over her.

Heading toward the mini-fridge, I took out a bottle of water that was stocked in every room and put it on the dresser beside her.

*You were always too good for me, Mae. I made myself unavailable to you by acting like a jackass. And you're still too good for me. But I'm selfish enough not to care anymore because I know what it feels like to lose you.*

Never again.

Tomorrow, I would do the unthinkable for this woman.

Because she was worth it.

# 28

## MAE

"You are absolutely letting us pay you for this," I said to Thayle as we walked into the cottage. "I know for a fact this is the best property. And how much it goes for."

Not only was it a four-bedroom lakefront property, but this was the only one with an outdoor hot tub too. Pia, Delaney and Jules oohed and ahhed as we brought our overnight bags in. On the kitchen counter? Two champagne bottles on ice with glasses surrounding them.

"And what is that?" Pia asked as she and Jules gravitated to the counter.

"You're not paying a dime, it was a cancellation. And that's a welcome from the owners," Thayle said. "The one on the left is for you."

Pia pulled it out and laughed. "Non-alcoholic. This is awesome. Ish. I'd prefer that one." She pointed to its partner that Delaney lifted from the ice.

"So would I but"—Thayle smiled—"I'm only pouring for the others. I'll be partaking in yours."

Everyone froze, took in that information, and offered a round of congratulations. They all knew Thayle had been to Grado Valley Vineyards throughout the years, but I was closest to her and gave her the biggest squeeze.

"Congratulations. That's amazing. When are you due?"

We popped open the bubbly, and the non-alcoholic one, celebrating Thayle's announcement. She and Pia got to talking all things baby prep and headed out on the deck while the three of us went about unpacking the char-cuterie goodies we'd brought for a light lunch. The event was due to start up at the main winery building at four with plenty of food, but in the meantime, I was starving.

We talked about the huge order Delaney had gotten thanks to a feature of her custom-made jewelry in a well-circulated Finger Lakes lifestyle magazine. We talked about Jules's dating life for a bit too.

When both of them looked at me, I tried to avoid the topic I knew they were curious about. One too complicated to put into words sufficiently. "I really have to remember not to skip breakfast so I don't eat everything in sight by noon," I said, reaching for my fourth serving of cheese and crackers.

"Speaking of cheese and crackers." Jules took a sip of bubbly. "What's the Beck status?"

"The Beck status, besides him buying the bar, is no status."

"Guess you're gonna pretend he didn't escort"—Delaney said that last word with more than a hint of suggestion in her tone—"you to your room the other night."

"I stayed at the inn," I explained to Jules. "After being strong-armed into drinking wine even though I was supposed to be drying out this week."

She nodded to my champagne glass. "You're doing a great job."

Delaney cleared her throat.

"Nothing happened," I said. "We talked a little. I fell asleep. He covered me and left."

And left a bottle of water by the nightstand which reminded me of the first time I drank too much. It was after a football game senior year of high school. Not only had Beck walked me home and covered for me by talking to my parents while I slunk off to my room, but he showed up at the window, courtesy of the tree right outside my bedroom, climbed in, and held my hair when I lost the contents of my stomach. That was before he lectured me about why I shouldn't be hanging out with Curtis Daniels, the football quarterback, and his friends. According to Beck, they were bad news. As if he and his buddies were angels.

"Well, that's just about the most boring report ever." Jules made a pretend sound of disgust.

"I feel like him buying the bar is something, right?" Delaney asked. "Maybe he really is turning a corner."

"You mean, becoming an adult?" Jules reached for a chocolate-covered raisin.

"Exactly," Delaney said.

"If being an adult means you have your act together, I'm not quite there yet. But I have been mulling around an idea."

"Oooh, do tell." Delaney rubbed her hands together eagerly.

"I spoke with Ellie, from that B&B last weekend, and she wants to move forward with an order. So I also talked to Pia a little yesterday morning, and she thought it was a great idea."

"It?" Jules drew her full eyebrows, one of her most striking features, together.

"The possibility of expanding the idea, to serve other inns, restaurants, whatever. Like the B&B. Could I get enough customers to make it a business?" I could tell the ladies were as excited as me about the possibility, and that meant the world to me. "It's all very willy-nilly. But between the festival success, and then Beck had the idea of putting the tarte tatin on the menu as a special... things like that. Could it be viable, without serving customers directly?"

"So you don't want a bakery or anything like that?"

"No," I said. "I had so much fun tailoring the perfect desserts. I want to experiment with recipes and bake."

"You could hire someone to handle customers," Jules suggested.

"I don't know," I said. "I envision more of a small-batch artisan dessert thing. But I have no idea if that's sustainable."

The ladies appeared thoughtful.

"Sort of a catering, but for desserts," Delaney said. "Yeah, that's definitely unique. What's the risk to try? Could you do it out of your house?"

"I'm not sure yet," I admitted. "There's more questions than answers at this point. But it's a thought."

"So," Delaney ventured. "You're wanting to stay in Cedar Falls?"

"Yes!"

That from Pia, who was just walking inside.

"She wants to be the most sought-after pastry chef in the Finger Lakes, her creations so in-demand that I've already put in a long-standing order. Then we've got her for taco nights and Wine Wednesdays, when I can drink again," she said, eliciting a nod from Thayle. "And not to mention making a man out of Beck."

"Have this all planned out for her, huh?" Delaney popped a piece of pepperoni into her mouth.

"In all seriousness," Pia said, her hand moving, probably unconsciously, to her stomach. "Did you not see them together the other night?"

"I did. And agree it's a different Beck since she came home. But this is Beck we're talking about."

"And you know as well as I do half, if not more, of his schtick is a front. He has a heart of gold underneath the jokes—"

"And womanizing?"

I watched Pia and Delaney like they were a ping pong match, wondering if they remembered I was in the room.

"That too."

"Um..." I raised my hand. "Hello?"

Thayle laughed. "You don't get a say," she teased. "But I will say this. We have a reformed playboy in our family too. When they fall, they fall hard. With the right woman, it's possible."

Jules reached for a cracker. "Really wish we had some popcorn. This is highly entertaining."

My pocket buzzed. Not wanting to attract more attention by taking it out, I excused myself. "While you guys analyze my love life, I'm hitting the ladies' room. Be right back."

Sitting on the toilet lid, I took out my phone and smiled.

> How's it going?

Aware I was smiling at my phone, and what that meant, I fired back:

> Just got here, so far so good.

> You?

I watched as Beck typed.

> All good. Working on something...

What the heck did that mean?

> Something?

Yep.

It wasn't like Beck to be so mysterious.

> So coy today.

Intrigued? (wink emoji)

> Lol, always.

Crap. Text sparring with him came so naturally, I hadn't even thought about how that sounded until I pressed send.

Good to know (wink emoji)

Friends. I was quite literally flirting with him. So much for the grand plan. It was just so easy with Beck, and even though it should be awkward, this limbo we were in, in a lot of ways, it was perfectly natural too.

I texted:

> TTYL

Couldn't stay locked up in the bathroom all day. Thankfully, when I made my way back out to the kitchen, no one commented on how long I'd been gone. I could have just as easily texted Beck in front of them, but they'd sniff that out in no time. And I couldn't make heads or tails of the situation in my own head, never mind trying to explain it to them.

I was just about to put my phone back in my jeans pocket when it buzzed again.

As long as you promise to think about me later.

I froze. A tingle of excitement ran through me, one that had no business making me feel as if the combination of an overnight with the girls, coupled with his flirty texts, was quite literally the perfect night.

"What is it?" Jules asked.

I looked up as all four faces stared expectantly at me.

Only one way to describe the situation.

"Ladies. I'm in trouble."

# 29

## BECK

*Earlier that day...*

Back into the lion's den.

Even though my parents only lived twenty minutes outside downtown Cedar Falls, I rarely saw them, especially with my sister off to college.

Elaine Claymont built her life, especially since Dad's bottling business exploded, around looking flawless. Socially. Emotionally. After she and my father's affairs ruined their marriage, she proceeded to curate their reconciliation like a reality show highlight reel.

Charles Claymont was worse. Wealthy, calculating, and impossible to please, he'd always treated people like negotiations. He valued control, legacy, and the illusion of a perfect family. He got back together with my mother purely for pride and PR. Reconciliation photographs better than divorce.

Staying grounded was only successful because of the guys, Mr. Bennett, Mason's dad, and growing up next to the O'Malleys. But I didn't escape completely unscathed, and sometimes I worried my sister might not either.

Pulling into the circular driveway, I parked my truck beside the perfectly manicured landscaping and took a few deep breaths as I climbed the stairs. My nervous system already unregulated, it spiked the minute I opened the front door as my mother was just making her way through the foyer.

"I thought that was your truck."

She'd never been particularly affectionate, but at some point during her and Dad's climb up the social ladder, she began kissing everyone, me included, on both cheeks in greeting.

"What brings you to our neck of the woods?"

A subtle dig that I never came home.

"I texted Dad earlier. He said he'd be here this morning."

She waved a hand toward the back patio. "He's outside with his coffee. But on the phone, I think. Probably sweet-talking some vineyard into doubling their order. Your father's been bottling charm as long as he's been bottling wine."

I refrained from "If you say so," not wanting an argument.

"How you doing?" I asked since I wouldn't know. My mother contacted me as little as I did her. Once she gave up on turning me into her Ivy League golden boy and realized pushing only made me dig in deeper, I became more of an occasional update than a son.

"Well," she said. "I was just heading out to meet Nancy. We're planning a founders' brunch for the Finger Lakes Historical Society."

Sounded about right.

"Don't let me stop you," I said, striding toward the back doors. "Tell Nancy I said hello."

When my mother didn't respond, I stopped and turned. She was studying me, so I knew exactly what was coming. Bracing for it, I reminded myself why I was here. And why this torture trip was worth it.

"Nancy's a new grandmother. Her son and his wife had twins. You remember her son? He's running for attorney general, was a year ahead of you."

Good for him.

I forced a smile. "I do. Tell her I said congratulations, in that case."

Before she could sneak in the next comment which was very likely to start a fight, I summoned years of experience dealing with my mother and walked away. There was a time I'd have thought it was rude, but after some soul-searching—and talking to Mr. O'Malley about the whole situation—I now filed it under the self-preservation umbrella.

Dad was leaning against the patio railing, coffee in one hand, phone in the other, wearing one of those crisp button-downs that screamed casual money.

"Beck," he said without looking up, like I was an expected delivery instead of his son. "You finally crawl out of whatever dive bar you've been hiding in?"

*Here we go.*

"Go grab yourself a coffee. I'll be about five more minutes."

I could easily sit down, ignore his directive out of spite for giving it, but that would have been as useless as trying to get my mind from replaying my kiss with Mae every hour of the day. So instead, I walked back through the exceptionally clean cream, like the rest of the house, living room, into the kitchen, and poured myself a cup of joe.

It was one of my father's luxuries I didn't mind. Single-origin Ethiopian beans brewed from a machine that cost more than my truck and poured like a European café.

Heading back outside, I waited for him to finish talking and focused on the coffee rather than the discussion that was about to take place. This was literally the one scenario I never wanted or expected to be in... asking my father for money.

Talk about a tail between your legs moment. Shoving my pride away, I took another sip.

"So. What's the favor?"

He sat on the wrought-iron chair across from me, putting his phone on the table.

*Hi, son. How are you, Beck?*

Too much to ask, I supposed.

Might as well rip off the band-aid.

"I'm buying O'Malley's bar. I don't actually need any money—"

"Good. Because if you think I'm funding your midlife crisis at thirty, pouring beers for locals who peaked in high school, you're out of your mind."

So far, it was going about as expected.

"Mr. and Mrs. O'Malley went down to Delray Beach to see if they liked the area for a second place. They ended up finding one already, a great deal, but if I wait to secure a loan they'll likely lose it. I just need some upfront cash to hold it for them while I get the paperwork in order."

He blinked. No reaction.

I told him how much I needed. Still, no reaction.

He might not have been a great father, but he was one hell of a business-man. And though I never wanted to go into the bottling business, a fact that my father would never get over, it wasn't for a lack of respect for what he'd built. And I was very much having a conversation with the business owner and not my father right now.

Last thing I was gonna do, though, was flinch. He hated weakness more than my life decisions. So instead, I waited with him. Stared back.

"A near-perfect SAT," he said finally. "And you're going to own a bar?"

It wasn't his words, but the derisive tone, that made me crack.

"Yeah, a bar. You own a wine bottling business. We'll both make money from the same industry," I said, not holding back my sarcasm. "Ironic, huh?"

"I could point out they are not the same industry. And that being the owner of a local pub and distributing to over a hundred high-end vineyards in upstate New York are, in fact, worlds apart. But you know that already, Beck. You're a smart kid."

*Deep breaths. Remember the goal.*

"I am not a kid, Dad. But you know that already, too. And yeah, they're worlds apart, but this"—I waved my hand toward the inground pool, its too-large poolhouse and all of the amenities one might need to host a perfect party at your perfect house—"has never been my world. Only yours. And Mom's. Some parents might be happy they became so successful and also managed not to raise a stuck-up prick."

His brows raised.

"Only throwing shade to some of your friends' kids. Not you," I clarified.

"Well," he said. "That's a relief."

He sat back, coffee in hand, and considered my request.

There was a fifty-fifty chance he'd do it. Dad had the money on hand and knew I was good for it. But giving it to me would, at least in part, go against his vow not to "fund my stupidity" as he so often put it. Bartender. Bar owner. Guess it didn't matter.

Even if a part of me, a tiny little part of me, wished it did.

He sipped his coffee again, then exhaled slowly like the decision was costing him something more than money.

"You'll pay me back," he said finally. "And not a cent goes to a sound system, neon sign, or whatever nonsense you think bars need these days."

That was as close to a yes as I'd get.

I nodded. "Done."

He studied me for a moment. "This isn't just about a bar, is it?"

I didn't answer.

The guy, if nothing else, was no dummy.

He picked up his phone, started texting and forced me to sit and watch him. Trying not to squirm in my seat, I again reminded my brain to concentrate on the coffee. It was really good shit.

"Done."

"Huh?"

"Saying 'huh' in a negotiation is generally frowned upon."

"Is that what we're doing?" I asked. "Negotiating?"

"What would you call it?"

He was giving me the money. Which made me just happy enough to let him hear the words, plain and simple, that I was certain he'd never thought to hear.

"A son asking his father for a favor."

The fucker actually smiled. More surprising, it appeared almost genuine. But hell hadn't frozen over, that I knew of, so maybe I just needed glasses.

"The money," he said, "is being deposited into your bank account as we speak."

Interesting. "How do you have access to my bank account?"

He sighed as if resigning himself to the fact that, despite my SAT scores, I really was stupider than I looked.

"It is the bank account your mother and I set up for you."

"That's still open?"

"Yes, Beck. It's still open."

"Hmm. Well, thanks. I'm heading there now to apply for a loan. You'll have it back soon."

Usually, my father was off to somewhere in a rush. And I had no doubt he would be before long. But for the moment, he didn't move, so I stayed there too. We sipped our coffee. Watched the water fall from an elevated hot tub into the pool.

"Thank you," I said finally.

His response was to lift his coffee mug, ever so slightly, before standing up and walking away, ending the conversation as abruptly as he'd begun it.

## 30

### MAE

Life was good.

As I lay down in the bed, I congratulated myself on washing off my makeup and downing a bottle of water. After a long night of wine tasting, tomorrow morning I would be thankful. If only two minutes ago I'd thought to turn off the lamp before snuggling deep into the soft bed. Dammit.

I'd turn it off. In a minute.

In the meantime, I picked up my phone and looked at the time. Just after one. Sighing, I gave a silent thank you to the universe for such good friends. I felt better than ever about the glimmer of a life plan I'd concocted over the past few days. For the first time since I'd come home... actually, since the disastrous dinner date with Mathieu when my life came crashing down around me, I didn't feel so lost.

With one (glaring) exception.

*Don't do it, Mae. You were the one who set the ground rules.*

*Screw the ground rules*, the devil on my other shoulder told me. It was just a little text. He'd be at the bar still.

One little hint?

And then waited. But instead of scrolling anywhere else, I actually stared at the screen. Yep, like I said to the girls, I was royally screwed.

*Put it down. Turn off the light. And go to bed.*

I actually began to sit up, to do just that, when a text bubble appeared. And then...

Still up, huh?

Slipping back down, repositioning myself in the middle of the pillow, I replied with a thumbs up.

Working?

Nope. Deep-cleaning keg lines tomorrow. Shut down early.

Did I wake you up?

Nope.

He was still typing.

And wouldn't mind if you did.

I sent a smiley face.

How was ur night?

Amazing. Will tell you about it tomorrow!

Looking forward to it.

My pulse raced as I realized... I was too. Looking forward to seeing Beck. Who would've thought?

Nite nite.

:( leaving me already?

It wasn't unusual. This entire conversation was one I could have had three months, or a year, or three years ago, with Beck. And yet, his words took on a whole new meaning now.

> Aren't you tired?

> Are you?

A few minutes ago, yes. Very. Now?

> Not really.

> Whatcha want to do?

> I mean, talk about?

The second text came through quickly.
I could ignore it. *Should* ignore it.

> Freudian slip?

My heart thudded as I waited for his answer. I was pushing it, but couldn't
seem to stop myself.

> No. Intentional.

Smiling, I thought about what to say next. I loved the ocean, but never
was a fan of swimming in it, always content to sit on the beach or dip my toes
in. But it felt as if I was wading into waist-deep water now with no idea what
was swimming around me.

> Options being?

I'd just taken a big step forward and was now in up to my chin.

> I'd elaborate, but it's against your rules.

> Which one?

Since there were only two, and kissing wasn't possible at the moment, I
knew exactly which one. Another step and I'd be above my head.

Pretty sure 'real talk' would break your crossing the line rule.

Real talk. It's what Beck and I used to say when one of us thought the other one was bullshitting. It was a way to say, "Spit it out," and get honest. We had some pretty deep conversations because of it.

How so?

You want me to answer that?

This was the crossroads. I could feel it. If I responded, "Probably not," we could end the conversation here. Proceed as planned. The other path had some pretty serious consequences. Mathieu was one thing. Losing Beck from my life would be devastation I wouldn't have the faintest idea how to come back from.

On the other hand, Jules's advice when I was hedging on going to France... "You don't get to rewrite a moment you were too afraid to live."

I do.

I was in the deep end now.

Option one, follow the rules, make small talk and say goodnight.

And option two?

We could play.

Ohmygod, ohmygod, ohmygod.

Meaning?

Truth or dare?

Was this really happening?

Truth.

> How many times have you thought about our kiss since Saturday?

I took a deep breath, the fresh cabin air from a slight breeze off the lake spilling into my bedroom window. How many times? I had no idea.

> Too many to count.

I got a smiley face for that.

> Your turn, truth or dare.

Truth.

Thank goodness. I had no idea what I would've dared him.

> When did this start for you?

Already a text bubble formed.

> A long, long time ago.

How was it possible? This wasn't far from our first "real talk," and yet all this time...

> Truth or dare?

Did I dare to go there?
*Memento mori* and all that. Here went nothing.

> Dare.

> Put your phone in your left hand.

Easy enough.

> Lick your middle finger, Mae.

Holy shit. But I did it.

> Now slip that down, into your pussy.

No, he did not.

There would be no going back after this. The thought of not doing it, though, left me... empty. A dare was a dare, after all. Though if I were being honest to myself, that really had nothing to do with the fact that I listened. Again.

> Imagine that's my finger, because it will be. Moving just how you like it. Don't hold back.

And so, I did.

For a second, there were no more texts. But I could tell he was typing. At this point, I'd have a hard time stopping, imagining just what Beck had told me to.

Oh, boy. So that's why it took so long. A voice text.

"There you go." His deep smooth voice played in my ear. "Close your eyes and circle your clit, Mae, as if I'm right there with you. Mmmm, that's it. Do you feel it building? Are you gonna come for me?"

I couldn't text back.

The very thought of what we were doing, what I was doing...

Another one.

"That's it. Think about how, the second I'm off this phone, I'm going into my shower, taking myself in my hand and imagining you lying on that bed coming apart for me right now. Go ahead, Mae, let go for me, baby."

It was the baby that did it.

I actually came, just like he told me to. Without a vibrator. Just by listening to his voice. I lay there for a few extra seconds, letting my breathing go back to normal. And then before I could think twice about it, I jumped out of bed, washed my hands, splashed water on my face and dried it, and then headed back into the bedroom. While I was up, I turned off the lamp and crawled back into bed.

Picking up my phone, I laughed at his confused emoji.

> Sorry. Took me a minute to recover.

From?

You know what.

Type it.

Awful demanding. Didn't hate it.

Coming, listening to your voice.

Good. Now it's time to put your phone down and dream of doing that with me there for real. Then maybe we can renegotiate our arrangement tomorrow.

Lol, I knew you had an angle.

Just winning you over. If that's an angle, guilty as charged.

Smiling, I sent him a smile and goodnight face, waited for the same, and put my phone on the nightstand. That was hot. Surprising. And most of all, whether smart or not, a tipping point.

Tomorrow would be... interesting.

# 31

BECK

It wasn't even dinner rush, and it felt as if today had lasted forever.

Between the bank, the lawyer, back and forth calls with Mr. O'Malley, and our cook coming down with the flu (in May?) it had been a full day. I had to promise my back-up cook two weekends in a row off if I wanted to avoid the kitchen myself, which I did. Not that I minded all that much, though I preferred front of the house more, but with everything else happening I couldn't be stuck back there.

"Round of shots, on me," Mason called.

I'd told the staff already, and the guys. Since I hadn't heard from Mae, I could only assume she hadn't talked to her parents yet.

It had taken some creative timing, an emergency wire transfer, and a hell of a lot of signatures, but by four o'clock, O'Malley's was officially mine.

"Four," he corrected when I poured three shots for us before looking around the bar to be sure no one needed a drink first.

"You drinking two?" I asked, grabbing another shot glass.

"I'll have his extra."

As if on cue, a buttoned-up Cole walked up between Mason and Parker and reached his hand over the bar.

I shook it, surprised, even though I shouldn't have been. So many people didn't get our friendship with Cole. He was very different than the three of us, especially Parker and me. But Cole Ford was one hell of a friend. And fun too, when he loosened up.

"Congratulations, buddy."

"How the hell did you assholes pull this together?"

Cole sat next to Parker. I thought he'd left a stool open for Delaney since the girls had to be back by now. They were stopping for lunch on the way home but Mae had confirmed she'd be here tonight.

I smiled, thinking of her brief text. Just a single line, classic Mae:

Behave till I get there.

"Only had one class this morning," Cole said, taking the shot I gave him. "Mason said it looked like everything was going through so, here I am."

He said that like it wasn't more than a five-hour drive, if Manhattan traffic cooperated.

"I appreciate it," I said, raising my shot glass, as did the others.

"To Beck," Mason said. "Welcome to the big boys' club."

Fuckers.

I downed it, the smooth golden liquid running through me. I almost got sentimental, having the three of them here like this to help me celebrate. Thankfully, the sight of Mae stopped me. It was hard to miss her. She was quite literally running through the bar toward me.

The guys turned to watch.

I barely made it to the bar opening when Mae was there, launching herself into my arms. If she hadn't been smiling from ear to ear, I'd have thought something was wrong.

"I can't believe you," she said.

She smelled as good as she looked. I could have stayed like that all day, even with the whistles and hollers we were causing from my regulars. Unfortunately, Mae pulled back.

"Talked to your parents?" I guessed.

"Yes," she said. "I was home getting ready when they called on the way home from the realtor's office where they left a deposit on their dream vacation place. Thanks to you."

"I'd say thanks to the hard work they put into this place."

She tilted her head to the side. "I don't know how you pulled it off—

bartenders must make a hell of a lot more money than I thought to have that kind of cash at your disposal."

A story for another time. Natives were getting restless.

"Come celebrate with us? Look who just got into town to celebrate."

She leaned around me to where my buddies sat.

"Cole? Holy shit, how did he get here so quick? My dad said it only came together this afternoon."

"Good question. He just surprised me too, about five minutes ago. Go say hello. I've got the bar."

I grabbed a few drinks and rejoined the others, slinging my arm around Mae's shoulders. I did it without thinking. But it was too late now to take back. Would just have to lean into it.

"Well, boys, you're looking at the new owner of O'Malley's and the woman who made it happen."

Mae all but snorted. "How did I make it happen?"

"He's a better man when you're around, Mae," Parker said. "You know that."

"Uh huh." She didn't sound convinced. Unfortunately, Lou the mechanic was empty. I reluctantly let her go and refilled him, grudgingly admitting it was my job. One I usually loved but, at the moment, was taking a backseat to a particular beautiful blonde standing a few feet away from me.

"Penny for your thoughts?"

She came up from behind me, reached past me, snagged a bottle from the speed rail, and poured a perfect whiskey neat like she'd been behind this bar a hundred times.

"Not bad," I said, watching her work.

She gave me a look over her shoulder. "You forgetting who taught you to pour without spilling?"

Fair point. And also... way hotter than it should've been.

"I'll give you one guess," I said, when she finished serving it.

"Your new bar?"

"Nope."

"The three amigos?" She nodded to the laughter coming from my friends. They were looking over Cole's shoulder at something on his phone.

"Try again."

She slid the glass across the bar, wiped her hands on a bar towel, then tossed it in the bin like she owned the place.

"I'm going to check the walk-in. Someone around here has to make sure the limes aren't molding. Besides, I think I already know the answer."

With that, Mae walked away, leaving me staring after her.

"Better pick your jaw off the floor, son," Lou said. "Before she comes back."

I shot him a look, ignored his chuckle, and rejoined the others.

"Ladies joining us?"

Mason shook his head. "Pia's at the inn."

"Delaney said she was going home to pass out. Sounds like they had a good time at Grado."

"So much for the pact," Cole mumbled, looking into his drink.

Mason put his arm around him. "Chin up, buddy. Think of what you can do with the extra cash."

"Wait a minute," Parker said. "Did you pony up?"

All three of them looked at me.

"Why would I?"

The look he gave me was classic Parker. Everyone called him "the nice one" but he could freeze a forest fire with his eyes.

"We're not dating," I pointed out. "Hang on a sec."

I flipped a shaker in one hand, poured tequila with the other, and slid a lime wedge onto the rim of a fresh glass, putting it, along with two beers, on Jenn's pass.

"Not yet, maybe." Mason lifted his empty mug, which I refilled.

"I told you, she put the brakes on us." Last night being one glaring exception.

"That didn't look like brakes," Cole said, swirling his drink around in his glass.

"It didn't," Mason agreed.

"Awww, fuck," I said, seeing three women walk in. One of them could easily cause me trouble.

Parker snorted. "Avoiding your past isn't possible," he said. "Just have to keep showing Mae it's not your present."

"Spoken like a man who left me stranded in a sea of plus-ones, quoting Nietzsche to the jukebox," Cole said wryly.

"They don't know who Nietzsche is," I pointed out.

"Sure we do."

I left Mason to argue that point to serve the newcomers.

"Looking good back there, Beck."

True to form, Laurie Lagan Hoban was dressed to the nines. A beautiful brunette, she was bubbly and fun, but not for me. Especially now.

"Pit stop for a girls' night out?" I asked them, avoiding her compliment.

"You know it," her friend, one I didn't recognize, said.

"What can I get you ladies?"

"Drink-wise or..." Laurie trailed off suggestively.

Despite the fact that our brief fling ended more than two years ago, Laurie never stopped trying to rekindle. She was tenacious, I'd give her that.

"Drinks," I said firmly, taking their orders.

And of course, because I couldn't catch a break where Mae was concerned, she strode toward the bar at that moment. Ignoring Mason's low whistle, I shot him the middle finger behind my back and greeted her.

"Hey, sexy," I whispered, since Mae was walking right past me. Couldn't waste the opportunity.

"You're a nut." She headed over to the guys.

I shook, poured and served the women.

"We're off to The Grapevine Bistro for dinner," Laurie said. "Have you been recently?"

She was as subtle as a Mack truck driving through my living room. It was where we went on our first date. As with all of my exes, it was only one of a few. Unfortunately I seemed to have left an impression on Laurie.

"Not in a while," I said, immediately turning away. Courting the line between appearing flirtatious and rude was never a strong suit of mine. I had a lot more practice with the former, but flirting with pretty women was firmly off the "to do" list.

Unfortunately, Mae didn't know that. She was trying to be subtle, but she'd noticed.

"How's the inventory going?" I asked.

"About as fresh as the guy who tried to sell us strawberries with mold on 'em."

"Ouch. The festival kicked my ass," I admitted. "But I didn't think it was that bad."

"No one to blame but yourself, boss," Parker teased. A reminder of why the gang was all here. It felt good. Really good. Sharing it with Mae? Even better.

"Fuck off," I said, nodding to his glass. "Big talk from someone whose glass is empty."

"I got you, Park." Mae grabbed it for him.

"Traitor," I muttered to her as she slid behind me. Hissing in a breath, certain that slight ass swipe was intentional, I caught Mason's gaze. He'd noticed and was grinning like a man who'd been there. Because he had.

We continued to chat for a bit until a voice I'd once thought was sweet but now grated through me called out, "Hey, Beck. Cosmos are running low over here."

Mae and I exchanged a look. I held my breath, wanting my good luck to continue until we could finally be alone. I couldn't wait to talk about last night, and what it might mean for us, but Laurie was a glaring stop sign for Mae, a reminder of why she'd put the brakes on us in the first place.

With a smile that could only be described as devious, she laid a hand on my arm, as if to excuse herself past me. But it would be hard not to notice how long she left it there.

"I got her," she said sweetly.

Mason barked out a laugh.

Parker grinned.

Even Cole smiled.

But as much as I loved these guys, and was grateful Cole had come up for the weekend to help me celebrate, the only thing I wanted at the moment was to kick them, and every other customer, out of the place and get Mae alone.

# 32

## MAE

Closed, finally.

If I'd ever second-guessed my decision *not* to take over the bar, co-managing it with Beck would have pushed me over the edge. I didn't mind hard work, or the customers (most of the time) but late nights would be the death of me. Unlike Beck, I wasn't a night owl most days. Unless the girls and I were out, of course. Or when I needed to be.

"How do you do it, night after night?" I asked, wiping the last streak of glass cleaner off the front door and tossing the rag onto the back counter.

Beck was behind the bar rinsing out the blender, his sleeves rolled up. He glanced at me with a grin, the kind that said this was his happy place... music low, lights dimmed, the air thick with the comfort of familiarity and spilled whiskey.

"I'd be happy to discuss that with you," he said as I approached, sitting on a bar stool. "But we have other, more pressing things, to talk about."

He reached under the bar and pulled out a bottle of my favorite prosecco.

"Where did you get that?"

"The liquor store," he said, dry as could be. I watched him expertly pour two glasses, his forearms flexing. Why were forearms such a *thing*? Beck's, especially. Seeing my expression, he winked. "Grabbed it for just this occasion. Although it occurred to me, after living in France, champagne might be more your thing these days."

He handed me a glass.

"In fact, I still like prosecco more. Funny how that works, isn't it?"

"What's that?"

"That sometimes, what we like most isn't always what we're supposed to." I emphasized the word "supposed."

"You're not kidding, there." He raised his glass. "To the end of an era and the beginning of a new one."

A shiver ran through me. "The bar, you mean?"

"That too."

I paused, trying not to make too much of it. But this really did feel like we were crossing some sort of invisible line. Not that we hadn't already last night. Or over the weekend, for that matter.

"Cheers," I said, taking a sip. Over the rim of the prosecco glass, I watched Beck who, in turn, hadn't taken his eyes from me. "I'm grateful for what you did for my parents, Beck. They're over the moon."

He leaned against the back bar. The sight of him, ruggedly handsome, sleeves up, hair tousled, drinking prosecco, made me smile.

"What?"

"I don't think I've ever seen you drink prosecco before."

"Not true," he said. "We've been to more than one wedding together."

"Fair point. But that's different."

"How?"

"Because you're in a suit then."

"I see." He took another sip. "And it wasn't just for your parents. I pretty much lived here anyway. It was just a matter of committing to being the owner. It's not a responsibility I take lightly, O'Malley's legacy."

"I appreciate that."

"Is there anything you'd like to talk about? Maybe we can avoid the topic a little more."

Chuckling, I tried to think of a way to do just that. "I never did tell you about the girls' night."

He shook his head slowly. "You're getting warmer but are not quite there."

"Thayle's pregnant," I blurted.

"Warmer."

"How is that warmer?"

His brows raised. "How did Thayle *get* pregnant?"

He was such a nut. "By having sex?" I ventured.

"Bingo."

I wasn't going to make this easy on him.

"What does that have to do with us? We haven't had sex."

"Keep it up, O'Malley, and I'll show you what that has to do with us rather than having a discussion about it."

My heart raced as I considered the next words that should come out of my mouth. Having sex with Beck, despite it being a recurring daydream these days, would unequivocally change everything. As much as I wanted it...

"Fine. Let's talk about it."

His smile was downright devious. "Enjoy yourself last night?"

"You know I did. Because you made me say it," I accused.

"Type it, technically, not to split hairs."

"Well, that was a good talk. So about—"

Letting out a little scream as Beck set down his glass and strode purposefully toward me, I did the same, placing it safely on the bar just in time. He grabbed my knee, pulled it open while simultaneously spinning me toward him.

A second later, Beck was between my legs, grabbing my face. It was the single hottest thing any man had ever done. But instead of kissing me, he stood there, looking into my eyes.

"Tell me you don't want to repeat Saturday night. That you want to keep following the rules. Because if you don't, Mae, I'm going to kiss you again."

My shoulders rose and fell, my heartbeat pounding in my ears. I couldn't tell him that. Not without branding myself a boldfaced liar.

This time, it wasn't as gentle. Our lips slammed together, Beck's hands inching from my face to the back of my head. Like the first, our mouths melded together as if they'd been made for each other. A flash of last night's antics ran through my mind as my body felt as if it had turned to jelly. His shoulders flexed beneath my fingers, Beck hard and unyielding.

Not that I wanted him to.

He was so good at kissing. Too good.

I forced the thought from my mind.

I could kiss him all night. But Beck seemed to have other plans. He pulled back, but not for long. His lips trailed a path from mine down my cheek to my neck. I lifted it, to give him better access, but the neck of my t-shirt didn't allow for much. Which was probably why Beck grabbed it with both hands, where the shirt was tucked into my jeans, looked at me with hooded eyes for a split second, and then yanked it up and off me in one smooth motion.

"Oh, God," he said, looking at me. "I've seen you this way before, but never just before I was about to rip off your bra. Dear lord, you are sexy."

His words. His tone. The way he stared at me. All of it together was a heady combination. I didn't utter a word in protest.

Resuming where he'd left off, I waited for Beck to reach behind my back and unclasp my bra. Instead, he kissed all the way from my collarbone to the top of both breasts. Still, he didn't attempt to uncover them.

When his mouth hovered over me, his breath on my nipple followed by a flick of his tongue through the lace, I clenched in anticipation. He did the same to both breasts, and I nearly reached back to undo the damn clasp myself.

Finally, his hands splayed across my waist on each side as he kissed a trail back upward. Arching into him, I let my head fall back.

"Mmm."

"Like this?" he asked, his tongue flicking against my skin.

"Mmhmm."

"Are you picturing my tongue on your bare nipple, Mae?"

How had he guessed?

I lifted my head to find him staring at me with the faintest hint of a smile.

His hands moved upward, Beck's thumbs sliding across my lace bra, stopping as he circled both nipples.

"I cannot fucking wait to get these in my mouth," he said, as both peaked under his ministrations.

Swallowing, the question at the tip of my tongue, I waited.

Nothing could have surprised me more when Beck suddenly reached down, grabbed my t-shirt, and put it back on. It wasn't until Beck smoothed my hair that had got tousled in the process that I said anything.

"Why... did you stop?"

"Good question." Leaning forward, he kissed me, softly, for what felt like the last time tonight.

"I stopped because I've been imagining seeing you naked, cherishing your body, for most of my adult life. This"—he waved his hand around the bar—"isn't how I pictured it. Besides, we could have an audience."

I thought of that. The front windows of the bar were covered in lettering, but it wouldn't be difficult for anyone walking by to peer in. Not that anyone was likely to at this time of night, and if they did, they probably wouldn't see much in the dark.

"But the other reason," he said, "is that I don't want to rush anything. I want to prove I can be patient for you, Mae."

Well damn, that was inconvenient.

Thoughtful. But inconvenient. Because I wanted nothing more than for Beck to tear my bra off, and my jeans too, and show me if he was as skilled a lover as he claimed.

Not that I really needed proof. Not after that kiss.

"And that's why I'm going to walk you home, now. Before I change my mind."

# 33

## BECK

"You look like hell."

"Thanks, buddy," I said to Mason, who ventured to the coffee maker, pouring himself a cup.

"It's early for you," he said, sitting across from me at the kitchen island.

"Lots to do today. I'm looking at a few apartments."

That got Mason's attention. "Why?"

"For the same reason most people look at apartments. To find one to live in."

He didn't say anything, so I stated the obvious. "Renovations are just about finished. Parker and Delaney's house will be done this summer. I can't live here forever."

"You can stay as long as you want, Beck."

"I know. But it's time."

Mason whistled. "You're not fooling around."

"I'm trying. But there's a lot of ground to make up. She didn't say anything about Laurie last night, but that's not gonna be the last time. Don't get me wrong, I'm thrilled Mae sees me as more than a friend too. But it feels like I'm walking on thin ice. There's a good chance I'll fuck this up."

Last night felt like a victory. It was borderline painful to walk home, and I kicked myself more than once. Everything I'd ever wanted was right there for the taking, but instinctively I knew Mae wasn't ready. She didn't trust me yet, and I couldn't blame her.

"You can't change the past."

"I know. Doesn't make it any easier though." I almost said the next part but couldn't, not even to Mason. Mae deserved the world. Had almost lived in France. And now I was offering her the life she'd always wanted to leave. Cedar Falls. Hitched to a bar owner. She respected her parents, clearly, but had never wanted to become them, and she'd made that clear.

Mason stood. "Don't self-sabotage, whatever you do."

With those parting words, he slapped me on the back and headed out, presumably to the inn. *Don't self-sabotage*. What the hell was that supposed to mean?

Finishing my coffee, I put the mug in the dishwasher and headed out, walking up the inn's long drive and toward town. I'd miss being on the lake, but that wasn't on the cards. At least not yet. I'd been smart with my money, made a few good investments, but the bar would set me back temporarily.

At the top of the hill, I watched as downtown Cedar Falls came to life. A father chased his young son through the grass toward the gazebo at the center of the square. On the four streets surrounding it, shops began to open. Tourists and locals alike wandered around with coffee cups, most from The Coffee Cabin.

The Big Easy, Jenkin's Hardware, Lakeside Pharmacy... I knew every one of the owners, and their families too. Unlike Mae, I'd never really been bored here. Was there more to do in bigger towns? Was an occasional weekend in Rochester or Ithaca warranted? Sure.

But this was enough for me.

Was it enough for Mae, too?

"Lost, son?"

I turned to find Emilio Russo, owner of a wine shop in town. He was straight off the boat from Italy, his accent still thick, even after all these years. His crazy white hair reminded me of Albert Einstein, a fact he found funny when I'd told him that.

I shook his hand.

"Just taking it all in," I admitted.

Emilio stood with me, staring into the town square.

"Do you ever miss home?" I asked.

"This is home for me," he sighed. "More than twenty years in Cedar Falls now."

"Of all the places in the world, why here?"

Emilio probably thought I'd been smokin' a little something. He didn't laugh though.

"It reminded me of home, but with more opportunities. There might be fewer men playing chess and smoking cigars in the piazza, but there are similarities too. Everything I need is right here."

"It's enough for me too," I admitted. "But there's a woman—"

"Always is," he said with a smile.

"I just don't know if it's enough for her too."

He was quiet for a moment, waving to Maggie LeBlanc across the square.

"Why here?" he repeated my question. "My wife and I lived in Brooklyn when we first came over."

"You did? I didn't know that."

"*Sì, sì,*" he said, slipping into Italian. "Worked in an Italian restaurant and met a couple from Cedar Falls. Visited it and liked it right away. It was different, that's for sure. But I liked the version of myself I was while I was here. My wife did too. And I realized… peace is not the same as boredom." He turned to me, his old eyes sharper than I expected. "You can't hold someone here with love alone. They must want this life too. Not the picture-perfect version. The real thing. Leaky roofs. Slow mornings. The same faces, every damn day. If she doesn't see beauty in that, she'll always be looking elsewhere."

Something heavy settled in my chest.

"*Capisci?*"

I nodded. "Yeah. I do."

Emilio patted my shoulder. "*Bene.*"

And with that, he shuffled off toward the wine shop, leaving me staring after him, the hum of town life pressing in like a wave I hadn't seen coming.

Thinking was hard. It was easier to get drunk, not have feelings for women, and enjoy each day. But that was just me putting off the inevitable.

*Time to adult, Beck.*

I just hoped, despite what Emilio had said, it meant Mae being mine.

# 34

## MAE

"Do you know how long it's been since I've had an ice cream cone?"

Beck walked beside me, taking a sip of his milkshake. I could never understand why someone would want to drink their ice cream.

"They don't have ice cream in France?"

"They do, but it's not the same. Smaller scoops, richer flavors, and no rainbow sprinkles in sight."

When Beck texted earlier to ask if I wanted to meet him in the square, I'd been researching starting a business. And checking my phone, wondering who would reach out first. If there was a guidebook on how to approach *potentially* dating your friend without destroying your relationship, I really could have used it.

"No rainbow sprinkles?" he asked, taking the path which led to the only public lake access near the square. "And you considered actually living there?"

It was a reminder that I had, a few months ago, been engaged.

"I was... caught up in the fantasy of it all."

His tanned bicep flexed as Beck lifted the shake to his mouth. A vision of that mouth grazing my nipple reminded me why I'd been tossing and turning all night. It was a different kind of unsettled than when I'd first come home. This was more like a nervous excitement, the moment just as you get to the top of a roller coaster. Fun, but a little scary too.

Miraculously, a lakefront bench was empty. On a Saturday, this time of year, they were prime seats. Grabbing it, we sat.

"What do you mean?" He crossed his legs. Beck wore a tee and jeans, his normal attire. The shirt was from a music festival we'd gone to in college when he'd flashed his ass out the back window of the car on the way home in traffic.

"Being back home reminds me of all the things I missed in France. But when I was there, I was content to forgot all of that for a... dream life. Or what I thought was a dream life at the time."

"You don't think so anymore?"

It was a question I'd been considering lately.

"I'm not sure. It just felt as if I had everything. But now?"

Without the proper words to explain the turmoil I felt, I licked my ice cream cone instead.

At Beck's groan, I stifled a grin and did it again, this time, more provocatively.

"O'Malley," he warned.

I gave him my most innocent smile.

"Yes, Claymont?"

"Keep it up."

"Or else?"

Instead of answering, he shot me a warning look and stared out at the lake. We sat in silence for a bit. That was one thing about us. The silence had never been uncomfortable.

"Could you be happy here?"

It was the one question I couldn't answer. For so long, my dream was to get out of Cedar Falls, not stay in it. I had enjoyed living in France. And probably would enjoy other places just as much.

But here? Where everyone knew your business and trying new restaurants meant driving at least forty minutes from home?

I looked at him, unsure what to say.

"You don't know."

It wasn't a question.

"What amazes me is how well we know each other, and yet all this time..."

His half smile meant Beck wasn't going to let me off the hook.

"You liked me," I finished, lamely.

"That's one way to put it."

He smelled so good. Looked so good. There was a time, way back in middle school, the younger version of me would have died for Beck to look at me the way he was right now. Before I realized he would break my heart if we ever "went there."

*Never date the neighbor.*

They really created a rule. For me.

This was too heavy for a sunny Saturday afternoon eating ice cream. I'd planned on telling him about my research but couldn't do it. Starting a business here meant I was staying in Cedar Falls. He'd asked if I could be happy here, and until I could answer that question with confidence, I wouldn't put us down that path.

"I found an apartment."

That brought me out of my reverie.

"Are you serious?"

"Yep. That's what I was doing in town. It's actually a double, three hundred block of Lake Street. Eventually I'd like to buy something, obviously, but in the meantime it's close to the bar and for rent."

"You're moving out of the inn?"

I was shocked. When Beck first told me about the arrangement, I'd teased that Mason would never get them out of there. It was like college all over again.

"It was never meant to be permanent. The renovations are just about done. Parker will be moving out as soon as the house is finished. And with the baby coming..." He shrugged. "It's time."

Holy shit.

The bar. An apartment.

He was really trying.

"Wow," I teased. "I honestly thought you and the guys would grow old there, sitting on the back deck with your cigars talking about the good ol' days."

"Don't rule that out," he said, finishing his milkshake.

Beck stood to toss it out, giving me a very fine view of his very fine ass.

"Caught you looking," he said, turning around quickly.

"You're ridiculous."

He tossed his empty shake like it was a three-point shot. Hit it, of course.

Beck was one of those guys that was good at every sport he tried, including basketball.

"Do you remember the time—"

"I kissed you?" he asked.

He sat just as I finished my cone. I thought of licking my sticky fingers, but that was probably not the best idea at the moment.

"How did you guess that's what I was thinking?" I wondered.

"Because I don't play a pickup game without remembering it. Mason dared me."

"I remember."

"You and your friends were waiting for us to come out of the gym. It was the week of our eighth-grade dance," he said.

"I pretended to be appalled, knowing everyone was watching."

"Pretended?"

"Mmm hmm," I murmured.

"You're gonna have to explain that one."

"Well." I wasn't sure how to phrase it. "Of course I wanted you to do it. Everyone, including me, knew you were the cutest guy in middle school."

"Oh yeah?"

I rolled my eyes. He was just looking for compliments now. "But I'd also made a bit of a show of not wanting to be another one of your fan club members. So I convinced my friends, and myself I guess, it was appalling. The idea of me and you, anything more than friends."

"I was a bit of a jerk," he admitted.

"A Casanova in training."

"Of sorts."

"Why?"

It was a loaded question. And I could guess at the answer. But I wondered if Beck had given it any thought himself.

"Why?" His gaze dropped down to my lips. A fact that was difficult to ignore. "I could blame my parents, I guess. Even then they were disconnected... so different from me, and from your family. But..." He shrugged. "I'm sure there was more to it than that. I got a lot of attention, and liked it. Leaned into it just a little too much. Insecurity, maybe?"

He was more self-aware than I'd have expected.

"I like this Beck."

"You would."

"What does that mean?"

One second, we were sitting beside each other on the bench. The next, he reached out, grabbed my hand, and entwined his fingers through mine. It was so unexpected, I didn't know what to say. Or do. Just that... it felt right.

"Do you remember when you asked me, when you first came home, why men suck?"

I thought back, and did remember it. I nodded.

His fingers tightened around mine. "I think I'm ready to give you an answer."

My breath caught.

But before he could finish, Beck's phone buzzed. He let go of my hand and pulled it out.

"Shit. I've gotta go. I'll see you at the bar. We have plenty of coverage. Come whenever."

"Beck? What is it?"

I wasn't sure if he heard me. He was still focused on his phone as he jogged across the grass back uphill, leaving me behind with no clue as to what had just happened.

## 35

---

### BECK

"Do you smell it?"

Spence and I stood at the back door of the bar in the alley. From here, the smell was unmistakable.

"I do. Head back in and tell Jenn to stop taking food orders. I'm calling the fire department."

"Got it, boss."

He was a good kid. I called it in, talked to the cook and prepared the staff for a possible night off. We weren't messing around with a gas leak, if that's what it was. Just as I headed out front, the fire truck arrived. Already people were gathering, the sight of the big truck on the small street the most exciting thing that would happen today in Cedar Falls.

Mae asked:

Everything ok?

Yep. Maybe gas leak at the bar. Fire dept. here.

I hadn't wanted to burden her. She'd dealt with plenty of headaches throughout the years because of O'Malley's Pub, and it was my problem now.

Of course customers stared as I walked through the place with two guys I'd known my whole life, one I'd played football with in high school. Waiting for them to check it out, I thought back to before we were interrupted at the lake.

*It was good we got cut short.*

Spilling my guts to Mae would only put pressure on her, and as much as I wanted our story to end here, hers wasn't written yet. It was selfish of me to think otherwise.

"Beck?" My old teammate snapped his fingers in front of my face.

"Sorry. What's up?"

"Thankfully you don't have a leak. It's a faulty pilot line."

"Meaning?" I had no clue about this shit.

"There's no imminent danger, but it's gonna require a shut off. Unfortunately we have to tag the system until it's fixed."

"Fuck," I muttered, glad it wasn't a leak, but the outcome would be the same. "Alright, thanks for coming out so quick."

"No problem. So I hear this place is yours now?"

"It is. Come back with your buddies, meal on me as a thank you."

"We'll take you up on that. Give Nate Coops a call. He should be able to get out pretty quick."

"Will do." I shook his hand and got to work. Unfortunately, Nate couldn't get out until tomorrow morning since he was out of town for the night. I called around but Cedar Falls wasn't exactly crawling with licensed gas techs.

I texted Mae back, told her we were shutting down and then took care of the staff and customers. By the time the place was empty, it was well into the afternoon. But since Mae and I were both supposed to be working tonight, I had an idea.

Plans tonight?

Nope. Not anymore.

She texted back right away.

Perfect.

Though part of me wanted to get out of here for the night, O'Malley's was actually perfect. I just needed some help.

Come up around six.

To the bar?

Yep.

She sent back a confused face, which I laughed at but otherwise didn't say anything. Then, closing down, I headed back to the inn where I found Pia arranging flowers at the check-in counter. Perfect.

"Can I have those?"

She looked at me like I was crazy. "Excuse me?"

"I know you always have fresh flowers around. I also need some candles. Any idea where I can get a bunch of them?"

Pia crossed her arms. "Can you please start from the beginning? You're making no sense."

I explained about O'Malley's and told Pia my plan. "I don't know if it's a good idea or not. The last thing I want is to pressure Mae into staying to have her end up bored or regretting staying in Cedar Falls. On the other hand, I can't let her go. Not without a fight. What do you think?"

Pia and I had bonded since she'd come to Heritage Hill. Mason's wife was warm and funny, fitting right in with us from the start. It had taken a bit to crack the hardheaded ex-army guy she called her husband, but she did it. And now I needed her help.

"First of all, let Mae make her own decisions. If she wants to stay in Cedar Falls, she will. If she wants to move to Manhattan or France or wherever else, no one knows what's best for Mae more than she does, even if she's a little confused at the moment. You know I love you, Beck, but there's nothing worse than a guy trying to 'save' a woman from a life she hasn't even asked to be saved from. Let her choose. Got it?"

I'd expected Pia not to pull any punches, but... shit. I swallowed.

"Got it."

"Second of all, as you're so fond of saying, I've been hearing about how much you adore Mae since I got here last year. From you. From Mason. The guys. There's a friggin' rule just for you. She's back. Sans a fiancé. And feels" —she cleared her throat—"more than just friendly feelings for you too. Obviously there's chemistry between you two. Stop overthinking it."

"I'm not," I insisted. "I'm trying to think of *her*."

"And you're doing it in the best way possible. By being the best version of yourself. You want her to choose Cedar Falls for herself, which is great. But you need to choose yourself because it's who you want to be. Not just for Mae."

"How the hell did you become so wise?"

Pia shrugged. "Therapy. Listening to people who know more than me. Which is why you need to listen to me now."

I laughed. "And so humble too."

She handed the just-finished flower arrangement to me. "Third of all, yes, you can have the flowers. We have a stash of candles in the second-floor storage room. Take as many as you need. But one thing... if you have to close down, is it safe for you to be in there?"

"It's safe. The line's shut off completely and tagged. No gas flowing in until the guy comes tomorrow."

"What guy?"

Mason walked in, and for a second, it was as if Papa Bennett had come back to life. His stride. His stance. I would tell him later. No doubt, his father would be proud to see what he'd done with the inn. If Mason could go from NYPD to an attentive husband and innkeeper extraordinaire, anything was possible.

"Bar was shut down, fire department had to come out after Spence smelled gas. Was just a faulty valve but we're shuttered until tomorrow morning when Nate Coops can come out."

"That sucks. Welcome to our world." He addressed Pia. "I was just in the Madeline room. You're right, there's a leak that'll need to be looked at."

"Parker around?" I asked, knowing he'd do it.

"I think he and Delaney went out to dinner. Speaking of, what are we doing?" he asked us both.

Pia looked at me.

"Not sure what you two are doing," I said, "but I'm off to Bella Luna's to grab some takeout after I raid your candle stash. Pia will explain."

I heard Mason ask, "What the hell was that all about?" as I walked off. He would think I'd lost my mind, but I didn't care. If I needed to buy every candle in Cedar Falls to make tonight special, that's what I would do.

Pia was right.

Mae could decide for herself what she wanted for her future, but I wasn't leaving anything off the table. I'd been pussyfooting around long enough.

Tonight, I would tell Mae exactly how I felt about her, how I'd always felt about her, and then it would be up to her to decide.

For better or worse, after tonight, we would be in Mae's hands.

# 36

## MAE

I could tell something was up as I walked toward the bar. Normally, unless it was dark, you could look straight in through the clear windows. But both were draped in black cloth, a "closed" sign on the door. It seemed an odd requirement. Why would a faulty valve require covering the windows?

I used my key to open the door, unsure what to expect. It certainly wasn't an entire room full of candles, the only source of light, and one table set for dinner in the center. Beck was, as usual, behind the bar. But he was wearing a different outfit than before, dressed more for... well, dinner. He looked so handsome in navy pants, a white button-down shirt with its sleeves rolled. For my benefit? Beck knew that was a "thing" of mine.

He came around the bar with two glasses of wine.

"Hungry?"

"Yeah, but... what is all this?"

"Dinner," he said, handing me a wine.

It was more than just dinner, obviously. I honestly didn't know what to think, but after spending the day doing more research, and trying to figure out my life, maybe I could *not* think just for the night.

I took a sip. "This is good. What is it?"

"I asked Emilio for his best red, and he gave me a Nero d'Avola a friend of his makes. It's a bit dense for what we're eating, but hopefully you like it."

"I love it."

"Good." He clinked my glass. "*Salute*."

"What are we toasting to?"

"Possibilities."

A shiver ran up me, both at his words and the way Beck looked at me. Sighing, I gestured to the bar. "It looks beautiful. Where did you get so many candles?"

"Pia had one hell of a candle stash."

I loved the way his smile reached all the way up to his eyes. Beck was always smiling, but when it was sincere... not flirty or him being silly, I could tell. Right now, he was genuinely happy.

"Sit," he said, heading to the table and pulling out my chair. "This was the best I could do to keep it warm."

Our plates were covered, but after I sat, Beck removed them. "Baked manicotti."

"Is this Bella Luna?"

"Of course," he said.

Their manicotti was to die for. I hadn't had it in years.

"This is all pretty incredible. I'd have thought, with a forced night off, you'd want to get out of here. Especially with no electricity and all."

"Just the opposite," he said as I began to eat. "It felt like the appropriate place to talk. The start of what I hope to be an exciting future as O'Malley's new owner."

"I like it," I admitted. "It almost makes me wish it was always like this. Maybe you should get rid of the lights and go for a 'pre-electricity' vibe."

"Jesus," he said, taking a sip of wine. "I'd have to get in an hour early to light all the candles. Flipping a switch is a hell of a lot easier."

"True."

We ate. Drank. Talked quietly about our day since meeting up for ice cream.

"Why didn't you tell me what was wrong?" I asked, the question having been on my mind all day. "I was worried."

"Sorry about that. I just... didn't want to burden you with the bar. Figured you'd come with me."

"It's never a burden. Being with you is... easy."

"Easy?"

"Uh huh."

"Is that it?"

"Fishing for compliments again?"

He winked. "Always."

"Enjoyable."

"That's better."

"There's more, but I don't think your head will fit through the door when we leave, so I'll stop there."

"Which head?" he teased, making me laugh.

"You're not that big," I managed. "Don't flatter yourself."

"How do you know?"

I didn't. But I wanted to. My thoughts on Beck might have been a jumbled mess lately, but that much was clear.

"I'm pleading the fifth."

His eyes widened. "Mae O'Malley. Did you cop a peek the night we went skinny dipping?"

How could I have forgotten that? A lakeside beer party took a turn the summer between junior and senior year in college.

"Absolutely not. Did you?"

"Hell yeah. Are you kidding me? One hundred percent."

He really was nuts.

*But he's my nut.*

The thought popped into my head before I could stop it.

"You said this was a perfect place to talk," I ventured. "Was there something specifically you were hoping to talk about?"

Despite the fact that my heart began to race as I asked the question, it was a necessary one.

"Yes," he said, matter-of-factly. "But first, in case things go sideways, there's something I need to do." Pulling out his phone, he changed the song as the first chords of "Tennessee Whiskey" began to play.

Without warning, he pushed back his seat and held his hand out to me. I took it, standing. Beck led me to the dance floor, a small area we cleared out on weekends, and pulled me into his arms.

As I laid my head on his chest, we moved to the slow chords. I listened to the words, knowing he'd put the song on for a reason. The bachelor pact rule. The bar. The apartment. His declaration.

Was it really possible Beck could be a different man for me than he'd been with any other woman all these years?

I looked up, to ask him that very question, when he leaned down and put his lips to mine. It was a kiss unlike any other. Slow. Sensual. Full of promise, and hope. We moved together in perfect rhythm, kissed like we'd been doing it for years.

His hand on my back tightened, pulling me closer just as the song ended.

Breaking the kiss, he continued to look into my eyes.

"I wanted to talk to you about us," he said. "I have been in love with you all my life, Mae. If I've acted like an immature idiot, it's because I never thought I could have the one woman I really wanted. Still don't."

I opened my mouth to respond, but he pressed a finger to my lips.

"It's a big ask. The biggest one there is. So until you know for sure, don't say anything. Think about it. Us. Me. Cedar Falls. What you want for your future. I know it's all tied together."

Wow. Sometimes I thought Beck knew me better than I knew myself.

I'd planned on telling him about my research. My business idea. But instead, I realized he was right. Committing to staying here was a big deal, especially because I would be committing to him too. And where I lived, which could be changed at any time, a relationship with Beck wasn't so straightforward. His life was here. At O'Malley's. With his friends nearby.

And mine?

Maybe he was right. Until I knew that answer for sure, not saying anything at all was probably for the best.

I wanted to respond. To tell him what I was thinking.

To tell Beck I loved him too, and not just as a friend.

But those were words I could never take back.

# 37

## BECK

"Whoa, didn't expect you back tonight," Mason said as I walked up the back stairs onto the deck. He, Parker and Cole had all gotten a head start, obviously. Pia and Delaney had said the same thing. They were watching a chick flick in the living room and had hardly looked up, except for Pia to ask, "What are you doing back so early?"

"Grab a beer." Parker opened the lid of a cooler.

"You lazy motherfuckers. The kitchen's right in there." I pointed inside.

"Yeah? You go in there and rattle a beer bottle around," Parker said. "See what happens."

The ladies had looked rather intense.

"And this is why living alone, no one to complain if you get a drink, is the way to go." Cole had his feet up on a wicker ottoman in front of him.

"You don't get lonely in that sparse-ass apartment?" I asked, using the bottle opener and taking my beer to the railing. The view was as good as it got, Mason's inheritance in one hell of a prime location. Unlike other places around the lake where the houses were on top of each other, he had enough land to actually afford a bit of privacy.

"Nope."

"Liar." Mason tossed a bottle cap at him.

"I get my needs met," he said, to which all three of us laughed. No doubt he did. Cole was a good-looking guy, especially if a woman liked the Clark

Kent-turned-Superman thing. He had more than his share of secrets that most people would be surprised to learn about.

"I'm sure you do," Parker muttered. "But there's something to be said for an actual relationship. I know we thought it was a bad idea—"

"It's a terrible fucking idea."

We all ignored Cole.

"But I think with the right person, marriage isn't as bad as we thought."

"How would you know?" I asked. He was engaged, but not married.

"We're close enough," Parker argued.

"That's the whole point, though," Cole said. "Our parents thought it was a good idea too. Until they didn't."

It was true. None of our parents had good track records. But that didn't mean a happy marriage was an impossible standard.

"Mason's parents were happy," I said quietly, not sure if I should go there. Thankfully, he didn't seem to mind.

"I think about that a lot," Mason said. "And get my dad more now than ever. If something ever happened to Pia, I can't imagine ever marrying again. But he wasn't as miserable after my mother passed away as I'd thought. He just missed her, a lot. There's a difference."

"To Papa Bennett." Parker raised his bottle, and we all followed suit.

"Look at Mae's parents," I ventured. "And Emilio and his wife. And Maggie. And—"

"Okay," Cole said, annoyed. "I get it."

"Why are you home?" Parker asked. "Mason said you had some big romantic date at the bar."

"Pfft," Cole scoffed. "A romantic date at O'Malley's."

My buddies backed me up by each giving our friend a death stare to which he frowned but said nothing.

"It's complicated."

As much as I hadn't wanted to leave her, and Mae had asked me over to her place, I knew without a doubt it was the right thing to do. I told her I was giving her space, and so I needed to follow through to show I was serious. As much as it killed me, I even broached the idea of hiring another person. Mae working there was temporary, and without her mother, who said she'd be happy to do the books until I got someone, I'd need some permanent help.

We agreed if the bar re-opened tomorrow she didn't have to come in. That would be two days not seeing her, since we were closed Monday. I was already miserable at the thought of it.

"Always is," Mason said. "Spill."

Where to even start?

"Bottom line is that Mae isn't sure about her future, including me, and doesn't want to ruin our friendship in the meantime. At first my plan was to go all in, Beck style, but then I realized, with some help," I admitted, "that's not going to win her over. Growing the fuck up, and doing it for the right reasons, is my only chance. In the meantime, I'm giving her space. Not because I want to, but she needs to be sure. Which is smart, I guess. I can't imagine getting involved and then Mae decides small-town living isn't for her."

"Isn't that why she moved to France in the first place?" Parker asked.

"That and getting into pastry school. But yeah, Mae always talked about moving to a bigger city, with restaurants that could appreciate the kind of thing she enjoys creating."

Mason shook his head. "I know a little something about the kind of decisions she's making. It's brutal. You're right to give her some space to figure it out."

"Mmm." Parker made a face, like he didn't agree.

"What?" I asked him.

"I get what you guys are saying, but neither of you know how good it can be unless you give it a go."

"Oh, it can be very good. I'm sure of it."

The guys laughed.

Cole was quiet, so despite myself, knowing his history, knowing very well he disagreed with the idea of marriage, I asked him what he thought.

"You're the big city guy now. Any chance she'll stay?"

I wanted him to say, "Sure," and that the city wasn't all it was cracked up to be. That there was a lot to do, but having the people that meant the most around you was more important.

"I wouldn't get your hopes up."

I waited, but that was it. Cole fielded a scowl from Parker and an eye roll from Mason by taking a sip of Scotch. The conversation moved on to talk of big city versus small-town living, but I wasn't in the mood to join in.

*I wouldn't get your hopes up.*

Thinking back to the day Mae was accepted into pastry school, I remembered her dancing around the kitchen table. Literally dancing, hugging her parents, and me, as excited as I'd ever seen her in my life. Living in Paris obviously appealed as much in real life as it had in her dreams. Mae had been prepared to stay there.

Paris. And I was trying to compete with the city of lights with a few dozen candles? In a bar she'd been going to since she was born? Suddenly my beer tasted bitter. I plastered a smile on my face when Parker busted my ass about a college prank they were reminiscing about. But it was forced.

I thought giving her space would help prove I was worth staying for. Now I wasn't so sure.

* * *

"I hear you had an exciting day in here yesterday."

I hadn't even seen Mr. O'Malley walk in. It was a busy afternoon, thankfully for the staff, after being shuttered yesterday.

He came behind the bar to shake my hand.

"Welcome back," I said, waving to Jenn to let her know the drinks were up. "How was Florida?"

"Better than expected, thanks to you."

"All I did was accept your offer."

"You did more than that," he said with a knowing look, although he'd never outright ask how I got that amount of money to him so quickly.

"Anyway." I re-directed the conversation. "You got out just in time." I told him about the valve and we talked about the closing while I worked. Or more precisely, while *we* worked. He probably didn't even realize he was serving customers, it was so automatic.

"Mae said she was off today."

At the mention of her, I stiffened. There was nothing I wanted more than to pick up where we'd left off last night. When we danced, I imagined it was our wedding night, and Mae was my wife. But today, that felt like a pipe dream.

"She's been living here," I said. "The festival went well." I grasped for topics that weren't solely related to his daughter. "We've had a steady stream of customers from it."

"That's great. I'm glad you two were able to pull it together so quickly."

Watching him working, something occurred to me.

"This is your legacy," I said. "You always have a second home in here."

"Thank you, son. I'll admit coming in here today, there's mixed feelings. I spent more time in this place than anywhere else, I think. Maybe my own home. Just remember to keep your priorities straight. The people here"—he waved a hand to the customers at the bar—"are like family. But they aren't family. Mrs. O'Malley and I had more than one growing pain until we finally settled in."

"I'll remember that, sir."

"The Mrs. will be in tomorrow to help out with the books until you find someone. Mae said you were looking to hire?"

"Yeah, know someone who might be interested?"

"Let me think about it. And of course, Mae can help out until she figures out what she's up to next. Although I think she might be onto something already."

I tossed a bar rag over my shoulder and had been reaching for a clean pint glass. My hand froze.

"Oh yeah?"

"She's been on the computer since we got home. Was looking at a pastry place in Brooklyn. I asked what she was up to, but she said it's a surprise."

I lined up a row of shot glasses like soldiers... anything to keep my hands busy while my mind spun.

Brooklyn.

It made sense. There were limited opportunities for her in Cedar Falls. That she was researching, and obviously excited about the possibility of leaving... I was such an idiot to think there was any possibility she might want to stay here.

*Could I go with her?*

I never imagined a life anywhere but Cedar Falls. More importantly, she hadn't even asked for that.

Putting a smile on my face, I joined Mae's father, pretending all was well. Pretending the woman I loved wasn't slipping through my fingers.

# 38

## MAE

"I love it. This is so exciting. But you need to eat."

I reached for a handful of popcorn when my mother slapped my hand.

"Real food."

"But it's white cheddar," I protested.

"Regardless. Take a break. You've been working since we got home. Your dad went down to the bar. Should we join him and grab some dinner?"

I gave her a look as my mother wiped the kitchen table for the hundredth time today.

"I can't eat popcorn but chicken fingers and fries is perfectly acceptable?"

"So much sass since you went to France," she teased. "I haven't had a chance to go to the store yet. Where do you want to eat?"

Not the bar.

Since last night, my mind was in overdrive. About Beck. About my future. As much as I wanted to see him... to text him... I held off. A day or two away would be a good way to clear my head.

I glanced at my laptop. "What if we get takeout?"

My mother looked at the laptop as if it were going to bite her. "You need a break from that thing. It'll hurt your eyes, staring at that little screen all day."

"Jules is screwed then," I mumbled. As a writer, she pretty much spent her life staring at a little screen.

"How is Jules?" my mother asked, sitting down for the first time all afternoon.

"Good. Just grinding away, living the dream." Actually that wasn't exactly true. "I'm trying to convince her to send her manuscript to an agent but she's terrified, for some reason."

"I would imagine she's put pieces of her into that story she's been working on for so many years. That has to be a scary, and very vulnerable, thing to do. Sharing it."

My mother, very much an older version of me, always said the wisest things. I thought maybe it was from meeting so many people throughout the years, collecting wisdom from them. Or maybe it was from her mother. Unfortunately, my grandmother had died before I was born. I wish I could have gotten to know her.

"Speaking of scary." I looked at the open page on my screen. "How do I know if I'm making the right decision?"

Mom sighed. "You asked me the same question when you went off to France. And again when you got engaged and decided to stay. Do you remember what I told you?"

I thought back to both of those instances. "That I could only make the best decision that felt right in my gut. Whether it was right or wrong remained to be seen. And at least one of them turned out to be the wrong one. Did you know that at the time and just not tell me?"

My mother reached for my hand. It was more wrinkled than I remembered, reminding me that our time together wasn't infinite.

"It wasn't that I didn't tell you. Did I think your engagement to Mathieu was quick? Yes. Did I worry about you? And want you to come home instead? Of course. But I also raised you to think for yourself. Be your own woman. Not a carbon copy of me. So it didn't work out. And what happened?"

I made a sound of disgust. "My life was upended. My heart was broken."

She didn't say a word. Was I supposed to glean some tidbit of wisdom from her silence? I had nothing.

"And then?" she prompted.

"I came home." And began to heal. And discovered that my best friend was in love with me. Part of me wanted to tell my mother, but I held back. My life was heading in a direction that, now that the boulder had been dislodged, was rolling downhill. I couldn't stop it. Didn't want to stop it, even though it was as scary as Jules sending her life's work off to someone who might tell her they hated it.

"You came home. Exactly."

"I feel like I'm missing something."

Mom glanced at my more than half-eaten bag of popcorn. "Probably lack of nutrients."

I laughed as she let go of my hand.

"I am getting a little hungry," I admitted.

"How about we go to The Big Easy? You always liked the red beans and rice special on Sundays."

My stomach growled. "Let me go change quick," I said, the sweats I was wearing not going to cut it for public consumption. I headed upstairs to my room, thinking about my mother's question.

*And then?*

It wasn't until I changed and was fixing my hair that her meaning came to me. I came home and began to heal. I surrounded myself with friends and family. Got involved, or whatever you called it, with Beck. I made the wrong decision, getting engaged to a man I didn't truly know. Not as well as I should have, to commit my life to him. It turned out to be the wrong decision, so I'd changed course.

And survived.

Was I making the right decision now?

That was yet to be seen.

\* \* \*

How was your day?

I waited until now to text Beck, wondering if I'd hear from him at all. But I guessed he was serious about the whole "give you time" thing. It just felt odd, to be a few miles from him and not talk at all. My mom wanted to stop by the bar after dinner, but I convinced her to have a proper girls-only night since Dad already ate at O'Malley's.

But enough was enough.

Busy, getting us back open. You?

I looked at the time, unsure if he was closing or not tonight.

Good. Spent the night with Mom.

He texted back immediately.

I heard. Red beans and rice?

I sent him a thumbs up.
Now what?
My plans weren't something I wanted to text him. We needed a real-life discussion for that.

Still at the bar?

He sent a thumbs down.
So not closing.

In bed?

Soon. Shower first.

Oh boy.
The thought of Beck standing in his bedroom, or bathroom, about to shower, was an image I didn't need just before I was going to attempt to sleep.
Wide awake now, I sat up.

Interesting.

I waited for his response, the same mixture of excitement and uncertainty as the last time making it pretty much a guarantee I wouldn't be sleeping anytime soon.

Oh yeah? How so?

So we were doing this.
Maybe we shouldn't.

Maybe it muddied the waters.

*Fuck it.*

> Just over here trying to picture where you are exactly.

He sent a devil so I fired back an angel.

While I waited for a response, a pic came through. Holy shit.

Beck was standing in front of his mirror, clearly naked, but he'd cropped the shot at his waist.

> Tease.

> Takes one to know one.

If I was doing this, might as well do it right.

Putting my phone aside, I tossed off my shirt, got under the covers, and pulled them up just enough. Then, angling the phone, I took the selfie and, before giving myself time to think it through... I sent it.

> FUCK.

And then...

> You're killing me, Mae.

It was only fair play, and I told him so.

> You got me off like this so... just trying to return the favor.

I waited. Thought back to the night at Grado Valley. It was just as much fun being on the other end, imagining Beck responding to my texts.

> Wouldn't be the first time.

Wait, what?

> First time...?

I've done this. Thinking of you.

Ohmygod. I wanted details. But first...

Are you touching yourself?

Did I really ask that?

Hell yeah.

Good.

I pressed record. "Do you know how hot you look, standing in front of that mirror? I wish I was there, in front of you. I wonder, have you ever imagined me on my knees, looking up at you..."

I sent that before starting another.

Maybe he was right. I was being a bit of a tease. And it was fun.

"I take your dick in my mouth, a little at a time. And then deeper, and deeper, and deeper. Your grip on my hair tightens as you pull me into you. But I don't mind because I know you're close."

Send.

One more.

"Finally, you can't hold on any longer, and you explode in my mouth. I take it. Every. Last. Drop."

Send.

I wait. Imagine him. And finally get a message in return. A voice memo.

"Jesus. Fucking. Christ. Are you for real, woman? Do you have any idea how hard I came just now? If you were here with me... damn."

I smiled.

I'd like to be there with him and told Beck so.

You sure we need this break?

It took him a few minutes to reply back.

Mae, I'm not sure about anything these days.

Join the club.

> We do need to talk.

Lunch tomorrow?

> If you want.

I do.

I wanted lunch. And to see him. And to do that again. Smiling, I lay back down. Big things were on the horizon, and I was more than a little afraid to make another life-altering decision when my last one proved to be a big-time mistake.

But it was time.

Tomorrow, I'd lay it all on the line.

Texting "good night," I put my phone on the nightstand and closed my eyes. Sleep was going to be elusive.

# 39

## BECK

"What time you heading out?"

Cole sat at the kitchen island, drinking coffee, looking every bit like the history professor from Columbia that he was.

"About an hour."

"You should stay. Classes are over for the semester, right?"

"Technically, yes. But I have some things to wrap up. I'm also co-authoring a paper and am meeting with a colleague about it Wednesday morning. It's a big one, so I want to be there in person."

"Any word on tenure?"

Making tenure at an Ivy League school, like his father, had been Cole's goal as long as I could remember. His family had moved from Cedar Falls to New Haven when we were twelve when his dad was offered a job at Yale. Not long after that, Cole started talking about doing the same when the rest of us were still toilet papering houses on Halloween.

I poured myself a coffee.

"Not yet," he said, tapping his mug. "But the committee's reviewing my file this summer. This paper could tip the scales."

"Do you ever wish you could stay?"

We'd asked him before. It was a question Cole typically evaded.

He rubbed the back of his neck. "Sometimes I wonder what it would've been like if I'd stayed here. Opened a history tour business or something ridiculous like that. But then I remember I'm two publications away from tenure..." He trailed off.

Someone must have spiked his coffee. It was the most I'd gotten from him in a long time, and it felt... important.

"Why is a history tour business ridiculous?"

He pushed his glasses up, as if needing to see to answer.

"In a place like Cedar Falls?"

"Or anywhere."

Cole shrugged. "I don't have any desire to move... anywhere."

"But you would come back here?" I pressed.

Sighing, as if the conversation bored him, even though that was just one of his tactics that signaled he was uncomfortable with the conversation, he didn't answer.

That was more like it.

For a second I thought I'd fallen down the rabbit hole and would see a tiny door appear any second. Maybe I was the one whose coffee was spiked. After last night, I didn't know up from down.

"I get why people move out. But for me, this town has everything I could need," I pitched. "The guys. Good beer. Good fishing. Good place to raise a family."

Cole's head popped up.

"What the hell has gotten into you?"

It was true that raising a family had never really been on my radar.

"Mae," I said. "This is going to sound like some Hallmark movie—"

"Oh, man, you've got the wrong guy to spill your guts to."

I forged ahead, not giving a shit if Cole wanted to hear it or not. "But I want to be a better man for her. That there's any possibility to be with her... she's just worth it."

He sighed, loudly.

"What the hell do I know?" he said finally. "Mason and Parker both seem happy."

"They are happy," I confirmed. I should know, living at the inn. Although Parker spent less time here now that he was with Delaney, and the renovations were almost done.

Cole stood and headed to the coffee pot, pouring it. Black. Like his soul.

I chuckled.

"What?" he demanded, his sport coat and crisp shirt so very... Cole.

"I was just thinking your coffee is black like your soul."

"Thanks."

Chuckling, I tried again. "Or what you want everyone around you to believe, anyway. Though for the life of me, I don't know why. Let other people see the fun Cole who would give his life for his friend."

Literally. Not figuratively. I should know.

"I'm good."

Biting back a smile, I sipped my coffee, thinking about... what else? Mae. And lunch. What she would say. What I would say.

"I'm not trying to be an asshole about the whole Mae thing," he said, quite unexpectedly.

"No? Could have fooled me."

"You're looking at me like I said Julius Caesar destroyed the Library of Alexandria."

Cole's lips hinted at a smile, but then apparently changed their mind.

"My parents were happy."

He said it so quietly, I almost didn't hear him. Cole stared into his coffee mug.

"Growing up, I can remember murmured voices when I went to bed. They talked, went to dinner, took me to the park. I don't know when it happened, exactly, but sometime between middle school and when I went to college, it just... eroded. They don't sleep in the same room. I don't even think they like each other." He looked up. "The idea of a bachelor pact, for me, was a reminder not to repeat their mistake."

I was pretty sure Cole had just used up his monthly allotment of words. At least, ones on a serious topic, about himself.

"I get it. Look at mine. They're a total shitshow. I agreed, we all did, for a reason. Our own reasons. But then we grew up." I grinned. "Some of us more recently. And took the blinders off to see... some relationships work. Some marriages work."

"And you think you and Mae would be one of them?"

I was about to say "yes" but paused. I would love that woman until the day I died. And would try like hell to make her happy. But could she be? Living here?

"What the hell do I know?" I echoed his earlier question.

"Apparently not who destroyed the Library of Alexandria."

"It wasn't Julius Caesar." But now I doubted my memory. "Right?"

"Right. It's a common misconception. The most widely believed cause was the destruction of the Serapeum and the actions of Coptic Christian Archbishop Theophilus."

Cole's master's thesis was on the subject, so I knew way more than I wanted to about the topic. But before he began nerding out on me, I stopped him.

"Appreciate the history lesson, but I don't have learning about Archbishop Theophilus on my to-do list today."

"No?"

"No," I said emphatically, eliciting a smile from him.

"Too bad. It was going to be a thrilling monologue." He smirked. "Despite what you think, I hope you don't get destroyed trying to work things out with Mae."

"Thanks. But that might be the worst pep talk in history."

Hopefully, it wasn't a sign of things to come.

# 40

## MAE

I looked around at the brick interior and barnyard wall accents, feeling like I'd left Cedar Falls. Beck said The Grapevine Bistro and Bar was one of the best new lakeside places to hit our town in years, and I had to agree. It definitely had a vibe, and I could easily become a regular at this place.

Looking at the door for the millionth time, there was no sign of Beck.

I couldn't wait to tell him what I'd been up to. As he walked in, I remembered him saying once, "Don't walk into a place as if you work there. Walk in as if you own it." That's exactly what he did now. Confident, but not overly so, he strode toward me. With every step, my body reminded me in little ways about last night.

About our kiss.

Reminded me this was no longer just my friend. Brakes or not, we'd begun to become much more than that, and denying it was silly.

"What's cooking, good looking?" he asked, sitting across from me.

We'd snagged a window seat, and though there was a deck, it was closed. The wind made it too chilly to sit outside. May in the Finger Lakes was like that. One day, it felt like summer. The next, I was cursing myself for not wearing a jacket.

"Something yummy. I think it's the steak behind me."

"Steak for lunch." He leaned over to see. "My kind of guy."

"Welcome to The Grapevine," our college-aged waitress said. She was pretty.

Young. And into Beck. Her smile was bigger for him than it had been for me, and she looked at him like, well, she'd be more than happy to jump his bones.

Not that I blamed her.

"Can I get you something to drink?"

"A Coke, please," he said. "Any lunch special today?"

While she rattled them off, I watched the exchange. He wasn't flirting, precisely, but Beck couldn't turn off the charm. It was ingrained from years of being fawned over. No doubt, by the time our meal was over, she'd be slipping her number to him on a napkin. Never mind I could be his girlfriend.

"I'll get your drinks while you look at the menu," she said to Beck.

"I might as well be invisible," I teased.

"Not to me."

He said it with a smile on his face, but Beck wasn't teasing me back. He was serious, and it occurred to me that I must have been blind all these years to miss the signs. Granted, we'd been separated in college, and then again while I was in Paris. But still.

"We have a lot to talk about." I took a sip of my diet soda, looking over the glass at him.

"Agreed."

Much too soon, the waitress was back. I had a feeling we were going to get excellent—maybe too excellent—customer service on this lunch. We ordered just as a boat cruised by.

"I think that's the Sunset Cruise. Its owner is married to Marco Grado. I met her for the first time at the girls' night."

"You never did tell me about that."

He was looking at me so intently. Beck had that way about him, always making you feel like you were the center of the universe when he looked at you.

"It was a lot of fun. Like I said, we met Rae and had a tour of the main tasting room. I'd been in the barrel room before, but we got to see more of the process. All while drinking wine, of course."

"Of course."

"It's an impressive operation they're running, ramping up production. Adding a brewery. Thayle said they've had two wines final in international competitions since they took over. Pretty impressive."

"I'll have to get back down there one of these days. And speaking of day trips, I was thinking about the bar you went to in Kitchi Falls. What's it called?"

"Boots and Brews?"

"Yeah, that one. I started cleaning out my things to take to the apartment and found my old cowboy boots."

"I haven't seen you in those in years."

"Seems like the perfect excuse." He grinned. "Maybe I'll hit the tattoo place too."

"You thinking of a new one?"

He had two, one on his arm and another on his back. They were sexy as hell, I didn't mind saying.

"I'm thinking of a sleeve."

Now we were talking. "Oh yeah? What would you get?"

"I have a few ideas. Thought I'd run them by you."

And he did.

We talked tattoos. Ate our sandwiches. But finally got to the important stuff.

"I have to tell you something," I blurted.

Why did Beck suddenly look like he was going to lose his lunch?

"I already know."

That took me aback. "You do?"

"About Brooklyn?"

Brooklyn? What the hell was he talking about?

"Your dad mentioned it. Said you were looking at a job there."

A job in Brooklyn? I was beyond confused.

"It was on your computer." He clearly picked up on my confusion. It dawned on me then, what he was talking about.

"My dad said I was looking at a job in Brooklyn?"

Beck shrugged. "Something like that. Said you were being mysterious but that's what it looked like to him. Guess I shouldn't have mentioned it."

I was about to clear things up when he added, "Kinda wish you did, though."

His tone was hurt. Defensive.

But honestly? That was bullshit.

"So you think I'm that much of a cocktease to rile you up last night, all while I was getting ready to leave town? Seriously?"

At least now I wasn't the only one confused.

"I don't get your meaning."

Maybe I was being unreasonable. But Beck should know better.

"That's not me," I said. "I'd never play with your feelings like that. I thought you knew me better than that?"

"Huh?" he asked, just as the waitress approached.

But suddenly, I wasn't in the mood for her either.

"We're good," I said, before she could start side-eyeing Beck again. If she was surprised by my change in manner, Beck was too. But he didn't say anything.

"I had a Brooklyn pastry catering business pulled up on my computer," I said. "And lots of others too. Because I've been researching the possibility of starting one of my own. With the bed and breakfast order, and a few other leads... I was trying to figure out the logistics of it. And if I could sustain that kind of thing here, in Cedar Falls."

To say he looked shocked was an understatement.

"You honestly thought I would lead you on and then skip town? Really?"

"Guess I should've known better. But people like you don't stay with people like me."

In one statement, he knocked down everything we were trying to build. I was behind the scenes, fighting for us, and he was just waiting for me to disappear.

"You've got to be kidding me?"

"Wish I was."

Beck doubling down wasn't a surprise. But that he so thoroughly got me wrong was. So much for honesty and vulnerability.

"God, Beck." I shook my head, hurt blossoming. "I was really hoping this would go differently." I was expecting today's lunch to be the start of something. Telling Beck about the business, getting his support... showing him I wanted this, or at least to try, despite the risks.

Instead, I was getting more of Mathieu. Emotional immaturity. The last thing I needed in my life right now. He looked like he meant it. Like that belief—people like me don't get to keep people like you—was tattooed on his arm. And it almost broke my heart. Almost. But I couldn't keep offering softness where there should be trust.

"I think," I said, picking up the napkin in my lap and folding it, "we should probably end this conversation before it gets any worse."

He paused.

Beck could have responded in a million ways. Instead, he did the most Beck thing imaginable and shrugged his shoulders as if it didn't matter.

As if I didn't matter.

"Can I get you guys anything else?"

By "guys" the waitress meant Beck since I'd been invisible to her since he sat down.

"I'll send you half of the bill," I said, standing. "I've gotta go."

The air felt heavy. Suffocating. Our waitress's small smile made me realize I had to get the hell out of there, now. Before I said something stupid.

"Mae," he called as I walked away, but it was too late.

*People like you don't stay with people like me.*

He thought I was leaving. Jumped to that conclusion based off a website my father noticed. What other false conclusions would he invent, thinking he wasn't good enough?

I wasn't walking away to prove a point. I was walking away because if I stayed, I'd start fighting for something he'd already given up on.

## 41

### BECK

I looked everywhere.

The house. Her office. The front room of the inn. I even opened the guest-book, but there were only two rooms rented for the night and both already checked in.

I could talk to Mason or Parker, but the latter was on a job and the former was currently digging shrubs. I'd already asked this morning if he needed help and didn't need to be told no twice. Landscaping was my least favorite form of manual labor. Besides, Mace was barely one step above Cole on "who to talk to about relationships." If Pia hadn't stormed into his life, he'd probably be as single as me.

*How could you have fucked that up so badly?*

By the time I paid the bill, Mae had been long gone. She wasn't answering her texts, and when I went to her house, Mrs. O'Malley said she hadn't seen her since before lunch.

I could text her. But another thought occurred to me. Someone that could help in this situation. Like the desperate man that I was, I couldn't wait. At this time of day, she was probably at the college. I only knew where Jules's office was because Mae had dragged me there once to pick up keys for some alumni event. I remembered the way mostly because I'd got a parking ticket.

Attempting to avoid another one, I parked legally this time and navigated Cedar Falls Community College campus, taking the steps of her building two at a time. There was a good chance she was teaching a class, but I had to start somewhere.

The door to the small office was partially opened. A good sign.

I knocked and then poked my head inside. Jules's black bob whipped around her head as she looked up.

"You scared the shit out of me."

"Sorry about that."

Not unexpectedly, she seemed pretty confused.

"Do you have a few minutes?"

Jules looked down at a stack of papers. "If it's not about why your opinion doesn't count as supporting evidence for a persuasive essay, sure." She gestured to the only other seat in the space.

"Nice view," I teased.

"Of the parking lot? Tell me about it. How did you know I'd be here?"

"Mae mentioned that Monday was your least favorite day of the week because you were required to stay on campus for office hours despite the fact that no one ever comes."

"Oh. Yeah. Well, it is." She waved her arms. "As you can see, loads of students are extremely concerned about the final grades."

"I'm surprised you're still in session. Aren't most colleges out by now?"

She smiled tightly. "CFCC is kind like that. To extend their calendar an extra week or so more than most. Is everything OK?"

"Actually, no. Did you talk to Mae today?"

I could tell before she even shook her head she hadn't. "No. I've been buried in essays. Is she alright?"

"Uh, yeah. I mean, physically. She's fine," I said, seeing her expression. "We had a fight."

Jules spun her chair around to face me and sat back. The epitome of an "artsy type," her outfit was wild, in a sort of non-matching but cool kind of way. I'd always liked her, though Jules definitely operated on a different wavelength than a lot of people.

"You and Mae? A fight?"

It was as unbelievable to me as it was to Jules.

We never fought. Ever.

"Yeah. And I'm pretty sure it was my fault?"

She laughed, and then immediately apologized. "You *think*?"

"Okay. I'm pretty certain it was. And she's not texting me back."

"Why don't you start at the beginning? I know you guys were having lunch today."

"She told you about that?"

"Uh huh. Was pretty excited too. To tell you about the business idea and all."

Shit. Shit. Shit.

I buried my head in my hands, mumbled something about not hearing much regarding the business and thought back to the entire conversation.

Looking up, I relayed it all to Jules.

"I honestly can't believe I came here," I said, realizing that I was sitting in Mae's best friend's office, at work, like a crazed man. "I couldn't find Pia. And the guys are…"

"Guys?" she asked, sardonically.

"Yeah. That."

"I'm glad you did."

She seemed sincere. But I still could kick myself, for the whole day.

"I'm no therapist," she said finally. "But I have been in a lot of it and know myself pretty well. Sometimes, asking questions about why we do the things we do are important."

I waited, but that was all she said.

"Specifically, why are you sabotaging your chances to make this work?"

"I wouldn't call it sabotaging, exactly—"

My mother couldn't have managed a sterner look, and she could be pretty stern. There was Mae's mom, the warm and fuzzy type, and then there was the exact opposite.

Aka, my mother.

"Fine, sabotaging."

Why was I sabotaging my chance with Mae? It didn't take a genius to figure that one out, even without years of therapy or whatever.

"I guess I pretty much laid it out to her when I said people like her don't stick around for people like me."

"Meaning?"

"Meaning, she's too good for me. Always has been. And don't you dare deny it. I've never been boyfriend material."

As expected, Jules didn't refute it.

"Alright, so one could argue you've been sabotaging your chances with her for a long time. Why?"

"I have to think about that one."

"Okay. That's a start."

"So you don't think I should try to talk to her yet?"

Jules tapped her nails against each other, thinking.

"No. I don't. Not until you know the answer to that question. Because if you don't fix it, you'll end up doing the same thing again for another reason. I'll tell her you came here. She'll know you care. Actually, Mae already does know that. But in order for the two of you to work, you've got to get on the same page. If you're waiting for her to walk, that's not good for either of you."

I got that but... "She's never wanted to stay in Cedar Falls," I argued.

"She never had a reason to," Jules responded quietly. And then added, "Sure, family is here. Friends are here. But she could visit us. Work somewhere else, come home when she wants. But we both know she's always wanted a partner in life, like her parents have. Who better than someone she's always known, who makes her laugh, who truly wants what's best for her?"

"I do, Jules. Honestly."

"I know you do. She does too."

I hoped she was right. If she was, I just needed to prove that to her somehow.

"Figure out why I've been chickenshit to tell her sooner. And then find a way to explain that, and show Mae how much I love her. Got it. Anything else?"

She laughed, good-naturedly, making me really believe Jules was on my side. Which surprised me, honestly.

"That's not enough?" she teased.

"I guess it is. Thanks, Jules." I stood. Had no plan. But at least I knew where to start.

"Anytime. I hope it works out."

I paused on my way to the door. "I can tell. Honestly," I admitted. "I'm a little surprised."

"Are you? Why?"

I shrugged. "I just figured you saw me as a fuck-up who's been with too many women to be serious about just one."

Jules leveled me another one of her laser stares. "You sure that's not how you feel about yourself?"

Damn.

"Not pulling any punches, are you?"

Her brows raised. "When it comes to my best friend? And potentially her future happiness? Damn right I'm not."

I wanted honesty, and got it.

"I see why she likes you so much," I said before passing through the half-open door. "Maybe if this doesn't work out you can get a therapy license. You're really good at it."

"Thanks. I'll stick to analyzing fictional people."

I remembered what Mae told me about Jules's stalled writing career. She'd given me great advice, so I owed her a bit back.

"Sounds like a good plan. Like I said, you're good at it. Maybe it's time to pull the trigger."

With a wink, I left, just catching Jules's dropped jaw on my way out.

With as much clarity as I'd had all day, my next stop seemed like an obvious one. The sun was out, and I had some thinking to do. Only one thing left to do with my afternoon.

It was time for some fishing to clear my head.

# 42

## MAE

"He went... fishing?"

"Apparently," Pia said. "He texted me earlier but I was at the doctor's office and just saw it. Routine checkup. Then Mason said something about him going fishing."

Mason was the one who sent me over here, to the inn side of the building.

I was glad everything was okay with Pia.

But...

"He went *fishing*?" I repeated, trying to decide if I wanted to laugh or throw something.

"I feel like there's more to this."

I began to pace in the reception room, meticulously re-decorated to give Heritage Hill a more modern feel but also capturing the small town, lakeside vibe that had always been here.

"Yeah," I said. "But I'm sure the last thing you want to do is re-hash mine and Beck's first fight."

"First? Come on. You must have fought before?"

"Teasingly, sure. But for real? Never. I guess that's what happens when you complicate something good."

"Your friendship."

It was not a question, so I didn't answer. Instead, I looked at the photos on the wall. Many of them were of Mason's parents and him when he was young.

Papa Bennett had been absolutely devastated when his wife died, according to my parents.

It was so sad. And a good reminder that I was wasting time being angry when today was just as much my fault as Beck's. Sure, he'd thought the worst of me. But how else was the guy supposed to feel when I'd been giving him mixed signals?

Brakes. No brakes.

"Yeah," I said finally. "It was always so easy before..."

"Couples fight," she said.

"But we're not a couple." I finally stopped circling the room and sat down. Pia joined me on the couch.

"Do you want to be?"

"If I could look into a crystal ball and know things will work out, and that we're not ruining a friendship trying to make it more than that, yes," I said with as much certainty as I'd felt in a long time.

"You know as well as I do, there are very few guarantees in life."

I thought about that for a second. "True. But we have a good thing, Beck and me. And look at today. Our first fight."

"Maybe you could have a better thing?"

"I still can't believe he's fishing," I said. "Like it's no big deal. I've been losing my mind all afternoon. I hate this. The only reason I didn't text him back sooner was because I didn't know what to say."

"And you do now?"

"No," I admitted. "But I know being mad at him feels horrible. I hate it."

"Seems like a good start to me." Pia smiled. "You're welcome to stay until he gets back."

"Thank you," I said sincerely. "I might head home. It's been a day."

"I bet. Want me to tell Beck you were here?"

"Sure. Thanks, Pia," I said, just as my phone rang. "It's Jules. I'll catch you later."

She waved as I made my way out of the inn and started walking to my parents'.

"You don't check your texts these days, or what?"

I pulled the phone away from my ear. Sure enough, Jules had texted "call me."

"Oops, sorry. I was actually just going to call you. I had the day from hell—"

"I know. He was here."

I stopped on the sidewalk. "What?"

"Beck. Was here."

Here? It was Monday.

"He came to the college?"

"Yep."

"Why?"

"Why do you think?"

Holy shit. "What did he say? I can't believe he came to your work."

"You and me both. Nearly scared the crap out of me since I didn't expect any students. Beck told me all about lunch, and that you wouldn't text him back. Apparently he looked for Pia but couldn't find her."

"She was at the doctor's office," I said, just as two kids went running past me toward the square. I watched him play kickball for a second and then kept walking. Baby. Kids. I wanted that.

Beck would be an amazing father, I had no doubt.

"Anyway, he wanted to talk about what happened. Asked for my advice."

This day just kept getting weirder and weirder. "I don't even know what to say."

"I did, apparently. Words just came out of my mouth, as if I were Carolyn. Maybe I have learned a thing or two from her."

Carolyn was Jules's therapist. She adored her and had been with her for years.

"So he told you everything?"

"He did."

"What did you tell him?"

She hedged. "I feel like that would violate patient confidentiality."

She was a nut. "Except, he's not your patient."

"True, but still."

That was one of the things I liked best about Jules, actually. She wasn't a gossiper. So I let her off the hook. "Fair enough. But since you know the whole situation, what are your thoughts? For me, specifically, Dr. Porter."

She cleared her throat. "Well, in my professional opinion..." I stepped onto my street. "I believe you two need a little space tonight to reflect. Talk tomorrow with clear minds and go from there."

"Wise words," I said. "I'm actually just walking into my house."

"Alright, will let you go. I'm considering dragging my butt to the gym."

"I have to get over there and join. Maybe we can convince each other to go."

"Do you know how happy I am that you're thinking to stay?"

"Yeah, well, to make that happen, I'm gonna need a whole lot of clients. We'll see how excited you are when I make you carry my cards to hand out."

"I will stand on the street corner in a croissant outfit and pass out flyers if you stay."

I laughed, trying to imagine Jules as a croissant. "I might take you up on that. Goodbye, you nut."

"See you later."

"Hey, kid. What's so funny?" my dad asked as I walked into the kitchen.

I still hadn't told Dad about the business. I wanted to firm up some things and then surprise him. I knew he'd be proud, and happy that I would be staying in Cedar Falls. He'd taken it really hard when I left for France, and even worse when I decided to stay.

"Jules," I said, evasively. "How's the bread-making going?"

"Not bad," he said, taking his latest masterpiece from the oven. "It's a good distraction."

I breathed in the smell of fresh baked bread and could already taste it. "I bet it's hard, huh? Not being at the bar?"

"Eh, it's not so bad. Specially since your mom and I are already making plans to go back and get settled into the condo."

"That's awesome," I said, taking butter from the fridge. "I can't wait to see it."

Dad turned off the oven. "I still can't believe we snagged it."

He looked at me, as if he knew something I didn't.

"What's the weird look for?"

"The money. For the downpayment. He went to his parents, didn't he?"

Wait, what? "Beck?"

"No, the other guy who bought the bar."

"Honestly, I have no idea. He didn't mention it. But..." That made sense. Sort of. It was a lot of cash to have sitting around. But the idea of Beck asking his parents for money? "If he did"—I shook my head and looked my dad in the face, already sensing the answer—"that would be huge. It'd kill him to ask them for anything, especially money."

My dad studied me. "I know."

Suddenly, this wasn't just about the condo. Or whether or not Beck had asked his parents for money. It was about his relationship with my parents, something that meant a lot to him. And us. I slunk into the chair.

"Dad?" I asked. Mom would kill me, that she wasn't the first to know. Only because there wasn't much to know, yet. "I think we need to talk. About Beck."

# 43

## BECK

"Afternoon, son."

"Thanks for coming, Mr. O'Malley. Can I talk to you in the back?"

I'd texted to ask him in, and the sooner I got this over with the better. "Spence," I called to the kid. "Man the bar?"

Without question, Spence took over as Mae's dad and I walked to the back office. Not wanting to drag it out, when the door closed, I dove right in, having thought about this speech all night.

"I'm sorry to spring this on you, since I'm sure Mae hasn't said anything about it, but..." There were nerves, like putting skis on for the first time in years and standing at the top of a double black diamond because your buddies were doing it. Or getting a call that your sister was in a car accident and in the hospital, the worst phone call I'd ever gotten, and only two days after she passed her driver's license test.

And then there was asking a man you respected to hand over most precious thing in the world to him.

"This is going to come as a surprise, I'm sure, but I've been in love with Mae for as long as I can remember."

He didn't flinch. But Mr. O'Malley did smile. A good sign.

"And I know what you're thinking... I'm probably the last man in the world you'd want to see her marry. But I've been thinking about it a lot since she came back, and I'm not excusing my behavior, but I think part of me pushed women away because I knew they weren't her. And I never really felt like I deserved someone as incredible as your daughter." I was talking fast, too fast. But I had to get it all in before he stopped me. "I knew the day she got engaged I screwed up, big time. But when they broke up, and she came home..." I took a deep breath. "It was the first time I thought maybe there was a shot for us. What I'm trying to say..."

Shit, this wasn't coming out the way I'd practiced.

"She has feelings for me too, but I honestly didn't think she wanted to stay in Cedar Falls. When she told me about the business, I was shocked."

That wasn't part of the speech at all. He was still smiling. Probably laughing at what a bumbling idiot he'd sold the bar to. *Get back on track, Beck.*

"I've been trying to think of ways to show Mae how much she means to me. The bar. An apartment. I'm ready to get serious with my life, and the best way I can think of to show her how serious I am about us, that is to say..."

Just. Ask. Him.

"I'd like your permission to ask Mae to marry me."

I could hear my heartbeat in my ears. This was an entirely different experience than sitting across from my own father. This man's opinion meant more to me than any other. He literally held my future in his hands. Mae was not the kind of woman you asked to marry you without the full support of her parents. I planned to call her mom too, but had to start here.

"Sit down, Beck."

Aw, fuck. It was a no.

I sat without even feeling the leather chair beneath me.

He did the same, Mr. O'Malley's hands on his knees as he leaned forward.

"Do you remember the day you moved?"

I did. Clearly.

"Yeah," I said, not sure what he was getting at exactly.

"You came next door, just before you climbed into the moving truck, and gave Mae a handful of daisies."

I'd forgotten about that.

"I remember."

"You hugged her, and then turned away immediately."

I remembered that too.

"But not before I saw your tears."

Oh, man.

"I also saw you take the long way around the truck so you could wipe your eyes first. That was the day I knew you loved my daughter. And once you see something, you can't unsee it. I'm just surprised Mae never figured it out, until now."

Talk about a curve ball.

"Why didn't you ever say anything?" We'd worked closely together for years. He'd had thousands of opportunities.

"It wasn't my place. People have to figure things out for themselves for it to mean anything. I'll admit, I almost did when she got engaged. I wanted to shake you, ask why you weren't getting on a plane to France."

Wait, what? He wanted me to break up her engagement?

"But I didn't, because I knew Mae needed to forge her own path too. I knew she loved you but had no idea in what way. And now I do."

What did that mean? How did he know how Mae felt?

He stood, so I followed suit.

"Do you have my permission to marry my daughter? Yes, you do. You're a good man, Beckham. And I hope you have a good plan for this engagement." He stuck out his hand.

"What?" I didn't even take it at first. "Are you sure?"

I extended my hand hesitantly.

"Let this be the last time you ever doubt yourself. The right question to ask," he said, shaking my hand firmly, "is 'how will I ask Mae to marry me?'"

Mr. O'Malley let go of my hand.

*Let this be the last time you ever doubt yourself.*

I wasn't embarrassed to have to wipe away a tear. I was expecting the worst. A lecture, at least. About my behavior these past years with women. How to treat his daughter. So many possibilities had run through my mind, but complete acceptance had never been one of them.

"Actually, I have an idea about that," I said. "But I need your help."

"Shoot."

I told Mr. O'Malley the plan, fully aware I'd only overcome one hurdle. The most important one was still very much yet to be determined...

# 44

## MAE

"You're sure you want to do this?"

Jules usually tutored on Tuesday afternoon, but since her client cancelled, I had a riding partner.

"Absolutely. I'm excited to meet her."

Last night I got a call from Ellie asking if there was any way I could meet her today. She had an "unexpected event" and wanted to place her first official order. After talking to my parents, I spent the rest of the night figuring out pricing since I was going to have to quote her. Between that and researching names and business cards... I was almost able to keep my mind off Beck.

Almost.

He texted me, said he was sorry he'd missed me at the inn. But his messages were short and didn't say anything about meeting up. I told him that I wouldn't be in today, and he said it wasn't a problem, that they were covered.

And that was it.

"I find it strange," I said now as Jules turned off my road. "Beck texted and called after yesterday's lunch, but since then, he hasn't said a word about meeting up."

"Yeah," Jules said. "That is strange."

"It doesn't feel like a conversation I want to have over text but"—I frowned

—"I'm thinking to have you drop me off at the bar later, but that's not really a great place to talk either. I just hate this place we're in."

Jules gave me a sidelong glance.

"How are you feeling about the whole thing today?"

I stared out the window. "The same as yesterday at lunch, I guess. But with a little more hesitation. I went there to tell him about the business. To tell him I was ready to see if this could work, between us. And then things went totally sideways. I don't know, maybe we're just better off as friends."

"Do you really believe that?"

I thought back to two nights ago.

"No. As evidenced by the dream I had last night. It was one of those you remember when you wake up, you know?"

"I do. Last week I had a dream I was renovating my house and forgot to install stairs so I couldn't get to the second floor. I still remember it clearly."

I did a double take. "That's weird. What do you think it means?"

Jules was as woo-woo as they came. She loved all the horoscope, dream stuff so I was certain she had an opinion on it.

"Obviously it has to do with my career. I know where I need to be but just can't get there."

I laughed. "Obviously."

"So what was yours?"

"Uh, new topic."

Jules's laugh was as deep and hearty as her personality. "That spicy, huh?"

"Beyond spicy. Honestly, it's like he woke up some part of me I didn't even know existed. At this point, if we don't have sex, I'll probably spend the rest of my life wondering what it would have been like."

She said nothing to that. In fact, it wasn't until we were a few blocks from the bed and breakfast that we talked about Beck again after I glanced at my phone for the umpteenth time and Jules mumbled something about me having it bad.

"I'm so nervous. It feels like I'm pretending to be something I'm not."

"Mae, you silly girl. You are an award-winning pastry chef. Ellie knows full well you don't have a business yet. Don't pretend, just be honest. You can always hear what she has to say and then quote her later. Just give her a good discount for being your first customer."

"Got it," I said as she pulled up. "You coming in?"

Jules looked around. "I'm just gonna circle the block since there's no parking."

"What about up there?"

"Looks like a handicap."

I didn't see any blue lines. Was it me or was Jules acting strange?

"Go, if I find a spot I'll be in. Good luck."

"Thanks," I said, grabbing my purse. I got out, looked up to the house, took a deep breath, and climbed the steps. Sure enough, Ellie was there to greet me, standing in the exact spot she was before.

"Well, hello there," she said warmly. "It's good to see you again."

"You too." I went to shake her hand but Ellie surprised me by going in for a hug instead. Okay then, a hug it was.

"Thank you for coming up on such short notice."

I'd wondered about that, at first. Why we couldn't do this over the phone. Probably a generational thing. Plus, it wasn't that far, and she was my first official customer.

"My pleasure."

I waited for her to take the lead.

"Before we talk details, would you mind taking a look upstairs? I've been thinking about adding a tea and pastry service up there on weekends, and I'd love your thoughts on the space."

I loved the idea. "Of course."

"So we've booked a rehearsal party, and they're interested in a brunch," she said as we walked up the stairs. A tug in my chest reminded me of that night. How quickly things had changed. One little kiss, and my life had turned upside down.

And I'd do it again.

"The bride is the daughter of a winery on Seneca, and they want to go all out. No expense spared, in their words."

I had ideas already.

"When is it?" I asked, a familiar hallway looming ahead of us.

"The last weekend of June. Do you think that might work for you?"

"Yes," I said, hoping I didn't sound too enthusiastic, even though I wanted to jump out of my skin. This was really happening. I couldn't wait to tell... Beck. It had always been my first thought when something good happened.

How could I not have seen the signs earlier?

"So this is the room."

The universe had a sense of humor, apparently. It was Beck's room from that night. The one I'd crossed the threshold into, having no idea what was in store.

I was surprised she wanted to turn it into a service room. It had looked recently remodeled, perfect for a bedroom.

"I'll let you go in first," she said.

Trying not to give Ellie a strange look, as it was an odd thing to say... or maybe it was the way she said it, I walked past her.

And gasped.

It was like a scene out of a movie.

Flowers everywhere.

Pink rose petals, my favorite color, everywhere.

In the middle of it all, Beck. The door clicked behind me as I stepped forward, unable to speak. He wore khakis and a white shirt, his sleeves rolled. He looked... handsome. And nervous.

"How—" I began as he stepped forward.

"I never meant to insinuate you were the kind of person who would lead me on. It's just that... I've loved you my whole life, Mae. And I was bound to screw up trying to make you understand how much. Truth is..."

This couldn't be happening. How was this even possible?

"You asked why men suck. Some of them just do. But others, myself included, were never taught the words to use to express emotion. Or worse, were taught not to do it at all. So then when we do, we mess it up royally. I can't speak for all of them, but for me? I pushed people away before they could decide I wasn't enough. Before *you* could. I didn't think I deserved the kind of love you wanted. Still don't know if I do. But I'm done self-sabotaging before I can find out."

I tried to process his words. They were as honest, and raw, as any I'd ever heard coming from Beck.

"You don't suck," I managed. "Not by a long shot."

"Good," he said. "Please keep that in mind when you give me your answer."

"Answer to—"

He knelt on one knee before me, eliciting another gasp. Opening a ring box, the most perfectly simple round diamond stared back at me. Beck was asking me to marry him.

"I might not deserve you, but I want you to be my wife anyway. I will spend the rest of my life proving how different I can be from the one you knew before. Mae O'Malley, I've loved you since the moment I realized a boy could love a girl. Will you consider becoming my wife?"

His wife.

I didn't know what to say.

It was the least expected question I could have imagined, coming from him. Which was exactly how I knew the answer. It was surprisingly easy.

He was my best friend.

I loved him too, and always had.

The chemistry between us was electric, and my heart raced as I realized the implications of the word I was about to say.

Looking into his eyes, so Beck could see the sincerity of my answer, I said, "Yes. Yes, yes, yes."

He couldn't hide his surprise, a fact I would have to rectify. I'd pushed him away out of fear, and he'd done the same.

No more fear. Just love.

My hand shook as he took it. "It fits, perfectly."

"Courtesy of your mom. She went with me this morning to pick it out."

He stood.

"My mom knew? You're full of surprises today."

"She did. And your dad too. I got his blessing last night."

Last night. He'd gone to the bar.

Ohmygod. He'd got my father's blessing. I was about to be a puddle but Beck pulled me into his arms. I'd been hugged by this man many times before, but never like this. Never as a lover hugs a person he's just asked to be his wife.

He held on to me as if I could save him from a sinking ship. And maybe I could. Maybe he could save me too. Being wrapped in his arms this way... I'd never felt safer in my life.

Never felt so... sure.

My heart raced as he pulled back to look at me. I understood what he was thinking. Disbelief that had just happened. Joy that the longest, and only, fight we'd ever had was over. Love. And also... knowledge of what would come next.

His gaze dropped to my lips.

Suddenly our text exchange came back to me, and I didn't want to wait any longer. I raised up on my tiptoes as Beck lowered his lips to mine.

Like the first one, there was no awkwardness. No learning curve. Our mouths melded and tongues clashed as if we had been kissing forever. My hands moved to the forearms I always stared at and wanted to touch. Now, I could. Running my hands along the muscles I'd watched flex as he made drinks, with Beck's lips on mine... I couldn't hold back a groan.

That seemed to set him off.

Beck's slow, lingering kiss became more insistent. And just like that, the slow seduction became an inferno of insistence and tossed clothing. First, he lifted my shirt, our kiss halting as it went over my head.

"Do you know how long I've dreamed of this?"

He reached behind my back, and easier than I'd ever managed, Beck's fingers unclasped my white lace bra. Thank goodness I'd worn a good one. Lifting it over my arms, he looked down, mouth opening, with the most primeval of sounds escaping from him.

"My God, you're fucking perfect."

He didn't waste another second. Both of Beck's hands covered my breasts as he kissed me again. I couldn't get his expression from my mind. It was pure... worship.

*Do you know how long I've dreamed of this?*

If I were being honest, I'd imagined it too. Many times. But had quickly put the idea out of my mind, certain we would never work. Certain Beck would only break my heart.

Who could have imagined the opposite were true? That it would be Beck who put it back together?

"I'm going to tear the rest of your clothes off," he said, pulling away. "Lay you on that bed, and worship every inch of your gorgeous body, Mae."

Before I could respond, he did just that. Kicking off his own shoes, so I did the same, he unbuttoned and unzipped my jeans and scooted them down. In nothing but a white lace thong, I was as impatient to see him too. Reaching up, I began to unbutton his shirt, Beck watching me.

"Do you have any idea how hard it was to walk away from you that night?"

I was nearly done unbuttoning. "Which one?" I asked, pushing off his shirt.

"Take your pick, but I was thinking specifically of the one at the bar."

Beck began to unbutton his pants.

"I'd have let you take me right then and there," I admitted. "Windows and all."

He pulled them off, taking off his socks too.

"I almost did."

"Beck," I said, when we were both down to our underwear. "We are about to see each other totally nude."

It might have been the most ridiculous thing I'd ever said.

"Mae," he responded, grinning like he'd just won the lottery, "I am fully aware of the fact."

With that, he lifted me, and tossed... literally tossed me onto the bed. Squealing, hoping there was no one in that adjoining room, I scooted up to the pillows as he crawled toward me. Biting one edge of my thong, and with one finger under the other side, he removed them.

With his teeth.

Watching him do it, I swallowed, hard. This was Beck we were talking about.

"Perfect," he said when finished. "Absolutely fucking perfect."

No one had ever looked at my body with such reverence before.

"That was hot," I admitted.

That smile. My breath caught.

"Yeah?"

Nodding, I watched as his head descended toward one breast, taking it into his mouth while simultaneously separating my legs. Knowing what he was about to do, I clenched, preparing. Waiting.

He worshiped my body, just as he'd promised.

As he kissed every bit of me on his way down, I reached for the head of hair I'd stared at so many times, wondering how he managed to make it look perfect when I knew for a fact Beck spent very little time getting ready.

Positioning between my legs, opening them wide with hands I'd watched pour a drink or toss a shaker into the air more times than I could count, Beck looked up at me.

"When I said worship, I meant it."

With that, he licked me from bottom to top. Pulled me open, and licked again. Cheekily, Beck looked at me, our eyes meeting.

I couldn't breathe. Let alone speak.

When he said worship, it wasn't a joke. With every touch of his tongue, Beck expertly made my ass jerk from the bed. The sight of him, the feel of him... "If you're trying to make me come," I teased, "it's working."

"Mmmm," was his response, as if Beck was licking a freshly baked croissant. "The first time you come," he said, abruptly stopping and kneeling up, "is going to be with me inside you."

With that, he sprang himself free. The loss of his perfect mouth, the sight of Beck between my legs, his dick full and hard and *right there*.

"Beck." My voice wasn't even my own. I lifted my arms, welcoming him into me. It seemed he needed no further encouragement. And just like that, Beck eased into me, holding himself up and studying my face as intently as I did his.

"I can't believe this is happening," he said, his voice thick. "God damn, Mae, you're so fucking tight. And wet."

"For you."

That put him over the edge.

When he leaned down to kiss me, a beautifully naked Beck thrusted deep as I grabbed his shoulders. We moved just as we'd kissed. With the rhythm and tempo of a well-practiced pastry chef crafting a perfect soufflé. Our bodies slammed together, and stilled. He thrusted and I met him at every turn.

When he lifted his head to look at me, it was all over.

This was *Beck*.

My life-long friend.

My future husband.

"Come with me," I pleaded. It was as if he knew exactly what to do, circling in the only way I could possibly come without any other stimulation.

"My pleasure."

He watched. Waited. Knew the moment the pressure had built and was about to explode. And then buried himself full hilt as the waves began, my ass cheeks clenched, and Beck roared with pleasure.

It wasn't sex.

Or even making love.

That was... magic.

## 45

### BECK

"We should have done that sooner."

It was hard to believe Mae O'Malley was in my arms, after having agreed to become my wife, and after what could only be described as the best sex of my life.

"Why didn't we?" Mae asked.

I ran my hand up and down over the curve of her hip beneath the covers. Because I could.

"Lord only knows," I said. "If I knew it would be that good…"

She turned her face toward me. I swore there was no woman as beautiful as this one.

"Are you always this smug after sex, fiancé?" she asked.

"Only when it's, as you say, that good."

Mae's sigh of contentment made me smile. "I wish we could stay here all night. What time do you have to get back?"

I scooted back to see her better. "What do you take me for, an amateur? I've got the bar covered all night. And opening tomorrow. Have to be back mid-afternoon."

That seemed to surprise her. "Who's closing? We have the room all night? But I don't have anything with me."

I tsked. "Mae, Mae, Mae. Give me some credit." I pointed to the duffle bag in the corner of the room.

"What the heck is that?"

"Your overnight bag."

I shouldn't revel in her complete confusion. But I was pretty proud of how we'd pulled it off.

"I distinctly remember *not* packing an overnight bag. And also, that's not mine."

"Close enough. It's your mom's bag she packed for you."

Mae sat up, giving me a stellar view. It took every ounce of self-restraint I possessed to keep my hands in place.

"Oh my God, that is Mom's." She lay back down in my arms and, regrettably, pulled up the covers. At least I could reach her again. "How did you pull that off?"

"Like I said, she packed it and put it in Jules's car before you knew she was there. Ellie's husband retrieved it from Jules when she dropped you off."

"Dropped me off? Shit. Jules. I completely forgot about her." Mae went to reach for her phone but I pulled her back.

"She's long gone."

Mae's face was all screwed up in confusion as the pieces slowly clicked together.

"That's why she was acting weird about parking."

"While you went in and talked to Ellie, her husband got the bag and walked right past the two of you and brought it up here."

"Get out of here?"

"Absolutely not. I've waited too long for this."

"But... so Jules is gone?"

"Yep."

"You got both of my parents, Jules and Ellie and her husband all in on this?"

"Impressed?"

"Yes, very."

"Good." I leaned down to kiss her. Mae tasted like sunshine and hope. A heady combination.

"I have to text everybody," she said. "Do the guys know?"

"They do. You think I'm smart enough to come up with this whole thing myself? Parker and Mason helped iron out the details."

Mae's brows raised.

"Okay, maybe with some help," I admitted. "I had the idea to do it here and Pia was the one who said I should call Ellie."

Mae actually looked slightly disappointed at that.

"What's wrong?"

"Nothing. It's just... there is no rehearsal brunch, I guess?"

"There is," I was happy to tell her. "When I called, Ellie was delighted to help out. Actually said she'd wanted to call you about the brunch anyway. We were a little worried you might not drive up to have the meeting, or put it off to another day, but we had a contingency plan for that."

"And the tea room?"

I shook my head. "That one was fabricated. Ellie wasn't sure how else to get you up here."

Mae's head shook slowly back and forth. "Beck, the romantic. Who'd have thought?"

"Not me," I admitted. "But you really do bring out the best man in me, Mae. I'll spend a lifetime proving it to you."

"No need," she said. "I already know it's true."

I kissed her on the nose. "My little business owner. What do you say we get dressed... I can't believe I said that," I muttered. "And head into town for some food. You can tell me all about your plans."

"I am hungry," she admitted.

As if I couldn't tell by the fact that Mae bounced out of bed and began to immediately dress.

"You coming?"

"Eventually. Just admiring the view at the moment."

She pulled up her jeans and stood at the foot of the bed, watching me. And then looked down at her hand. "This is so surreal."

"In a good way?"

"In the best way imaginable."

I wholeheartedly agreed.

"Glad to hear it, because I have another surprise for you."

Mae loved surprises. "What is it?"

I got out of bed, reluctantly, reveling in the way Mae's appreciative glance scanned me from head to toe.

"If I told you, it wouldn't be a surprise."

Ignoring her "harumph", I dressed, pulled a sheet of paper from my duffle, folded it and put it in my back pocket.

In some ways, I was as nervous to show it to her as I was to ask Mae to marry me. I'd convinced myself if Mae had committed to staying in Cedar Falls, I shouldn't question it. Or sabotage us by second-guessing her decision.

On the other hand...

Old habits died hard. Despite myself, there was a small part of me that wondered if the next surprise was one Mae would welcome.

\* \* \*

Most wineries didn't serve hearty lunches, just charcuterie. But thanks to a conversation with Ellie, after she congratulated us and talked shop with Mae about the rehearsal dinner, we found a perfect spot.

Right on the lake, serving drier wines than most Finger Lakes wineries, our late-lunch spot also had a decent-sized menu.

"I think I'll do a tasting since I've never been here."

"Sounds good," I said as Mae chose her wines. "Let's get some food in too."

We ordered, a perfect view of the lake reminding me of our last lunch. As much as I didn't want to bring it up, it felt necessary to get out of the way.

"We've never had a hard time communicating," I said. "But obviously it's a different dynamic than we're used to."

"Just a little," Mae said with a secret smile tugging at her lips.

"The last thing I want to do is spoil the mood, but it's important for me to apologize for our last lunch."

"Beck—"

"Just let me get it out there," I said, having thought a lot about it. "You know there's not a lot of things I'm insecure about. But being good enough for you is one of them. Pia told me it's important to talk to you about that. To make sure we communicate rather than shutting down, even when it's uncomfortable."

She paused as her wine, and my beer, were served.

"I agree." Mae tucked a strand of hair behind her ear. "I shouldn't have left like that."

"This is about me—"

"No," she said. "It's about us. Neither of us are perfect, and we're bound to make mistakes. But I agree with Pia. Communication is so important. We just need to keep talking."

I took a sip of beer, silently agreeing. "And having mind-blowing sex," I added.

"There's the Beck I know and love. The sentimental one is gonna take a bit of getting used to."

"Eh, no need. He'll only make an appearance here and there."

One of those appearances came not much later, after we ate. Hesitantly, I took the sheet of paper from my back pocket just as my phone buzzed. Glancing at it, I saw it was our group chat.

"Looks like Mason's demanding I add three hundred bucks to the pot."

"Ouch. That seems like a lot."

"I'll have to argue the technicalities of it later. But the guys are claiming I broke three rules."

Mae looked like the cat who ate the canary. "Never date the neighbor? I still can't believe you made a rule just for me. And never told me."

"Would have been a dead giveaway if I had." I read the text. "Number one, two and three."

"Never fall in love, never date the neighbor, never stay the night. Seems like three hundred bucks to me. Which one are you refuting?"

"Technically speaking... we never really dated. We sort of went from friends to fiancés."

She made a sound of disbelief. "Yeah, good luck with that one. This feels an awful lot like a date."

"Does it though? We've been going to lunch for a long time."

"After sex?"

The mere thought of it made it necessary to shift in my seat. I was going to have a near-permanent boner for a long, long time.

"No. But that feels irrelevant."

"I think you'll need to find a good attorney to argue that one."

A perfect transition.

"Speaking of attorneys." I unfolded the paper. "So, about that surprise."

"Usually people seem excited about surprises. You get this way when it's about something serious. Like you're trying to talk yourself out of it."

She knew me well.

"That's what I want to say first. This is just an idea. Feel free to knock down any part of it. I was going to save this one for later—"

Mae's eyes lit with amusement. "But you have the patience of a guy holding fireworks and a lighter."

"Exactly."

Here went nothing.

"I bought your dad's bar."

She peered at me from above her wine.

"You did."

"But it's called 'O'Malley's.'"

"Yes," she hedged. "It is."

"So it would seem to make sense to me, if we're going to get married, that an actual O'Malley should be part-owner."

Her eyes widened.

"Before you say anything, I'm hiring someone to do the books, thinking maybe an assistant manager so I can have someone else to open and close and run things when we're away."

"Will we be away a lot?"

One of the reasons Mae had never wanted the bar was because of how tied down to it her parents were. "Yes," I said firmly. "That'll be important to making this"—I gestured between us—"work. Time away from that place. Especially if you like this idea."

I handed her the paper and held my breath, waiting.

It was a sketch Parker made for me last night. The top sheet was a sketched layout of the bar's kitchen. On the right side, marked in pencil, was a separate workspace labeled *Pastry Prep*.

"He can't work on it for about a month, so you'd have to use your home kitchen in the meantime. But he said it's totally doable. If," I added quickly, "that's something you want. If you want your own place, that's fine too. I know how you feel about the bar..." I stopped and tried to remember what else I'd wanted to tell her.

"We talked about featuring some of your things on the menu and have had so many people asking about them since the festival. I just thought, if you wanted to do that too... but really, whatever role you wanted to take in the bar. Or none."

She cut me off by reaching across the table for my hands.

"I love it."

Honestly, I hadn't expected that.

"You do?"

"I do, truly. I never wanted to own the bar, for all the reasons you already know. But co-own it? With my husband? My best friend? With a built-in place to run the pastry business? This is amazing. I'd been looking at options and... honestly, this couldn't be more perfect. I don't even know what to say."

I squeezed her hands. "Yes?"

She broke into the widest grin. "Yes. A thousand percent yes."

I almost asked if she had any hesitation at all. Going from "putting on the brakes" a few weeks ago to engaged and owning a business together... it was a lot. And quickly.

Yet it wasn't. We knew each other inside and out.

No more doubting myself. Doubting us. I would take Mae at her word, trust her to make decisions for herself, and just be happy she'd said yes.

"But I do have one question."

"Shoot."

We pulled our hands back as the waiter cleared our lunch. "Thank you," I said.

"Where did you get the money for the downpayment?"

"My dad," I said simply.

She didn't seem surprised. Maybe had already worked out the answer.

"Why didn't you tell me?"

That was an easy one. "Because I didn't want you to think I was buying your dad's approval—or buying *you*. I just wanted to keep the bar in the family. Even if it meant going back to mine."

"I can't believe you did that. I can only imagine how hard it must have been."

It was hard. But worth it.

"For you? I'd do it every day."

Mae shook her head gently back and forth, as if in disbelief.

"He didn't make it easy, as you can imagine. But he gave it to me. And when I went to the bank, there was actually twenty thousand more in the account than I needed. It's a loan," I clarified. "I was already approved for my own, but I didn't want your parents to lose their place and it was the only way to get it so quickly."

"Wow." She took the napkin from her lap and put it on the table. "And he gave you twenty thousand more?"

"Yeah. I called to ask him about it. He said if I tried to pay that back, he would only re-deposit it."

She looked as confused as I had been.

"It was a gift. For the bar. One I had planned on giving back, but I've decided to suck up my pride and use it instead on the kitchen renovations."

"Beck—"

"I'm still sole owner," I reminded her. "And I won't put your name on there until it's done if you give me a hard time."

"You're a real winner, you know that?"

"I do," I said sincerely. "Today, it feels like I just won the greatest prize in the world."

# 46

## MAE

It had been a whirlwind twenty-four hours.

From a business meeting turned engagement, to a day (and night) I wasn't going to stop fantasizing about for a long time, and then back home to celebrate with my parents who were, quite literally, waiting on the doorstep, I stopped short before heading into the bar.

Was this him? Again?

A sparkly silver "congratulations" banner adorned the entrance. At this point, I should probably not be surprised. To say Beck had gone all out these past two days was the understatement of the century.

*My fiancé.*

The only hesitation I had wasn't related to Beck at all. Every doubt had been erased; his assertion that I was different than the other women wasn't just words. He'd shown that to me, and I believed it. Knew he loved and would cherish me.

It was my decision-making that gave me pause. To think I had agreed to marry Mathieu scared me a bit. The difference between the two men—their motivations, character and actions—could not have been more stark. When I called Jules to thank her and tell her the good news, she quoted her therapist, as usual.

"You made the best choice you could with the information and self-worth you had at the time. That doesn't mean it was wrong. It means you've grown."

Thank goodness for that.

I was about to start a night shift, one I might have groaned about a few years ago when I'd helped my dad out at the bar between CIA and France. But now? I couldn't wait to work alongside my fiancé, especially since it meant meeting up with Parker, who was coming up later to show me his plans for the kitchen renovations.

I pushed open the door to a round of applause.

At the bar, the entire crew. Including a hotter than hell bartender who apparently planned to live in button-down shirts now after I'd teased him about saying yes to his proposal thanks to his attire. It was Beck's forearms, I'd said, that sealed the deal.

He grinned, probably knowing exactly what I was thinking as he more vigorously shook the ice shaker in his hand. I blinked, forcing myself to focus on the people sitting and standing in their usual corner of the bar.

Mason. Parker. Delaney. Pia. Jules. Only Cole was missing. A round of congratulations met me as I hugged each one of them and everyone talked at once.

"I wasn't surprised at all," Delaney said. "You two were meant for each other."

"Tell your fiancé he still owes us three hundred bucks." Mason nodded to the man in question, who quipped back, "Two hundred."

"What do you think?" he asked me.

Beck poured martinis for two women at the other end of the bar. Ones I might have been threatened by, especially as they both looked at him with stars in their eyes, if it weren't for the absolute certainty that Beck wasn't interested in them.

"I think you need an impartial second opinion, and I'm not your girl for that."

"Three hundred." Parker raised his beer glass to me in greeting.

"Pretty sure you're not considered impartial either," Jules said.

"Hey, pretty lady."

Every head turned as Beck addressed me.

"Nice shirt."

"Thanks."

That's when I noticed Jenn. "I thought she was off tonight?"

"She was," Beck said. "But I figured you could celebrate easier, and talk to

Parker about the kitchen plans, if you didn't have to worry about customers. So you're off the hook."

"Awww," Pia swooned. "Why did you warn me away from him when I first came?" Pia asked Mason. "He's a sweetheart."

Parker nearly spit out his beer. "Not the word I'd use."

Sidling up to the bar on my newly minted night off, I met Beck's gaze.

"I don't know what I'm in the mood for," I said in my most overly flirty tone. "Can you help me decide?"

"Well, beautiful," he said, as smooth as ever. "How are you feeling tonight? We'll go from there."

"Hmmm." I leaned my elbow on the bar, pretending to think. "I'm feeling happy. And excited too."

"Ah yeah? Why's that?"

I deliberately stared overly long at his forearm before meeting his eyes, sighing dramatically.

"It's a guy."

"Ooof, must be one hell of a guy to catch the attention of a woman like you."

"Oh, he is," I assured him.

Without hardly even looking away from me, Beck noticed the same thing I did, that Lou was on empty. Without missing a beat, he said, "Let me think about it a sec," and headed off to refill him.

"So I hear we're working on some renovations together?" Parker asked.

I turned to the group.

"I can't thank you enough for squeezing it in. With the business, and your own house, I know you're slammed."

"It's no problem at all. Though like I told Beck, it'll be about a month before I can get to it. I want to clear at least a week so there's minimal disruptions to the kitchen."

I exchanged a look with Delaney, girl code for "you've got a good one here."

"I appreciate it."

"When you get your drink, how about we go back and take a look? I have some updated plans."

"Sounds great."

Beck was back.

"So about that drink. Two options for you. First is a Velvet Night. Blackberry, gin, hint of spice. Just enough bite to keep you curious, like the look you gave me five minutes ago."

Oh man, he was good.

"And the second?"

His slow smile said it all. "A Slow Burn. Whiskey, honey, and a splash of chili syrup. Starts sweet, finishes with a kick. Kind of like what I've got planned for later."

Holy shit, Beck.

This working together thing was going to be tough. Gathering myself, I forced a leveled, and still flirty, voice. But this time, with a seductive spin.

"I'll take the second one. Feels more in line with my mood."

"Oh yeah?"

"Hmm hmm."

Beck let out a breath, smiled as if to say "you're killing me", and began to make the drink. I watched every move with a different kind of anticipation than I had when walking into the bar.

Turning back to the group, I forced my mind from Beck. After all, he was closing, so the slow burn was an appropriate choice.

"Like Pia's sign?" Delaney asked.

"Ahh, so that was you?"

"I had it hanging around the inn. I hope you don't mind. Jules said you were telling everyone."

"Mind? I love it. And I love you guys too. Seriously, thank you for everything. Welcoming me into the fold, putting up with Beck and me these past few weeks—"

"Mostly Beck," Parker said to laughter.

"You made it easy to want to stay in Cedar Falls."

Mason handed me my drink. I glanced back at Beck, who winked at me, and then turning back to the gang, I lifted my glass.

"To Cedar Falls."

They lifted theirs too, and we drank. To the town that had brought us all together.

# EPILOGUE
## BECK

"Why don't we bring these into the kitchen?"

Mae and I followed Ellie from the front room into the bed and breakfast's kitchen, our arms both laden with trays of desserts. Placing them on the table, I watched my beaming fiancée as she hugged the woman who'd gotten it all started.

"Thank you," she said. "If it weren't for you, Mae'd from Scratch might not even exist."

"I'm certain," the older woman said, "it would. But I insist on an invoice."

Mae had refused to give her one, telling Ellie her thriving pastry business was thanks to the start Ellie had given her.

"Absolutely not." Mae stood firm. "You were my first customer and this is my way of thanking you for believing in me before I even had a business card."

Ellie's displeasure showed clearly on her face. "Then I insist you stay the night, on me."

Mae and I exchanged a look.

"We weren't prepared to stay," she began.

"And don't have overnight bags with us," I finished, my mind racing. We had the bar covered for the night, but I had to open early tomorrow. Not that it was an issue since we weren't that far away. Ellie was our only delivery today, so technically...

"I have your room."

That seemed to do it for Mae. I could tell by her wistful expression she was thinking of the last time we'd stayed in that room. As I was.

"Let's do it," I said.

"You were planning to check on the bar later."

"Only if we ended up back in town," I said. We'd already planned to walk around town and possibly stay here for dinner. "It's not necessary."

O'Malley's had been running like a well-oiled machine thanks to our hire who not only handled the bookkeeping but was an excellent server. I'd promoted Spence to manager, a role he'd been so proud of that his entire extended family had come in to celebrate. And he was damn good at it.

She'd already decided but just wanted me to confirm. I knew her, not from being engaged to Mae this past month, but from growing up with her. Now, there was just a whole new layer to our relationship. One I was already looking forward to exploring tonight.

"Deal," she said to Ellie. "We'll have to go into town to get some things."

"No need for toiletries, we have those. Now, about this taste test you mentioned."

Just as her husband walked in, Ellie opened one of the trays. They fawned over Mae's mini almond croissants and apple cardamom crumble cups, my personal favorite. Word hadn't spread about Mae'd from Scratch only because of the support she'd gotten from Cedar Falls businesses—from Mason and Pia to Maggie at The Big Easy to Bella Luna and Cedarwood Bar and Grill—but because her creations were damn good.

After finishing with Ellie, we headed into town to get a few things and make dinner reservations. By the time we returned, our room was ready to check into. The second I opened the door, memories flooded back.

Our first kiss.

Our engagement.

"I can't believe it's been just over a month," Mae said as I closed the door. She looked at the bed. "Do you remember the first time we had sex?"

Had she lost her mind?

"Remember? I fantasize about it daily."

"You do not."

"Calling me a liar?" I teased, pulling Mae toward me.

"Yes. A blatant one."

"Not nice," I said, reaching up to undo the first of her two braids. "May have to punish you for that one."

"Oh yeah? What are you planning?"

One braid done. Onto the second.

"Maybe a nice slap on the ass. Or two."

"Big. Fat. Liar."

"Taunting me now, are we?"

I spun my fiancée around, pushed her hair to one side, and took advantage of the spaghetti strap dress she wore. "The first time I saw this," I said of her tattoo, "I wanted to trace the lines with my tongue."

Doing exactly that, I relished the sounds Mae made. Whimpers that got me every time.

"You like that?"

"I like everything you do."

"Good," I said, spinning her back and pushing the straps down. "I think sundresses should be your required apparel of choice from now on." It slipped down easily, revealing the fact that Mae wore no bra. Of course, I'd known that already.

"I think I'd be a little chilly in this in January."

My hand slipped beneath her underwear. "What if I warm you up?"

Mae couldn't answer because I covered her mouth with mine. With my tongue and fingers working the same rhythm, I willed her to come. The sound of her pleasure had become my new favorite thing, next to seeing Mae's face as she orgasmed. If I thought the fantasy was hot, it paled in comparison to the real thing.

She was close.

I was hard as a rock already, but this was about my fiancée. A full circle moment for her business, and for us too.

I rubbed her clit while teasing Mae with my tongue until the telltale pulses around my finger, and wetness that I couldn't wait to sink into, told me I'd reached my goal.

For now.

There would be more to come. And there was, more than once.

It was only later, when we sat across from each other at dinner, that I looked into the eyes of the woman I loved, my best friend, and reveled in... well, all of it.

"I love you," she said, beating me to it. "Always have."

"That's my line," I said as she took a sip of wine. "Sometimes I curse the time we wasted—or specifically, I wasted. But I think everything happened the way it should."

"What do you mean?"

I shrugged. "I was still too immature, before you left, and probably would have fucked things up if I'd told you then. Seeing Mason and Pia, and then Parker and Delaney, gave me hope. It made me realize, even though I probably already knew by then, the pact we took was nothing more than four guys who were scared to repeat their parents' mistakes. Or in Mason's case, scared to lose someone he loved."

"I think about it a lot too," she said, this conversation one we'd had more than once but in different ways. "What would have happened if I hadn't gone to France. I needed that, I think, to be where I am today, with the business."

"Agreed." I twisted my lips. "I could have done without Mathieu, though."

"Same. But you know... even that taught me something. I think regrets are pretty useless. We are where we're meant to be when it was meant to be."

"You think?"

"I do."

Like she said, it didn't matter either way. The past was behind us. The future was uncertain but filled with possibilities. The present was really all we had, and I for one didn't want to waste a minute of it.

"I remember distinctly coming up with the rules when Mason blurted, 'Oh, and another one... never date the neighbor.' Every one of them looked at me, already knowing the rule was for me alone. I never even argued it. They knew what I did... Any interest from you and it was all over."

"That's still so unbelievable, that you all kept it from me for so long."

"They knew the stakes. The guys can be a bunch of assholes sometimes, but they'd never have risked ruining our friendship. It was, and is, too important to me."

"Cost you three hundred bucks," she teased.

"Try five fifty. Remember we each pitched two fifty to start."

"Ouch."

I reached across for Mae's hand, the one with a ring on it. "Let's not wait." Prepared to explain what I meant, that I wanted to marry her now... yesterday... I opened my mouth to do just that.

"Okay."

"Okay, what?"

"Let's get married. This summer."

There were benefits to marrying someone you'd known your whole life, who could almost read your thoughts.

"Done." I squeezed her hand. "Rule number five. Marry the neighbor. Stay forever."

\* \* \*

## MORE FROM CISSY MECCA

Another book from Cissy Mecca, *Tempted Hearts*, is available to order now here:

https://mybook.to/TemptedBackAd

# ABOUT THE AUTHOR

**Cissy Mecca** is the author of the American small-town romance series such as *The Bachelor Pact* and *The Boys of Bridgewater*. She also writes spicy roman-tasy under the pen name C. L. Mecca. She lives in Northeast Pennsylvania with her family.

Download your exclusive bonus content from Cissy Mecca here:

Follow Cissy on social media here:

facebook.com/MeccaRomance

instagram.com/meccaromance

tiktok.com/@clmeccaauthor

# ALSO BY CISSY MECCA

**Cedar Falls Series**

Fallen Hearts

Desired Hearts

Protected Hearts

Tempted Hearts

**Cissy Mecca writing as C. L. Mecca**

**Heirs of Elydor Series**

Whisper of War and Storms

Tide of Waves and Secrets

Fate of Echoes and Embers

Realm of Stone and Starlight

# Boldwood
# EVER AFTER
xoxo

JOIN BOLDWOOD'S
**ROMANCE
COMMUNITY**
FOR SWEET AND
SPICY BOOK RECS
WITH ALL YOUR
FAVOURITE
TROPES!

SIGN UP TO OUR
NEWSLETTER

HTTPS://BIT.LY/BOLDWOODEVERAFTER

# Boldwood

Boldwood Books is an award-winning fiction publishing company seeking out the best stories from around the world.

**Find out more at www.boldwoodbooks.com**

Join our reader community for brilliant books, competitions and offers!

Follow us
@BoldwoodBooks
@TheBoldBookClub

Sign up to our weekly
deals newsletter

https://bit.ly/BoldwoodBNewsletter